Life and Death of the Wicked Lady Skelton

Life and Death of the Wicked Lady Skelton

Magdalen King-Hall

with notes and an introduction by Rowland Hughes

UNIVERSITY OF HERTFORDSHIRE PRESS

First published in Great Britain in 1944 by Peter Davies Ltd.
This new edition published in Great Britain in 2016 by
University of Hertfordshire Press
College Lane
Hatfield
Hertfordshire
AL10 9AB
UK

British Library Cataloguing in Publication Data
A catalogue record for this book is available from the
British Library

ISBN 978-1-909291-34-8

Design by Arthouse Publishing Solutions Ltd
Printed in Great Britain by Charlesworth Press, Wakefield

CONTENTS

INTRODUCTION

When it was first published in 1944, Magdalen King-Hall's historical novel *Life and Death of the Wicked Lady Skelton* was an immediate best-seller. The novel is set in the late seventeenth century, and tells the story of Barbara Skelton, a beautiful, aristocratic young woman who, to escape the tedium of married life, disguises herself as man, takes to the road as a highway robber, and carries on an adulterous affair with a fellow criminal. King-Hall's book was reprinted twice in little over a year, and the rights were almost immediately purchased (for the sum of £5,000) by Gainsborough Studios, one of the most successful British film studios of the 1940s. By the early spring of 1945, a film adaptation was in production. Directed by Leslie Arliss, and starring Margaret Lockwood, James Mason and Patricia Roc, *The Wicked Lady* premiered at the Gaumont cinema, on Haymarket in London, on 19 November 1945. Despite a fairly dismissive critical reception, it went on to become the highest grossing movie of 1946 at the British box office.

The film nearly suffered disaster at its very first public showing, however. The première, a charity event, had been promoted for weeks in the press. It was the first glamorous, star-studded movie première to take place in London since the end of the war, and it was due to be attended by Queen Mary, the widow of George V and grandmother of Queen Elizabeth II. On the morning of the screening, the first reviews were published, many of which suggested that the lurid content of the film was far too shocking for the Queen Dowager to see. Marlborough House requested a private screening from the studio, and an equerry was despatched to watch the film before deciding whether it was suitable for Royal eyes. After an anxious couple of hours, the equerry emerged and agreed to allow Queen Mary's attendance, and Lockwood later recalled that they spent the film watching her from behind, trying to gauge whether she was offended or not.[1] She wasn't, but despite that, *The Wicked Lady* retained its salacious reputation, to the extent that the devoutly Methodist J. Arthur Rank, owner of the Rank Organisation which distributed Gainsborough films in the UK, refused to sanction a sequel to the film, despite its massive commercial success, because he found its depiction of criminal behaviour and extramarital sex too disturbing. However, the film is now regarded as the quintessential example of the period costume melodrama in which Gainsborough specialised during the 1940s, and which proved immensely popular with cinema audiences, particularly women. As such, although critical opinion of its cinematic merits still varies, its status as a classic of British cinema is assured.

The story of Barbara Skelton is a fictional re-imagining of the legend of Katherine Ferrers, a long established piece of folklore from the English county of Hertfordshire. Born in the mid-seventeenth century, Ferrers was a scion of a respectable and wealthy family and heir to a considerable estate. According to legend, having married young and being poorly treated by her husband, Katherine supposedly donned men's clothing and became a highwaywoman (in some versions of the story, she did so in the company of a low-born lover). While committing one of her crimes, she was shot and, having ridden home, died of her wound on the steps of her family home in the village of Markyate. The narrative does not end there; for it is claimed that Katherine's restless spirit proceeded to haunt her house and neighbourhood for several centuries. It is impossible to tell how long the story has been circulating orally – in textual form, it dates back only to the nineteenth century – but the tale of Katherine Ferrers is still relatively well-known in Hertfordshire to this day. Indeed, a pub by the name of The Wicked Lady stands at the end of Ferrers Lane, on the edge of Nomansland Common, near the village of Wheathampstead, reputedly the scene of many of her crimes.

Although both legend and film have endured, King-Hall's novel has almost disappeared from memory, despite the fact that it belonged to the same significant cultural and historical moment as the film and clearly spoke with equal power to a predominantly female audience just emerging from the Second World War. This critical edition of the novel aims to recover King-Hall's work from its relative obscurity and introduce a modern audience to a hugely enjoyable novel that is sometimes startling in its progressive attitudes towards gender and sexuality, and which, when understood in relation to its genre and its historical context, tells us much about the hopes, fears and anxieties of a generation living through a period of profound transformation. Many modern retellings of the legend (in newspapers, tourist brochures, and on the internet), feature details which are lifted wholesale from the novel and the film, so that the line between history, tradition and fiction has become increasingly blurred. The story of the Wicked Lady is an interesting example of how folk tradition can continue to evolve once it has been appropriated by other media, and even draw new energy from this appropriation. To understand how this has happened, this introduction will focus on the women at the narrative's heart: the historical Katherine Ferrers, around whom the legend grew; the author, Magdalen King-Hall, a popular and talented novelist whose work is now little read; and the fictional Barbara Skelton, King-Hall's re-imagining of Ferrers.

Although Katherine Ferrers is supposed to have been shot and killed in the mid-1600s, there is no textual record of any scandalous rumours attached to her name until much later. Henry Chauncy's *Historical Antiquities of Hertfordshire* (1700) simply mentions her as the brief owner of the manor of Flamstead; Robert Clutterbuck's *The History and Antiquities of the County of Hertford* (1815–27) similarly makes no mention of the legend. This is not conclusive, of course; the authors of such monumental, serious histories may have had no interest in scandal, gossip or superstition. Given the explosion of print culture in the late seventeenth and eighteenth centuries, however, and the public taste for lurid tales of crime, the total absence of the legend from the printed record during this period suggests that it is of a more recent genesis, almost certainly nineteenth-century.

Although it is impossible to say how long the story had been in circulation, it was certainly well-established by 1855, when Frank E. Smedley published a narrative poem entitled 'Maud Allinghame: A Legend of Hertfordshire'. The author claims that the poem is 'founded on a story current in the part of Herts where the scene is laid'.[2] The poem itself is a piece of doggerel, telling the tale of the eponymous Maud, sole heir to the Allinghame estate, who resists the entreaties of various suitors during the day, and takes to the highway at night. After various adventures, the town council sends to London and hires 'bold Jonathan Blaker/ The famous thief-taker'; he pursues and shoots Maud, who dies on the steps of Allinghame Hall.

A couple of decades later, in the third volume of his three-volume *History of Hertfordshire* (1870–81), John Edwin Cussans provides a full summary of the legend which, 'in the present year, 1878, is religiously believed in by the majority of the inhabitants of Markyate Street', and has remained the basic outline ever since:

> It is said that, in the disguise of male attire and mounted on a coal-black horse with white fore-feet, she robbed travellers on the highway, but at length was fatally wounded at No Man's Land when so engaged. She was found lying dead outside a door leading, by a secret staircase, to a chamber where she changed her dress. The doorway was built up, and so remained for certainly a hundred and fifty years.[3]

A further detail is added, namely that after a fire in 1840 the owner, Mr Adey, wanted to re-open the doorway but could not get any of the local workmen to do the job for fear of the ghost of the Wicked Lady, having to send to London for labourers instead. Moreover, he mentions that some of the labourers witnessed an apparition of Lady Ferrers dangling from a tree and 'took [it] upon themselves to saw the branch off, and were greatly surprised that they were not handsomely rewarded by the owner for their zeal'.[4]

What exactly do we know about the real Katherine Ferrers, the young woman whom folklore has associated with the figure of the Wicked Lady? Drawing on the work of assiduous local amateur historians, we can be fairly certain of the bare outlines of her life, and unfortunately those details are not easily reconciled with the legend itself.[5] Katherine was born in the village of Bayford in Hertfordshire, on 4 May 1634, the daughter of Knighton Ferrers and his wife Katherine (nee Walters). The Ferrers family were of distinguished lineage, and had been substantial landowners in Hertfordshire since the reign of King Henry VIII (1509–47), who had awarded the manors of Flamstead, Markyate, Ponsborne and Bayford, amongst other properties in the county, to Katherine's great-great-grandfather George Ferrers (c.1500–79), as a reward for his loyal service. These had remained in the Ferrers family for more than a century. When Katherine was only six years of age, in April 1640, her father died. Five months later, her grandfather, John Ferrers, also died and the young Katherine became the sole heir to the considerable Ferrers fortune. Her mother quickly remarried Sir Simon Fanshawe, of Ware in Hertfordshire, and it is clearly no coincidence that this marriage took place on 21 September 1640, a mere four days after her grandfather's death and four days before he had even been buried. By marrying the elder Katherine,

Fanshawe gained indirect control of her daughter's newly acquired wealth; when Katherine senior died in Oxford in February 1642, the young heiress was made a ward of court, on payment of a sum of £1200 by the Fanshawe family, and she was left in their care.

For the next six years, while the Civil War raged around the country, she lived with her stepfather's sister, Alice Bedell, in Hamerton, Huntingdonshire (now part of Cambridgeshire). In April 1648, when not quite fourteen years old, she was married to Thomas Fanshawe, the fifteen- or sixteen-year-old nephew of her stepfather, in what looks very much like a marriage of convenience. The Fanshawes were Royalists, and their staunch support of King Charles I in the English Civil War had cost them much, leaving them in desperate financial straits. Following the passage of the Sequestration Act in 1643, Parliament had the power to confiscate the income and property from the estates of known Royalists and place them under the control of local commissioners, and Ware Park, the Fanshawes' home, had suffered this fate. According to John Barber, by 1650 its contents and furniture had largely been stripped out and sold to fund Parliament, and even when Thomas Fanshawe Sr (Simon's brother) successfully petitioned to have the estate returned, the family were on the point of financial ruin. It had become both a necessity and an inevitability that the Ferrers family estates would be sacrificed to restore the Fanshawe family fortunes.

Katherine conveyed the title of her properties to her new husband on their marriage, in accordance with the common-law doctrine of coverture, whereby a married woman could not own property herself, and indeed had few, if any, legal rights of her own. One by one these properties were sold. Markyate Cell, the supposed base of her operations as a highwaywoman, and the scene of her death in the legend, was sold by 1657 to one Thomas Coppin, who had actually been a tenant in the property even earlier, certainly by 1655. It seems certain that Thomas and Katherine were not resident in Markyate at the time of her death in 1660, and possibly may never have lived there at all. As Colin Field points out, '[o]wnership did not imply occupation'. 'Had the Ferrers family lived at Markyate,' Field suggests, 'there would be entries in the Caddington registers to prove it. There are none, apart from three very early entries in 1558, 1576, and 1580'.[6] From 1610 onwards, the house seems to have been rented by a family called Norton, and then by the Coppins; the Ferrers themselves resided at Bayford, just south of the county town of Hertford in east Hertfordshire, where Katherine was born, like her father before her, and where both her father and grandfather were buried.

Death and burial records indicate that Katherine Fanshawe died in 1660, and was buried at Ware on 13 June. An account in the memoirs of her aunt, Lady Ann Fanshawe, suggests that her death may have occurred in London, in childbirth, rather than from a bullet-wound suffered during a failed highway robbery. Lady Ann was in London for the triumphal re-entry of King Charles II on the occasion of his restoration to the throne, on 29 May 1660. She notes that 'My niece Fanshawe lay then in the Strand, where I stood to see the King's entry with his brother, surely the most pompous show that ever was; for the hearts of all men in this Kingdom moved at his will.' Although, as Field notes, the phrase 'my niece Fanshawe' does not unambiguously apply to Katherine, it probably does; and it seems highly likely that Thomas Fanshawe would have been in London for the restoration of his monarch, given that he had been a staunch supporter of the exiled King, and would have expected and desired to be rewarded for that loyalty. Lady Ann makes this self-interest apparent when she continues, 'The next day I went with other ladies of the family to congratulate his Majesty's happy arrival, who received me with great grace, and promised me future favours to my husband and self.'[7] Again, Field argues persuasively that 'it would be incredible for Catherine not to have been there'.[8] If she were there, as self-interest would seem to dictate, and if 'my niece Fanshawe' really does refer to Katherine, then the phrase 'lay then in the Strand' might seem to indicate that she was pregnant, as the phrase 'lying in' was commonly used to describe the period immediately before and after a woman gave birth. Both Barber and Field note that Thomas Fanshawe had taken part in Booth's Uprising, a Royalist conspiracy to overthrow the Protectorate which had taken place in 1659. On the failure of the uprising, Fanshawe was imprisoned between September 1659 and February 1660, so if Katherine was pregnant, and had been with Thomas shortly before his arrest, then she might have been nearly full-term. If she had not been with Thomas the previous autumn, then she could have been no further along than four months. Even so, it seems likely that Katherine was in London for the Restoration at the very end of May 1660, and possibly was pregnant. By 13 June, she was being interred in the family tomb in Ware. It seems highly improbable that in the intervening time she left London for Markyate, where she had never lived, took to the highway, and was shot and killed. Death from complications resulting from childbirth or a miscarriage is the more likely explanation.

Despite the lack of evidence to support the truth of the legend, it was certainly widely believed and reproduced from the late nineteenth century onwards. It was Cussans's version of the story, to all intents and purposes, which was retold by Christina Hole in her book *Haunted England* (1940), and as the title of her book implies, Hole was most interested in the supernatural elements of the tale. She recounts the story of 'Mr Adye' (sic) and his reluctant workmen, before bringing the legend up to date:

> The discovery of her secret room had no effect upon Lady Ferrers' spirit, for she continued to wander for many years afterwards, the last record of her appearance being early in the present century, when she was seen by a number of people at a parish tea.[9]

Although brief, Hole's account in turn provided Magdalen King-Hall with the idea for her fictionalisation of the legend, as she acknowledges in the 'Author's Note' at the beginning of the novel.

Before discussing the novel in detail, it is worth pausing to place it in the context of King-Hall's life and career.[10]

Magdalen King-Hall was born on 22 July 1904 in Chelsea, the youngest daughter of Admiral Sir George King-Hall, and his wife Olga (née Ker).[11] The family had a distinguished naval history, dating back to the late eighteenth century. She spent her early years in London, before moving to Australia from 1911–13, where her father was appointed naval commander-in-chief of the Australia station. The family then returned to Britain upon the Admiral's retirement, and settled in Hove, near Brighton. Having relied on governesses for a rather informal education until this point, King-Hall was sent to boarding school at Downe House in Berkshire, and then to St Leonards school, near St Andrews in Scotland. She spent some time in Switzerland and France, learning to speak French fluently, before returning to live in Hove. It was here, between 1923 and 1924, that she wrote her first novel, though her father bought a house on Tite Street in Chelsea, and the family moved back to London shortly before its publication in 1925.

This novel, *The Diary of a Young Lady of Fashion, 1764–5*, made an astonishing and unexpected impact, and would remain King-Hall's most successful work until *Life and Death of the Wicked Lady Skelton* two decades later. It is a playful but convincing recreation of the intimate diary of a young Anglo-Irish woman called Cleone Knox, purportedly written during her travels around various European countries in the mid-eighteenth century. The prefatory material to the diaries claimed that they had been discovered and edited by Knox's descendent, the equally fictional Mr Alexander Blacker-Kerr. King-Hall's publisher, Thornton Butterworth, was responsible for the book's careful marketing and publicity. King-Hall's name was not attached to the book, so that it appeared, at first glance at least, to be a genuine diary. It was taken as such by a number of reviewers, including Lord Darling in *The Sunday Times*, who hailed it as an important literary discovery. After these enthusiastic pre-publication reviews appeared in the autumn of 1925, the canny Butterworth postponed its release while more copies were printed, and when it finally went on sale in December it became a bestseller. Experts in eighteenth-century literature quickly questioned its provenance, however, and over the next six months speculation turned to the true authorship of this literary 'hoax'. On 24 June 1926, a headline on the front page of *The Daily Express* declared it the 'Cleverest Hoax of the Century', while the front page of *The New York Times* read: 'Girl Tricks the World with Literary Hoax, Intended as a Joke'. King-Hall – who had never intended any such deception when she wrote the book, and had relied only on her own general knowledge, and what she could glean from Hove Public Library – found herself propelled into a brief period of literary celebrity.

King-Hall capitalised in a modest manner upon this small degree of fame, working as a journalist during the next few years, and producing several more novels which did not garner the same degree of attention. In 1929, she married Patrick Perceval Maxwell, actually a distant cousin, who was working for the Sudan Cotton Plantation

Syndicate. For the next three years, King-Hall spent winters in the Sudan and (wives being forbidden from remaining during the hot season) split her summers between London and Ireland, where her husband's family lived. When not in the Sudan, she continued to write, both novels and journalism, and when a family inheritance allowed Patrick to quit his job, they returned to live in Chelsea. Her first son, Richard, had been born in 1930; her second son was born seven years later, and a daughter three years after that. In 1938, the family moved again, this time to County Down in Northern Ireland, to run a farm close to the Perceval Maxwell family home. It was here, after producing only three modestly successful novels during the 1930s, that King-Hall entered her most prolific period of authorship, and that she wrote *Life and Death of the Wicked Lady Skelton* – the novel for which she is most often remembered today.

During the 1940s, packages of books would regularly arrive at their Irish home from the London Library, which supplemented her own library to form the basis of her research. According to her son, Richard, her method of composition was remarkably relaxed: she did not insist on scholarly isolation, instead writing longhand, in pencil, while sitting in the company of her family, if they were at home. However, the children were looked after by an Austrian nanny, and later sent away to boarding school, so she did have time to herself to devote to writing.

In 1953, the family relocated again, to County Waterford in Ireland, where King-Hall continued to write quite prolifically. In the late 1950s, however, she began to manifest signs of Parkinson's Disease, and the last of her twenty books (seventeen novels and three non-fiction works) was published in 1962. Following the death of her husband Patrick in 1968, Magdalen King-Hall spent the final three years of her life living with her son Richard's family in King's Langley, Hertfordshire, and she died in Hemel Hempstead hospital on 1 January 1971.

King-Hall's works were always historical novels, though there was ostensibly little consistency or pattern to her choice of subject matter – unlike her friend and contemporary Margaret Irwin, for example, best known for her *Young Bess* trilogy of novels about Queen Elizabeth I. Like Irwin, however, her attention was inevitably caught by stories of women – the character of Barbara Skelton has a forerunner, for instance, in her novel *Lady Sarah* (1939), which fictionalises the life of the notorious eighteenth-century aristocrat, Lady Sarah Lennox. King-Hall was inspired partly by locations with which she was familiar – several of her novels have an Irish setting – but more commonly she would read widely in history and folklore and keep her eyes peeled for interesting stories which she might embroider into fiction. At the time she wrote *Life and Death of the Wicked Lady Skelton*, King-Hall had no direct knowledge or association with Hertfordshire, though she would end her life there. Indeed, she transplants her protagonist's home from Markyate in Hertfordshire to the fictional Maiden Worthy in Buckinghamshire, just across the border.

Her facility at embellishing the kernel of a good idea can be seen in *Life and Death of the Wicked Lady Skelton*. The account of the Wicked Lady legend in Hole's book is only one page long, summarising the version of Ferrers' life drawn from Cussans. The considerable flesh which she attached to these bare bones emerged almost entirely from the imagination of King-Hall, and the endurance of the legend into the twenty-first century owes much to the richness of her invention.

The success of *Life and Death of the Wicked Lady Skelton* was perhaps no surprise, as King-Hall was by this stage of her career an experienced and skilled popular historical novelist. The genre in which she worked has not always been afforded the critical respect or attention that it deserves, but in recent years feminist critics have recognised that King-Hall and her contemporary writers of women's historical fiction provided a crucial reflection of, and outlet for, the desires, hopes and anxieties of their largely female audience. The marketplace was relatively crowded. Some of the best-selling books of the years immediately before, during and after the Second World War were historical novels written by women: among them were Margaret Mitchell's *Gone With the Wind* (1936); Daphne du Maurier's *Jamaica Inn* (1936), *Frenchman's Creek* (1941) and *The King's General* (1946); Kathleen Winsor's controversial *Forever Amber* (1944); and Margaret Irwin's *Young Bess* (1944).

The popularity of historical fiction at this time can be explained in a number of ways. As Diana Wallace has pointed out, the appeal of historical fiction 'can be situated within a wider popular appetite for history, especially social history': G.M. Trevelyan's *English Social History* (1942), for instance, was also a best seller.[12] Such interest in the English past was clearly a response to the pressure of wartime, as many readers turned to the past to establish or renew their sense of English identity and values, for which they were fighting. Many readers picked up historical novels out of a desire to learn about the period in which they were set, and an easy means of dismissing much 'popular' historical fiction was to focus on its 'inaccuracy'; du Maurier, for example, was so eager to avoid this pitfall that she collaborated with the eminent historian A.L. Rowse when researching her Civil War novel *The King's General*. Although her research was much more informal and less exhaustive, King-Hall also demonstrates a high level of historical knowledge, conjuring a vivid sense of the seventeenth-century setting not merely by dropping the names of significant historical characters, but by depicting the rhythms, patterns and rituals of day-to-day life. The novel is rich in detail about seventeenth-century traditions and practices: wedding customs, music, dances, card games, recipes for perfumes and folk remedies.

And yet, as Wallace notes, traditional non-fictional history writing had tended to exclude women, who, with a few exceptions, tended to feature only as the wives or daughters of 'great men' who shaped major historical events. In the hands of many women writers, the historical novel offered an opportunity to produce an alternative version of history more reflective of the everyday life and experience of women. However, in Wallace's words, 'any historical novel always has as much, or perhaps more, to say about the time in which it was written' as about the period in which it was set – indeed, even the choice of period setting can often tell us much about the meaning of a novel.[13] The Restoration period in which *Life and Death of the Wicked Lady Skelton* takes place is notable for perhaps two important factors. Firstly, it was a notoriously licentious age, when the 'Merry Monarch', King Charles II, presided over a court in which decadent behaviour and sexual promiscuity were the norm. The novel abounds with passing references to this – and it is notable that many of the real historical personages who fleetingly intersect with the fictional characters are women, such as the two mistresses of King Charles, Lady Castlemaine and the Duchess of Portsmouth, who are said to have been former victims of the highwayman Jerry Jackson. Barbara Skelton's frustration at the grinding tedium of life at Maryiot Cells is heightened, one feels, by the tantalising proximity of a more glamorous, luxuriant life at court, which yet remains inaccessible to her. For a novel concerned with rampant female sexuality, the Restoration world is the ideal stage.

Secondly, Restoration England was a society in which the memory of a relatively recent war – the English Civil War – remained strong. The story of Barbara Skelton commences in 1678, three decades after the end of this devastating conflict, but there had been other major catastrophes in more recent times – the Great Plague of 1665 and the Great Fire of London in 1666 – which haunt the text, imbuing it with a sense of the fragility of life and happiness, just as Barbara's ghost haunts the house itself. This 'haunting' is often subtly, almost invisibly embedded in the text by intertextual quotation and allusion, as when the effects of a devastating cold snap in the 1680s are evoked using the diarist John Evelyn's description of the plague.

For a readership living through another devastating war, the sense that the characters inhabit a vibrant world that has survived conflict and catastrophe may have been additionally appealing. King-Hall emphasises the historical continuum between the past and the present with a series of framing narratives at the beginning of the novel. The history of Maryiot Cells is linked to a contemporary context by a preface, ironically titled 'Finis?', describing the destruction of the house by a German bomb in 1942. We then travel back through time, in a series of 'flashbacks', each of them focusing on earlier female inhabitants of the house from the eighteenth to the early twentieth century. Though each of them struggles to come to terms with the spectral presence of Barbara Skelton, these chapters suggest that the past is not entirely segregated from the present; we can trace our current identity as individuals and as a nation back to the past which is described in the book. Moreover, these framing narratives privilege the experiences and authority of women, suggesting an alternative model of social and domestic history.

Despite King-Hall's determination to make her readers aware of an historical continuum between the seventeenth-century and the present-day, many of her readers would have picked up the novel looking for a temporary escape from the bleak reality of a world at war, rather than a reminder. There is much in the text to satisfy this desire, and King-Hall's Restoration world is mostly rather glamorised and sterilised. The depictions of Barbara's wedding festivities, or of her performance as Diana in a ballet before the King, would seem utterly fantastic and luxurious to readers for whom both food and clothes were rationed. This type of historical novel became known, for good reason, as 'costume fiction' (just as the many film adaptations were known as costume melodramas), and King-Hall shows an expert knowledge of fashion, and a fascination for what her characters – both men and women – are wearing.

This focus on outward display, however, should not be taken as a mark of frivolity; it allows King-Hall to temper her escapism with gender politics. Historical fiction provided a 'safe space' for many writers, particularly women, to explore subjects that were taboo in any other context. The immorality of Barbara Skelton – robber, murderess, and adulterer – was shocking enough in its historical setting, but it was safely contained and distanced in the past. To explore such transgressive behaviour in a contemporary setting would have been difficult, almost unacceptable, for a woman writer; as Wallace puts it, 'the historical novel has allowed women writers a license which they have not been allowed in other forms'.[14] Barbara's rebellious, subversive exploits, her rejection of the pre-ordained path that a patriarchal society has laid out for her, had a vicarious appeal for women readers in particular.

Women in the 1940s were also testing the boundaries of their prescribed gender roles. The war had required many women to take on roles that had once been the preserve of men, to become factory workers or agricultural labourers – jobs that required them to dress like men, too, in trousers rather than elegant dresses. Moreover, as Maroula Joannou has suggested, '[t]he day-to-day disruption of their lives as well as the loss of their loved ones made it impossible for women to plan for the future and expedient to live for the moment. Many took sexual risks that they would not have done in more settled times…'.[15] For many women, extra-marital affairs were more conceivable and achievable during wartime than they had ever been before; but the end of the war led to a resurgence of conservative ideology, as men resumed their customary place in both the workplace and the household, and women were expected to return to their domestic confinement. The refusal of Barbara Skelton to toe this line is both a reflection of changing patterns of female behaviour during wartime; and, for readers after the war, a reminder of a type of freedom that has suddenly vanished. Barbara's sense of stifled frustration, if not her cold-hearted self-interest, would have struck a chord with many of her readers.

That such identification occurs between reader and protagonist is remarkable, given the litany of crimes she commits. Clearly, though, she is no conventional heroine, and the character of Barbara Skelton crystallises the fears and anxieties of conservative society about the consequences of affording women more freedom, particularly sexual freedom. One of the paradoxes of the war years, as Joannou notes, was that while the war effort meant that many established forms of gendered behaviour were broken down and reordered, 'the importance of beauty in lifting individual women's spirits and enhancing their self-esteem was heavily accentuated in advertising and in newspapers and magazines.'[16] Propaganda demanded that women should retain their 'womanliness' ("Keep your beauty on duty!", as an advert for Ivory soap put it) in order to protect not only their own morale, but that of their absent husbands, brothers and sons. However, though women were encouraged to continue making themselves beautiful (cosmetics were never rationed, though they were highly taxed), such propaganda tried to strike a balance, so that female beauty was presented as wholesome and domestic, rather than alluring.

In this context, it seems particularly significant that it is not only female clothing which is fetishized by the novel; in fact, it is the act of cross-dressing, of donning her 'suit of men's riding clothes, boots, hat, belt, pistols, all the cherished accoutrements' of Barbara's alter-ego, which give her the greatest thrill, for these have become 'the symbol of her partial emancipation from the dragging reality of life'. In a memorable moment, Barbara gazes adoringly at herself as she puts on her highwayman's outfit:

> With the impatient but deft movements characteristic of her, she stripped off her Indian gown and silk nightrail, smiling down at her beautiful naked body, before clothing herself in her man's attire. When she was ready, the long heavy boots pulled on, the over-large belt girded round her elegant waist, her wide-brimmed hat set jauntily on her head, she sat down at the table and gazed at herself in the mirror.
>
> She loved her face in all its moods, but never better than in this strange, bizarre aspect; the green eyes wide and wild with excitement, the curious nostrils poised – you might almost say! – for flight. Her face looked back at her, daring her to bold and dangerous deeds, and it was then that she resolved to try her luck on Watling Street. (p. 122)

What is striking about this passage is that it manages to eroticise Barbara without objectifying her; the gaze which admires her naked body is her own, and conveys her self-sufficiency and independence. She does not need the approbation of a man to enjoy the possession of her own body. Barbara's beauty, here and throughout the novel, is marked by an oddness – her unsettling feline gaze, her quirky, flaring nostrils – which problematizes stereotypical associations of femininity with submission and weakness. These features have an uncanny quality which attracts and repulses simultaneously; they are contrasted quite markedly with the more conventional prettiness of her hated cousin, Henrietta Kingsclere. Even when Barbara does take a lover, the highwayman Jerry Jackson, she retains control. Barbara's appraising eye evaluates Jackson for his physical appearance much as a woman would normally be measured: 'a handsome enough, lively-looking man' with 'all the self-complacency of the fine male animal in his expression' (p. 133). Later, as Jackson tears open her coat to reveal 'her lovely woman's body to his ravished gaze', King-Hall's phrasing empowers Barbara (p. 136). *She* is not being ravished; rather, it is Jackson's helpless gaze which is victimized by her powerful sexuality. And it is Barbara who sets the rules for the conduct of their affair, insisting on Jackson's local fidelity to her, and punishing him mercilessly for what she perceives to be his betrayal, in an inversion of typical patriarchal paranoia about female sexual incontinence. For all of her narcissism and self-interest, then, I would argue that it is Barbara's willingness to embrace and relish her sexual power that lies at the heart of her – and hence the novel's – appeal.

King-Hall's depiction of the institution of marriage, by contrast, is strikingly critical. From the first, Barbara has a very pragmatic, unromantic sense of marriage: shortly before her wedding, we are told that she regarded it as 'a means of escape from the trammels of maidenhood – the only means open to a young woman of quality' (p. 79). But that dream of escape quickly evaporates, and Barbara finds that, in fact, marriage is profoundly constraining rather than liberating. Even at the moment of her union with Sir Ralph, 'something wild and innocent in Barbara cried out in panic, "No, this can never be my fate! Escape before it is too late!"' (p. 84).

King-Hall depicts the oppressive patriarchal system within which Barbara is trapped with bleak irony, noting, for instance, during the wedding ceremony that 'The bride, being the weaker vessel, naturally came in for the larger slice of Mr Belcher's advice' (p. 84). Barbara's wedding night foreshadows her fate, and it is made fairly clear that, for all the flaws in her personality, she is also a victim, and her downfall has a certain inevitability to it. She stands 'like a forlorn and resentful ghost' (p. 90) as she waits to enter her marriage bed, and she feels as though her bridesmaids are preparing her for her execution rather than the consummation of her marriage. The crushing disappointment and inadequacy of her sexual relationship with her husband are conveyed in the restrained but withering line, 'She submitted to Sir Ralph but did not enjoy him' (p. 92). This inadequacy results in the shocking declaration that after five years of tedious married life, Barbara 'would have welcomed the distraction of a lover' (p. 99). King-Hall is careful to frame this more as a desire for interest and stimulation than as a calculating decision to betray her husband. It is the featureless boredom of married life, and the limited prospects available for an intelligent, energetic woman, which are really being critiqued here: 'Inside herself she led an intense impatient life, all her thoughts concentrated on her own personality, and always watchful to seize the opportunity for self-expression that must surely come to her before long' (p. 101). The expected life of a genteel lady offers her no such opportunities, making it inevitable that she must transgress that role.

The prospect of women continuing to exercise their sexuality outside of marriage was a source of paranoia for many men, perhaps with good cause; and in mainstream discourse such behaviour was characterised not only as immoral, but also unpatriotic. In this context, perhaps, the story of Barbara Skelton acts as a reassurance and a warning – that women who indulge their desires and refuse to conform to their expected role will be punished, by fate if not by the legal system. However, the novel's later chapters, in which Barbara falls in love with Kit Locksby, the fiancé of her sister-in-law Paulina, are arguably the least convincing and least interesting section of the novel. After seducing him almost instantly, her sudden, overwhelming need to reform in order to make her lover happy seems forced, and the ending rushed. King-Hall was constrained by the inherited 'plot' of the legend, of course, which required Barbara's death; but the attempt to generate extra pathos – by having her resolve to submit herself to male control shortly before she dies – falls rather flat. It seems to me, then, that the moralistic message articulated in the closing chapters fails to dislodge the much more potent image of a woman who relishes the freedom and power afforded to her by her cross-dressing disguise, and the indulgence of her desires.

For a novel which has, until now, been largely forgotten, *Life and Death of the Wicked Lady Skelton* can lay claim to a significant cultural legacy. It was one of a number of popular and influential historical novels written by – and largely for – women in the 1940s, providing a crucial imaginative outlet for their hopes, fears and desires. Diana Wallace has noted that many women writers and critics who grew up in the post-war era 'have attested to the importance of women's popular historical novels in their emotional, intellectual and literary development', so that, she suggests, 'it is perhaps not too far-fetched to argue that the roots of second-wave feminism itself can be found [...] in the popular historical fiction read by these women'.[17] Many of these texts were adapted into equally popular films, and if people think of the costume melodrama today, they are most likely to remember *The Wicked Lady*, which in many ways was the high point of the genre which it came to define.[18] Finally, it seems likely that the success of the novel and the film effectively reanimated the original legend, imbuing it with a cultural energy which has ensured its survival. In 1907, W.B. Gerish, an antiquarian and folklorist, visited Markyate in pursuit of the legend, but noted that in the last forty years 'the believers in the apparition have nearly all passed away'.[19] It is perhaps not too fanciful to suggest that without King-Hall's intervention, the ghost of Katherine Ferrers might have finally rested in peace. We should be grateful that, fired with the rebellious spirit of the green-eyed Barbara Skelton, she seems destined to ride the highways of Hertfordshire for a little longer yet.

Rowland Hughes

AUTHOR'S NOTE

MY GRATEFUL ACKNOWLEDGMENTS are due to Miss Christina Hole's book, *Haunted England* (Messrs B.T. Batsford, Ltd.), which records that there was once a seventeenth-century lady of quality who took to the Road, and subsequently haunted the family mansion.

To that extent this novel is founded on tradition, but the adventures and crimes of Lady Skelton are fictitious, and my apologies are due to her prototype the Wicked Lady Ferrers for the liberties taken in this book.

M. K.-H.

To Jock and Phoebe
With my love

FINIS?

AT MIDNIGHT ON April 3rd 1942, a Nazi bomber, seeking to escape from the just vengeance of our night fighters, unloaded its bombs on the peaceful Buckinghamshire parish of Maiden Worthy. One of the bombs fell on the village of that name, destroying a row of cottages and burying several families beneath the ruins. Another made a harmless crater in a field. Yet another hit the ancient manor house of Maryiot Cells.

The house was so deep among the trees, lying furthermore in a hollow, that it was some twenty minutes before a reddish glow warned the villagers that it was on fire. Soon antlers of flame trembled against the sky; sparks shot upwards; the place was ablaze. By morning the house was a smoking, blackened shell.

Maryiot Cells was unoccupied by any human tenant. Its owner, Sir Hugh Skelton, had closed it some years before the outbreak of war. It had been requisitioned during that past winter as a convalescent home for A.T.S. girls[1] but, for some reason or other, perhaps because of its lack of modern amenities, and its notoriously clammy coldness, it was soon empty and shuttered again.

What more natural than that the villagers, occupied as they were on that disastrous night with the task of rescuing the living, searching for the dead, succouring the wounded and comforting the bereaved, should have no time and little thought to spare for Maryiot Cells?

Yet Maryiot Cells had been the dominant house of the locality since the Middle Ages, first as monastery, later as manor house. Even in times of war, when human lives are poured out like water on the ground, the destruction of buildings, hallowed and made lovelier by time, is mourned with an acute and personal sense of loss.

Not so with Maryiot Cells. A stranger, knowing nothing of the house and its history, would have noticed a singular lack of regret among the country people, though few of them were as explicit as the landlord of the Red Lion, who declared that 'those Nazi —s did one good job, anyhow, when they put a finish to that house.'

But tradition dies hard in England. Once recovered from the shock of the bombing, the local people paid Maryiot Cells a tribute which doubtless would have been more acceptable to the begetter of its uneasy reputation than any sentimental lamentations.

There was a vigorous revival of the rumour, which had already been the talk of the neighbourhood, to the effect that the A.T.S. girls (stalwart and intrepid young women though they were) had flatly refused to convalesce in a house where the sound of slow dragging footsteps could be heard across the floors, and lights seen in the windows of unoccupied rooms; where mysterious rappings, sighs and whisperings disturbed the stillness of the night hours.

More than that, there are several reputable people, in the neighbouring village of Abbots Worthy, who are ready to state on oath that passing by the short cut across the beech avenue of Maryiot Cells (a midnight walk that would have been favoured by few in normal times, but these were A.R.P. workers[2] and hurrying to their duties), they heard the thud of a horse's hooves galloping down the avenue, approaching nearer and nearer to them, passing so close that they sprang back alarmed into the ditch, receding into the distance and into silence – and not a horse nor rider to be seen.

Something of this kind was to be expected, whichever way you look at it. 'Suggestion – aural illusion – collective hallucination' (nourished by centuries of local legend and superstition) – the arguments are familiar.

On the other hand, how typical of the insensate egotism of Barbara Skelton, dead and buried these two hundred and sixty years, to thrust her fading entity into that night of twentieth-century horror and woe.

The crimes that earned her the title of 'The Wicked Lady Skelton' seem those of a dilettante beside the vast, organised evil of the Nazis, the impersonal but deadly malevolence of a German bomber. Has this greater violence by destroying Maryiot Cells, her earthly habitation, brought release to her distracted spirit, or will her form still appear at the gaping windows of the ruined house, with no audience but owls and foxes, her spectre horse still gallop down the overgrown and deserted glades?

It is too soon to say. Meanwhile there may be some interest, if not edification, in casting a backward glance through time at some of her better authenticated manifestations, till Barbara Skelton the living woman herself and her misdeeds shall be revealed.

PART I

THROUGH A GLASS, DARKLY[1]

'I would therefore willingly know if you are of the opinion that phantoms are real figures…or are empty vain shadows raised in our imaginations by the effect of fear?'

Pliny the Younger: Concerning Phantoms[2]

1

LADY SKELTON AT HOME

'The thin habit of spirits.'[1]

IT WAS BEAUTIFUL weather that day, August 1911, for Lady Skelton's garden fête at Maryiot Cells in aid of the Umweulu Mission Fund. This was almost to be expected. Lady Skelton was so efficient. One might fancifully imagine that she had ordered the fine day from the Clerk of the Weather at the same time that she had ordered the ices, the marquee and the band.

Few people, in staid fact, came in contact with Lady Skelton without paying her some tribute of intimidation or respect. Her more flippant neighbours had nicknamed her 'Boadicea' and there was something reminiscent of the warrior queen about her monumental but comely person, her imposing nose and firmly modelled chin, and her head of hair which, in her late thirties, was still blonde and abundant, though a trifle faded. But one imagines that Boadicea lacked Lady Skelton's formidable graciousness; the Iceni were probably more fractious than the villagers of Maiden Worthy, the Romans less amenable than Lady Skelton's county neighbours. There was no need for Maud Skelton to career about in a chariot with wildly streaming hair. She had only to smile, to suggest, to command. She got her own way every time.

How fortunate for the Umweulu Mission and the young African convert whose education was the special charge of the parish of Maiden Worthy, that Lady Skelton had decided to take their affairs in hand.

There had been signs of late that the interest of the parishioners in their African protégé was flagging. This was not altogether surprising, as they had been subscribing to his upbringing for some forty years. Presumably he had grown up by now and entered into his labours, other dusky young converts taking his place; but this had never been clearly explained to his benefactors, with the result that he (or rather they) had in the minds of the parishioners assumed the guise of an African Peter Pan, who would have to be sustained to the end of the ages by annual bazaars and parish teas.

The old rector, Mr Chambers, had very wisely cast his worries, spiritual and financial, on this score at Lady Skelton's feet, and she had promised her assistance, a promise of which this garden fête was the fulfilment.

Lady Skelton never did things by halves – she was not built that way – and this fête was one that would be remembered for some time in the neighbourhood. The locals – hot and respectful in their Sunday best – were to be admitted to the park, the yew glades and the kitchen garden for the sum of one shilling. There was to be lemonade, ginger beer and bath buns for their refreshment; for their entertainment, a Punch and Judy show, the band, skittles, bowls, a fortune teller's tent (with the rector's sister Miss Chambers disguised as a gipsy) and a regatta on the river.

The 'county', before driving up the long beech avenue in their carriages and pony traps, or snorting up it in their motor cars, would pay the entrance fee too. There was a kind of piquant absurdity in handing their shillings to old Hatch the lodge keeper, who had so often touched his hat to them when they had arrived for house parties and shoots.

'Good day, me lady. Good day, Sir Thomas.'

'Fine day for her ladyship's fête, Hatch.'

'Yes, indeed, sir.'

But, once arrived at the house, they could have a chat with Arthur and Maud, smoke one of Arthur's excellent cigars, or be taken up to Maud's bedroom to titivate (according to sex), and generally collect themselves before emerging into the hot August sunshine to listen to the Bishop's opening speech.

For them, and for the lesser lights of the county – old, rather mad Miss Moffat, who dressed like a scarecrow and yet maintained an unmistakable air of withered gentility, genial Doctor Wilson and his wife and three bouncing daughters, Colonel and Mrs McRoberts, old Mrs Horley, the late rector's widow, and the like – there was tea and ices and sugared cakes in the marquee, and the run of the rose garden and the picture gallery. Lady Skelton had secured for her fête the presence of two distinguished though very different visitors, the Bishop of Chiltern and Lady Ansborough, Lord Ansborough's young and lovely bride. The Bishop could be relied upon to give a suavely sacerdotal air to any gathering, while Lady Ansborough, however much one might disapprove of her fantastic hats, hobble skirts[2] and general air of frivolity, would certainly give it the stamp of fashion. Thus everything seemed propitious, set on the smooth and successful course that

Lady Skelton's projects invariably took. The first intimation that anything out of the usual might disturb events occurred at midday, before the guests had arrived or the fête itself had begun.

Lady Skelton's three children, Gwendolen, Joyce and Hugh, in charge of their governess Miss Parsons, had been dispatched by their mother on one of those errands with which the children of county families are only too familiar.

First they were to go to the farm with a message to the dairy maid that Mrs Wheeler, the cook, would require three more pints of cream. Then, circling round the demesne, they were to call in at the Rectory and remind old Mr Chambers, who was notoriously absent-minded, and at the moment was submerged reams deep in his treatise of *Ancient English Chalices,* that the fête was to be opened by the Bishop at 2.30 sharp today. Up the beech avenue and home in time for luncheon. Such was the programme outlined for the Skelton children by their indefatigable mother, and which they accepted with dutiful resignation. After all, there was always the chance that Mr Chambers, who was fond of children in an abstracted way, would regale them with *petit beurre* biscuits or ginger-snaps.

The little party set off across the lawn which sloped down to the smoothly flowing and murmurous river, crossed the narrow stone bridge (Hugh pausing as usual to throw a stone into the water) and straggled along one of the yew glades. Gwendolen and Joyce – thin, lanky children of twelve and ten years old, in their white *broderie anglaise* frocks, their long legs in black stockings, their long straight hair well brushed under their straw hats trimmed with wreaths of summer flowers. Hugh, aged five and a half, his sturdy little figure in a white piqué suit with a lace collar, a large straw hat set well back on his head, framing his round, obstinate face and kitten-eyes. Miss Parsons, who wore a grey flannel coat and skirt and a straw boater, carried a basket for the cream. Her red tie was fastened with a brooch in the form of a dog's head, and her pince-nez snapped back in a very fascinating way into its case which was pinned on to her bosom. The yew walks, or rides – for they were wide enough to justify the larger name – were a notable feature of the demesne. Six in number and each about a quarter of a mile in length, they converged on to a clearing adorned with a carved urn on a pedestal, the significance of which, if it had any beyond that of mere decoration, was the subject of various local legends but was, in fact, not known to this generation of Skeltons. The high walls of clipped yew were backed by closely growing beech and ash trees, so that even on the brightest day these sylvan paths had a feeling of almost aqueous coolness and remoteness.

The yew glade, facing the bridge, into which the Skelton children and their governess entered, was certainly quite startlingly cool and dim after the August midday glare. Overhead the light filtered uncertainly through the branches; the grass was mossy and damp underfoot.

This much may be conceded, but by no stretch of the imagination could the yew glade have been described as cold on such a very hot day. When, therefore, Hugh began complaining of the cold as soon as they had entered the glade, Miss Parsons, who knew that her youngest charge had an excellent circulation, replied with a kindly but firm,

'Nonsense, dear. It's very pleasant to get out of the sun for a while.'

Hugh's sisters jeered, 'If you're cold, why not run, Podge?' As was to be expected their gibe had the effect of slowing down their young brother's pace almost to a standstill.

Though he could move with lightning speed when engaged on his own errands, Hugh had brought dawdling to a fine art. Adjurations of 'Come on Hugh!' 'Walk up dear.' 'Hurry up slowcoach!' invariably punctuated these schoolroom walks.

It was no surprise, then, to Miss Parsons or the girls to find, on turning round, when they reached the juncture of the glades where the carved urn stood in sunlight, that Hugh was still some way down the shady green tunnel from which they had just emerged. There was nothing odd in this, but there was something odd in his behaviour. Instead of ambling along with his usual bland and determined slowness, he was stopping constantly to turn and stare back down the yew glade, then breaking into a quick jog that seemed to betoken some unusual excitement. When he had reached the end of the glade, he gave one quick look over his shoulder, galloped towards Miss Parsons, his hat falling off as he came, threw his arm round her petersham belt and pressed his chubby face against her stomach.

Hugh was an undemonstrative child as a rule. Miss Parsons, though secretly a little flattered, was surprised.

'Why Hughie, whatever is the matter?'

Hugh, his face flushed, replied shortly, 'Nuffin.'

'Well, then, pick up your hat and come along, or we shall never get all our little jobs done before luncheon.'

It was not till they had left the clearing and had again entered the sombre walls of yew that Hugh announced:

'Somebody's coming after us.'

Miss Parsons glanced back. 'No dear, I don't see anyone.'

'I did,' said Hugh. 'I kept seeing somebody.'

'What sort of a person? A man or a woman?' asked Joyce.

'I don't know,' said Hugh. 'Like both, I fink.'

'Well, there is no one in sight,' said Miss Parsons briskly, peering dubiously across the dazzle of the clearing to the dimness of the glade by which they had come. 'So I expect you were day-dreaming, dear.'

'No, I saw somebody,' Hugh said stoutly. 'It was there and then it wasn't there. It was coming this way. I fink it's still coming.'

Miss Parsons felt a curious sensation in the region of her spine, as though someone had lightly run an icicle down it.

She was, of course, aware of Maryiot Cells' dubious reputation. Everyone in the neighbourhood *knew,* and most people were eager to tell. But Lady Skelton did not encourage speculation or tittle-tattle on the subject. Paranormal activity had no place in Lady Skelton's well-regulated life. She had made the interior of Maryiot Cells almost cheerful with chintzes and hot-house flowers and signed photographs of royalty in silver frames.

Unaccountable noises were firmly attributed to mice and hot-water pipes. Nervous young maidservants were severely snubbed by their seniors when they tried to recount creepy experiences. One or two who would not be silenced (such as the Irish scullery maid who insisted that she heard 'a smart foot-step travelling through the house') were given a month's wages and dismissed. Yes, it must be admitted that Lady Skelton had the supernatural well in hand.

Miss Parsons knew that it would be as much as her post was worth to speak of such things to her charges. She saw that the two girls were staring at their little brother with eyes widened by curiosity. Questions that had better remain unasked trembled on their parted lips.

Miss Parsons said resolutely, and with a touch of severity, 'Now dear, no more of that. You must not say things that are not true, even in fun.'

This was unfair, and Miss Parsons knew it. Hugh, who accepted the aspersion on his probity with the extraordinary resignation of childhood, was a singularly truthful and rather unimaginative child. But the situation had to be reined in somehow.

Miss Parsons added cheerily, 'Let's see which of us can reach the end of the glade first. Walking as fast as we like, but no running.'

No, it would never do to run. That would be too suggestive of panic, of flight from the indescribable something that Hugh's infant eyes had discerned moving along in the shades behind them.

Placing a hand behind Hugh's lace collar, she propelled him vigorously forward. It would never do if he turned round and began staring again. Miss Parsons had not realised before quite how still and dim it was in these yew glades. Six of them. Too many, too long, and too old. It occurred to her that there was something slightly morbid in an enthusiasm for topiary-work indulged in to excess. It was quite a relief to emerge again into the hot sunshine. It greeted them like a friendly tap on the face.

Miss Parsons felt Hugh's forehead. It was cool. She thought, 'Perhaps a little dose at bedtime.'

It was as gratifying to Lady Skelton, as it would have been bewildering to the young African at Umweulu, for whose benefit this fête at Maryiot Cells had been organised, to see the substantial crowd that had assembled on the lawn to listen to the Bishop's opening speech.

The setting was ideal – the sombre but picturesque background of the old house itself with its bayed windows, its turrets and its tall multitudinous chimneys; the brightly filled flower beds on the terrace, shaped in crescents and stars like floral jewels; the shady, well-kept lawn sloping down at the side and back of the house to the glossy, softly singing river; the old stone bridge and, across the bridge, the yew glades.

On the lawn to the side of the house, just below the terrace, a small platform had been erected, draped in red bunting and a rather puzzling collection of national flags, for the accommodation of the Bishop and his wife, the rector Mr Chambers, Sir Arthur and Lady Skelton, Lady Ansborough and a few other notables. A tumbler and a carafe of water on the table suggested that some test of endurance on the part of both the speaker and the audience might be looked for.

There were several rows of chairs in front of the platform for those who, without being immediately concerned in the opening ceremony, were too important or too elderly to stand. The rest of the audience, county, country town and village, clustered round the platform and flowed out across the lawn.

On all sides there were parasols, large hats with flowers and feathers, white spotted veils, top hats, grey homburg hats, straw boaters and white panamas, black Sunday suits, girls in muslin frocks, boys in knickerbockers, and old ladies defying the heat in feather boas.

The buzzing voice of the crowd, its aimless, fluid movement, was stilled in sudden expectancy as Lady Skelton sailed on to the platform in full heliotrope rig, followed by the Bishop of Chiltern and the other guests.

With a surprising air of decision the rector, vague old Mr Chambers, stepped forward and, imposing silence with a raised hand, invoked a blessing on the proceedings, the Bishop listening with bent head and closed eyes and the air of paying due tribute to spiritual etiquette.

Mr Chambers's moment was soon over. Lady Skelton swam to the fore and, surveying friends, acquaintances, tenants and strangers with a gracious smile, proceeded to address them in the masterful tones of one who had spoken at countless bazaars, parish teas and committee meetings.

It was so delightful, she said, to see so many happy faces here today, and to feel that so many friends, known and unknown, had rallied loyally round her to make this fête a real success. They all knew that the Umweulu Mission was Maiden Worthy's own special mission. It was very wonderful to feel that for forty years the good, dear people of Maiden Worthy parish (she paused) . . . . Nor must she forget the kind parishioners of Little Worthy who, in conjunction with their big sister parish, also contributed towards the Umweulu Fund. Well, it was very wonderful and inspiring to feel that for forty years they had been supporting this splendid work and helping to maintain and educate a young African lad of the Umweulu tribe. How they all wished that they could be transported to Umweulu and see for themselves the good work going on amid the dense African jungle with its lions and crocodiles and other marvels of nature. She was sure that then they would realise what a really *worthwhile* work it was. As it was they must be content with Maryiot Cells, and the very warm welcome – not quite tropical, but very warm for all that! (Laughter) – which she and Sir Arthur extended to them one and all. Now she knew that they had not come here to listen to her (polite murmurs of dissent from those on and around the platform) so she would, without further ado, invite his Grace, the Lord Bishop of Chiltern, to address them.

The applause which greeted the close of her speech drowned a savage growl from Colonel McRoberts, 'Confounded nonsense, in my opinion, all this business of trying to turn niggers into Christians. All that happens is that they drink your whisky and steal your best pair of riding boots like that rascal of a Ujojo boy that I had out in Kulanga in '82.'[3]

But before he could enlarge further on his African experiences to his neighbours, there was another outburst of applause as the Bishop rose to speak.

With his imposing height, silvery hair, ascetic but benign features and rich voice, he looked so exactly all that a

Bishop ought to be that it would have been difficult to have mistaken him for anything else even without his gaiters. He was justly famed for his eloquence, and his listeners, agreeably conscious that they were combining something of the spiritual benefits of a service at the Cathedral with the mundane entertainment of a garden fête, settled down to give him their full attention.

He began by addressing them in light, even whimsical vein, getting up speed, in a manner of speaking, before soaring towards sublimer things. He had been speaking for about seven minutes and a half, and had begun, with the dove-like gentleness and serpent-like cunning enjoined by Scripture, to introduce a more serious note into his speech, when it seemed to him that a sudden change had come over the day. It was not only that a passing cloud had obscured the sun, as often happens on the finest summer day, giving a somewhat livid appearance to the verdant lawn and the people collected on it, but surely there was a sudden and noticeable drop in the temperature too?

The Bishop felt extraordinarily chilly. His hands, with the fingers lightly interlocked across his apron, as was his wont when speaking on a platform, had become stone cold. He was conscious of an odd sensation of 'pins and needles' all over his body.

Perturbed as he was – for he believed that he had suddenly been taken ill and, like most active and conscientious persons, he had a dread of illness – his words continued to flow out with the smoothness of the accomplished orator. He was speaking of service and fellowship, was actually saying the words, 'We cannot live unto ourselves alone,' when he saw the figure standing under the beech tree.

It was the figure of a woman – of that he had no doubt, for though its attire was masculine, with long skirted coat and breeches and broad-brimmed hat, there was a distinctly feminine appearance about the face and form.

Moreover, this person who stood there with closed eyes was a young woman. 'Beautiful and well favoured' were the words that came into the Bishop's numbed mind, but it was not a beauty that would commend itself to a Bishop, nor, for that matter, to any God-fearing man. The expression on the face was malign, predatory, doleful, and altogether most disquieting.

The archaic costume might have suggested someone decked out in fancy dress for the occasion of the fête, but no such comforting supposition came to the Bishop's aid. Something undefinable in the figure's looks and demeanour assured him with horrid certainty that this was no human being that he gazed upon, but an apparition. Rigid with fear, it seemed to him that he was enclosed with this unhallowed thing in a sphere apart – a sphere of icy coldness and a menacing stillness. The people on the platform beside him, the upturned faces beneath him, had receded from reality, were as meaningless as images painted upon glass. Enclosed together, and yet – final horror! – she was unaware of him, wrapt in some state of being beyond human comprehension.

Shutting his eyes, the Bishop clutched at a prayer. The wave of terror subsided, leaving him faint and sweating. He became aware of his own faltering voice, his wife looking at him in anxiety. He cleared his throat, poured himself out a glass of water with a shaking hand. In the moment's respite which this action gave him, he glanced leftwards towards the river.

Upon the narrow stone bridge was a figure on a horse – the same figure which but a few seconds ago had stood upon his right hand some fifty feet distant under the beech tree.

The glass of water dropped from the Bishop's hand. He staggered and collapsed on to his chair.

They said it was the heat. They said it was his heart. They said it was overwork. The Bishop himself said very little, apologising to his host and hostess for the trouble that he was causing them, begging that the fête might proceed as though nothing had happened, and – when he was lying down in Sir Arthur's shaded dressing room – murmuring to his wife:

'My dear, pray do not question me at present, but I should like to leave this house as soon as possible.'

Both the prelate and the child had been vouchsafed a glimpse of the unseen, and, in consequence, had suffered some emotional disturbance. The gross unfairness of life must be a continual source of distress to the sensitive-minded. They gave the Bishop a tot of Sir Arthur's Napoleonic brandy, but little Hugh got Gregory's Powder.[4]

2

THE RETICENCE OF MISS ISABELLA SKELTON

'Evil thing that walks by night.'[1]

As far as can be ascertained, the following experience was the only really startling one that occurred in Miss Isabella Skelton's placid and blameless life. There may have been others – though hardly, one imagines, of a like nature – but if so, there is no record of them either in the known facts of her life or in family traditions or journals.

Born in 1855, the youngest but one of the six daughters of Sir Wilfred and Lady Skelton, Isabella's existence pursued the sheltered course which might have been expected from the circumstances of her class, period and virginity.

Her childhood in the large and well-filled nurseries of Maryiot Cells was a cosy one. It could hardly have been otherwise with Nanny Callaghan, stout, comfortable, yet somehow superb, in her cap with streamers and her voluminous white apron, as their presiding genius. Nanny Callaghan was never flustered, never at a loss. To see her sitting before the fire in her rocking-chair you would suppose her nearly immovable, or at the least slow-moving. But let some nursery crisis occur – Miss Florence bellowing from the cupboard into which she had been bolted by her angel-faced toddler sister Miss Lucy, Miss Charlotte shrieking at having thrust a marble up her nose, the adenoidal nurserymaid dropping a kettle of scalding water over her foot – and Nanny Callaghan was all speed and commanding movement.

She had a store of sagacious maxims which her charges accepted as hardly less sacred than scripture:

'A sad child is a sick child.'

'It is good to be helped.'

'Of saving cometh having.'

'With patience and perseverance you can drive a snail to Jerusalem.'

Nanny's sayings, the high, polished fire-grate, muffins for tea, the battered rocking-horse, the dolls' house, syrup roly-poly on winter Sundays, roast chestnuts and apples for Hallowe'en, a cuckoo clock which Aunt Bessie had brought back from Switzerland – these and innumerable other trifles were woven together to form a nursery pattern of rich security and happiness for Isabella and her sisters.

Living in the same house, but in a world somewhat apart, there was Papa and Mama, Papa with his beautiful side-whiskers, cravats and frock-coats – a magnificent being to be revered, a little feared but nevertheless adored. Ecstatic moment when he took Isabella on his knee at dessert and, smoothing out her frilled muslin frock and her silk sash, fed her with cherries. Or (there was a meet on the lawn at Maryiot Cells) bent down from his chestnut horse in all the splendour of his scarlet coat and white buckskin breeches, and lifted her on to the saddle.

Dear Mama suffered from delicate health. She spent a good deal of her time lying on a sofa. From their earliest years it was impressed on Isabella and her sisters that they must not make too much noise on their visits to the drawing-room because of 'poor Mama's head'.

A photograph of that same head (crowned with a luxuriant coil of hair) shows that Lady Skelton had the expression of a fretful if inoffensive sheep, but Isabella never noticed this. To Isabella her mother was something precious and fragile that might be snatched from the family circle at a moment's notice by singing angels. Nor did the fact that Lady Skelton lived to the age of eighty-five greatly alter her daughter's conception of her.

Childhood passed into girlhood. Nanny Callaghan was painlessly superseded by governesses and retired into the housekeeper's room, from whence she ruled, nursed, bullied and comforted the household. There was the mild discipline of lessons, good works, and 'good' books, regular church services, sacred music on Sunday evenings, sketching and pianoforte lessons, relieved by picnics, skating, charades, drives in the brougham and games of croquet.

The evening came when Isabella wore her first ball dress of white satin trimmed with Valenciennes lace,[2] and long white kid gloves, and attended her first grown-up ball. There is no reason to suppose that she was not a success either then or on her subsequent appearances in society, and her continued celibacy was certainly dictated by her own choice. It is known that she had several suitable 'offers' and, though by no means a beauty, there were elderly gentlemen, in later years, who were ready to assure the younger generation that 'though your aunt Blanche was the handsome one of the family, your aunt Bella was a very pleasant-looking girl.'

If some secret unsatisfied fancy, some frustrated romance, nipped like a belated November rosebud before it came to full blossom, prevented Isabella from fulfilling her woman's destiny, it must have been a mild and fugitive one, for there is no evidence that it impaired her contentment or her spirits to any marked degree. When girlhood was left behind and all her sisters married, she settled down cheerfully to the role of what Lady Skelton described as 'our home bird'. She was her father's companion, her mother's right hand, and so active in parish affairs that the rector used to declare that she was worth two curates to him.

When her father's and, years later, her mother's deaths left Isabella to face middle-age alone, she was neither idle nor lonely. She lived on in the small dower house with a devoted maid. Her life was filled with good works, gardening, and the interests of her large band of nephews and nieces and, later, their children (her drawing-room was so thick with family photographs that there was hardly room to put down a cup of tea). She made one or two trips to Switzerland and the Italian lakes with a friend, another maiden lady, enjoyed herself, admired and sketched the scenery, but was glad to get back to Maiden Worthy where everyone spoke English.

Every Sunday, wet or fine, her neat little black-clad figure, growing more bent as the years went on, could be seen trotting, umbrella in hand, up the avenue of Maryiot Cells, for it was an understood thing that she always took tea on Sunday afternoons with her cousin Arthur and his wife.

When she died in her sleep in her late seventies, she was sincerely mourned, by her relations and regretted by the village people. During her lifetime some of the more recalcitrant parishioners, habitual drunkards, faithless wives, unmarried mothers and the like, had resented her gentle but persistent interference in their affairs (she had a supply of text cards, decorated with lilies, violets and other devout-looking flowers which, in her opinion at least, were effective weapons against every form of spiritual wickedness that might flourish in the parish). But when she was gone, these irritations were forgotten in appreciation of her many acts of benevolence.

A placid colourless life, one would say, and a placid colourless personality. True, yet Isabella Skelton's reaction to the one extraordinary and alarming thing that happened to her, indicates that her conventional, timid nature possessed reserves of self-control that would have stood her in good stead in grimmer times.

It happened in 1873, and at a time when Maryiot Cells had so many people packed under its roof that not a single bed, far less bedroom, was unoccupied. The occasion was the marriage of Sir Wilfrid's and Lady Skelton's eldest daughter Blanche. The bridegroom was a young Irishman, William Allen of Castle Allen and his widowed mother, and his numerous sisters and younger brothers had been invited to stay at Maryiot Cells for the ceremony, only Mr William Allen himself being obliged, by a curious convention that supposed that the most temperate bridegroom's desires would prove too much for him on the wedding eve, to put up at a neighbouring country house.

Consequently even the rabbit warren of attics at Maryiot Cells was occupied by a bevy of young and giggling Miss Skeltons and Miss Allens, and by schoolboy cousins who tormented the young ladies by making them apple-pie beds,[3] or, invading their maiden privacy in whooping gangs, tying them together by their stay-laces.

The young men of the party were accommodated in the rooms over the stables where the under-footmen, grooms and pantry boys usually slept. Where these underlings had been banished it would be as well perhaps not to enquire.

The match was a most propitious one. Blanche was a good and beautiful girl, while William Allen did not appear any less amiable or personable for being one of the largest landowners in the North of Ireland. Even Aunt Lizzie could find no sourer criticism to offer than to remark that she doubted if 'poor William would make old bones'.

The atmosphere of the house-party was redolent of goodwill, coy, innocuous little jokes about matrimony, and vicarious excitement. The tenants of Maryiot Cells presented the young couple with an illuminated address[4] and a Sheffield plate dinner service which included a venison dish suggestive in shape and size of a baby's bath.

Judging from the family album of this date, a heavy leather volume with brass clasps, the photographer of the local town must have reaped a rich harvest from this notable family gathering. It seems likely that he was summoned, camera, black velvet cloth and all, to Maryiot Cells, for it is hardly probable that the Skelton (to say nothing of the Allen) clan – from the Dowager Lady Skelton, a frail wistful figure with her lace cap, white corkscrew curls and black and white striped dress, to little Arthur Skelton (who in default of a direct male heir was to succeed to his uncle Wilfrid's title and estates) in his muslin dress with tartan shoulder knots and sash – could have undertaken the trip into the county town.

At any rate, thanks to the photographer's labours, it is possible to have a clear idea of the family party, collectively as well as individually.

There is, of course, the group of groups, taken on the wedding day. There are what the French unkindly describe as 'déplorables groupes de famille', seated on the terrace steps or clustered round the front door – Father in shepherd's plaid trousers and dark jacket, Mother in a bustled, beruffled walking-dress, their offspring in braided clothes, striped stockings and buttoned boots. All of them wearing hats that appear to modern eyes to be too small for their heads. There are the bachelor groups – young men wearing foulard cravats and a mildly rakish air, seated with their arms on the backs of chairs. Mother and child groups, with younger matrons propping up limp-looking infants in décolleté frocks. There are schoolboys whose pugnacious expressions are set off rather than disguised by their turned-down collars and somewhat long hair. There are small consequential girls with long ringlets and tiny pork-pie hats...

To identify them all would be tedious and difficult, perhaps – at this date – impossible, for, with a touching belief in the permanency of their memories and of the golden security of family and class which enwrapped them, no names have been written beneath the photographs. But the resolutely good-looking young man in hunting kit, with side-whiskers and an impeccable profile, is almost certainly Desmond Allen, younger brother of the bridegroom who, if family tradition is to be credited, won more than a small part of Isabella's heart (he died three years later of consumption).

There is Isabella herself. She is wearing a dark dress with ruffles at the throat and wrist, and is seated at a table gazing down pensively at a very artificial-looking rose which she holds in her hand. She has a round, childishly earnest face and smooth, demurely parted hair. Thus she must have looked, only with the addition, no doubt, of a little round hat or small bonnet and a jacket, when she set off for that evening stroll which was to bring her so shocking an experience.

It was the eve of her sister's wedding day. All that day, and for many days previously, Isabella had been assisting with the multifarious preparations which a wedding entails – answering letters for Mama, unpacking and making lists of wedding presents, helping to amuse the children of the party, attending to the comfort of the older ladies, training the village choir in the nuptial hymns, making white satin favours for the gentlemen, helping fellow bridesmaids to try on wreaths, cutting out frills for the candlesticks, walking down to the garden with a message to the gardener about the white chrysanthemums. Whenever anything needed doing, a cry went up of 'Where is Isabella?', and Isabella, whom one of her aunts truly described as 'a bright, active girl', never failed to respond.

But at last it seemed to her that her duties were at an end, or at any rate the more pressing of them. She decided with a gentle spurt of rebellion not to think of the others, and to indulge herself in an hour's rest and relaxation. This was unobtainable in the crowded, bustling house, and so, putting on her outdoor clothes, she slipped out of a side door and across the lawn.

The evening was fine. The light of the setting sun was tangled low in the trees. Where the sunlight did not catch them, their trunks and branches had a smoky hue. The ground was powdered with the dull gold of fallen leaves. She paused for a few moments on the bridge, resting her small gloved hand on the stone parapet, and gazed down at the lustrous, smoothly gliding waters. It fascinated her now, as it had fascinated her since childhood, to see how the water for ever changing was yet for ever constant, forming itself even as it flowed away into the same pattern of ripples, swirls and eddies, ceaseless movement thus creating perfect immutability. Isabella's mind, devout by nature and training, tried to find some religious significance in this, but she was a little fatigued by the fuss and excitement of the last week, and had to leave the river's symbolic meaning to look after itself.

Its secretive, singing voice soothed her, and glancing back across the lawn at the familiar outlines of Maryiot Cells, its clustered chimneys, obelisks, and turrets sombre against the water-pale sky, its many windows bright with gleams from the sinking sun, she felt a rush of affection for her home. She felt too a sentimental pang for Blanche at having to leave these dear accustomed scenes, though from all accounts Castle Allen was a beautiful place, and dear William was such a fine, good fellow. She was sure that she would weep tomorrow when she saw her beloved eldest sister being married; it would be the first break in the family circle. There was something just a little sad, Isabella thought, about weddings, but it was a pleasant, really rather beautiful sadness, and the tears which everyone (at least all the near female relations) shed at them were as agreeable and mild as dew.

When she had crossed the bridge, Isabella did not enter one of the yew glades. They were uninvitingly dark and damp under foot at this season, and Isabella was sure that Mama would not approve of her risking a chill by walking there on this autumn evening.

Instead she turned to the right, and followed the path which ran parallel to the river. It was one of her favourite walks. The sound and sight of the river gave her a feeling of companionship. The trees which grew there formed a canopy of branches over the path; in some parts dipping down to the water's edge, as though intent, Isabella thought, on imparting to it some secret. At intervals along the river were three pools, whose quaint names, The Abbot's Pool, Purgatory and Hell, were reminiscent of the days when Maryiot Cells was a monastic foundation. Here, where the river lay in topaz-brown repose before cascading on again over the flat stones, the trout lay basking. In the old days the monks had evidently enlarged these natural pools into fishponds, for there were still traces of low stone walls, long since fallen into decay, on the river banks.

It was in a pensive, quiet, cheerful mood – in this lull, as it were, in the swirl of the wedding preparations, not unlike the quietness of the pools in the swirl of the river – that Isabella Skelton strolled by the river on this fine autumn evening. It is necessary here, even though it means a digression, to emphasise that there was no apprehension nor nervousness in her mind. It would be ridiculous to deny that Isabella knew that her home was not as other people's homes; that there was a queer atmosphere about it, an abnormal and sinister tradition that made it an object of morbid interest to visitors and to the locality. In plain words, that it was 'haunted'.

It is impossible to say at what age, exactly, she became aware of this. That she should become aware, however, was inevitable, in spite of Nanny Callaghan's unceasing vigilance. There had been a period, in fact, in her childhood, when she was about eight years old, when the obscure forces that lurked in the background of her home had obtruded themselves most unceremoniously upon her childish consciousness.

It is said by those who occupy themselves with psychical research that these supernormal phenomena occur, if not in regular cycles, at least in periods of varying intensity. Dormant for a number of years, they become suddenly active, for no ascertainable reason.

Something of this kind must have happened at Maryiot Cells at this time. The details, as far as they can be gathered from family diaries and recollections, are blurred, but it appears that several guests curtailed their visits abruptly; there was a rapid succession of kitchenmaids (then as now highly impressionable creatures); pet dogs behaved in a hysterical manner; a carpenter was summoned to find out why doors opened that should have remained shut, and what combination of loose boards, wind or rats could cause a sound resembling 'six quick young footsteps' (the phrase is from Sir Wilfrid's journal), rappings, something stirring and rustling, uncouth whisperings and mutterings.

It was about this time too that a window in one of the turrets was blocked up. The room which it illuminated was only used for storing trunks. Even so, its deliberate darkening might have seemed a senseless action – what more aggravating than to stumble and rummage about among trunks and portmanteaux with a candle? The fact was that a good deal of silly talk was being spread around in the village about the light that shone out mysteriously from that window near the midnight hour.

Sir Wilfrid himself, muffled in an ulster,[5] and accompanied by the butler carrying a gun (rather an unnecessary precaution in the circumstances, one would have supposed) had waited for several hours one night between the entrance court and the beech avenue, and the light had been clearly visible to both master and man. The 'nasty, unaccountable thing about it', as the butler had confided to the housekeeper next day, was that the light had wavered and moved, for all the world as though whoever bore it had passed several times before the window. And this though the trunk-room door was locked beyond all doubt, and the key lying in Sir Wilfrid's vest pocket.

The nurseries at Maryiot Cells were situated in the more modern, that is to say late eighteenth century, wing of the house, which may explain why Isabella, naturally knowing nothing of these singular disturbances which were perplexing her elders, was not made aware of them till a measles epidemic caused a temporary change in the family's sleeping arrangements. Blanche, Charlotte, Florence and little Lucy caught the infection and were nursed by Nanny Callaghan in the nursery or (as it was now called in honour of the older girls' status) the schoolroom wing. The fourteen-year-old Alice and Isabella were accommodated as a precaution in the chintz room, at the end of the passage from their parents' bedroom.

It may have been the change of bed and the excitement of sharing a room with big sister Alice (it was certainly not the onset of fever, for neither of the girls caught the measles) which made Isabella sleep so uneasily during the first few nights in her new bedroom.

Whatever the reason, Isabella – a child who slept like a dormouse as a rule, and whose digestion was excellent – was troubled by curious and disagreeable dreams. For such, her elders assured her, were the experiences that she related to them in the morning. And as such Isabella, a biddable child who seldom disputed the sacred conclusions of grown-ups, accepted them, secretly qualifying the acceptance however by calling them her 'wake-up dreams', for it certainly seemed to her that she had been wide awake at the time.

The first night she had been woken, she thought, by the sound of music. A queer, tinkling music, brittle as pieces of glass – something like dear Mama's pianoforte, and yet again most unlike. The music was insistent, dulcet and alluring, but the startled, listening child did not like it. She liked it so little that after a few moments she cried out, 'Alice! Alice!'

A grunt from Alice's bed was blessedly reassuring, but when Alice asked, 'What's the matter?' and dismissed Isabella's, 'I hear music' with a good-natured, 'Silly! Go to sleep,' Isabella had to admit the justice of the rebuke, for the music had ceased – swallowed up in the profound nocturnal silence of the big house.

The next night Isabella was not aware that she had fallen asleep, though of course she must have dozed off as Mama and Nanny said so. She had only been in bed some ten minutes, it seemed to her, when her attention was caught by a swishing sound, as of a silken skirt, coming from the direction of the turret staircase at the end of the passage. This might have been Mama (there were no lady visitors staying at that time in the house), but the footsteps moved in a stealthy way that brought no comforting sense of recognition to the scared child. Her skin tingled with fear as she heard a rustling or scrabbling noise outside her door. There was no sound of the door opening, but the room had grown noticeably colder. All of a sudden she felt an icy pressure on her forehead. The sensation lasted for only a few seconds, passing as swiftly as it had come. Isabella lay stiff with terror, then she broke into loud screams. Before long, she was being hugged to Nanny's capacious bosom, was sobbing out her incoherent alarm.

The next night the two girls were given a night-light. As things turned out it might have been more agreeable for Isabella if the room had been in total darkness, for when she woke up with a violent start, feeling chilled in spite of her warm coverings, she was able to perceive by the little lamp's dim but steady light, that a figure stood at the foot of her bed. It was not Mama, nor Papa, nor Alice, nor Nanny, nor any of the maids, but utterly unlike them or anyone else that Isabella had seen in her short life.

'Matthew, Mark, Luke and John,
Bless the bed that I lie on.'

Something told Isabella unmistakably that this dreadful, unknown visitor was not one of the kind apostles, nor the guardian angel who, Nanny assured her, watched over good little girls' slumbers.

Isabella yelped like a terrified puppy and dived under the bedclothes. Again Alice woke to find the room in its normal condition, though this time she had to get out of bed to soothe her frightened little sister.

But if Lady Skelton and Alice, following her mother's lead, were kindly complacent about 'Silly little Goosie's dreams', they were to experience a rude awakening.

The following night, whatever invisible influence was disturbing that part of the house was extraordinarily active. It was Isabella this time who slept through the most violent of the manifestations, though fitfully, her sleep shot through with nightmare images and sounds. When she woke up suddenly she saw by the glow of the night-light that Alice's bed was empty, the bedclothes tossed back, her bedroom slippers still by the bed, the door of the room open.

Impelled by an unreasoning terror, Isabella scrambled out of bed and fled down the passage towards her mother's room. Here she came upon Mama – a shawl thrown over her nightgown, her long hair in two plaits, a candle in one hand, the other thrown round the clinging Alice. Both her mother's and sister's faces were sharpened with an expression of fear that made them look quite unlike themselves.

Alice whispered, 'Oh Mama dear, what can all this noise be? Isn't it terrible?' To which Lady Skelton replied, in the same scared, breathless tones, 'Oh dear, oh dear. I can't think what it is. I am sure it will disturb Papa.'

This larger apprehension made all three of Sir Wilfrid's womenkind glance towards the door of the dressing-room where he had retired to an early bed with a toothache and a glass of whisky, hot water, lemon, nutmeg and sugar.

Bemused with sleep, confused by the lateness of the hour and the strangeness of the scene, ignorant of what had happened, her thoughts momentarily diverted by the allusion to Papa, Isabella only caught the tail-end of the really appalling noises, which sounded as though something was pouncing down from step to step of the great staircase, but which ceased, a moment afterwards, with unnerving abruptness. She caught Alice's terrified whisper, 'Mama, who is it?' Lady Skelton shuddered violently. 'Hush! I don't know, dear.'

She shepherded her young daughters into her bedroom, made them get into her bed and, though she was in a shocking state of tremor, stood for a moment at the communicating door of the dressing-room – but luckily Sir Wilfrid slept on.

Lady Skelton always had a little spirit lamp and a saucepan handy in her bedroom in case she should feel faint in the night, and the episode which had opened in such blind terror for Isabella ended as a midnight picnic, with hot milk and biscuits and the unparalleled privilege of sleeping, snug and secure, between her mother and sister in the huge walnut bed.

Next morning, it all seemed like a nightmare, but this time it was a nightmare that she shared with Mama and Alice, as the cups and crumbs of last night's repast testified. But her enquiries on the subject of the disturbances themselves were gently discouraged.

‘Mama, was it burglars making the noise last night?’

‘No dear, not burglars. Old houses do make odd noises at night, you know.’

‘Old houses do make odd noises at night.’ Certainly Maryiot Cells seemed to do so, though fortunately for the peace of mind of its inmates, whatever or whoever was responsible for this particular outbreak appeared to have spent itself.

The recollection of that strange night became blurred in Isabella’s memory. Unsatisfied curiosity soon died. No unusual experiences came her way, except the unrelated, untoward noises and happenings that the Skelton family – if not the more timid of their visitors – had come to accept as an unmentioned feature of their home life.

And so there was no reason why Isabella Skelton should feel apprehensive or alarmed as she took that evening stroll on the eve of her sister’s wedding day. Her thoughts, in fact, were occupied with her bridesmaid’s dress of pale blue figured silk trimmed with forget-me-nots and fine lace, as she passed the Abbot’s Pool and walked along the path, a little narrowed here, that led to the pool called Purgatory. No sensitive antennae of her consciousness warned her, ‘Beware! Beware!’; no shadow of approaching horror fell across her innocent and trivial meditations.

She observed that she had come to the great oak – Lady’s Oak, it was traditionally named – one of whose boughs, thick as a man’s wrist, overleaned the path. Her glance dropped to her small, neat elastic-sided boots whose progress through the heaps of fallen leaves made a pleasant rustling sound. She raised her eyes again and there, immediately before her, there swung the body of a hanged person.

'Swung' – no, that was not the word, for the figure hung in a stillness and rigidity that was utterly preternatural as though, in its dark outlandish male attire, it was violently superimposed upon the harmless evening air. Though so still, so lifeless, it was full of menace. Was the face, lolling upon the body, male or female? Enough to say that it was loathsome to behold, congested, the swollen tongue protruding leeringly from the mouth....

Isabella gave a low moan, clutched at a tree for support and, leaning her head against its trunk, battled with closed eyes for her reason and her life. Sheer animal fear of death had blotted out all else from her reeling mind. Her heart was like a horse that had broken loose and was galloping wildly away. If she could not stop its panic flight she knew that it would gallop her out of life itself.

It was in this dire extremity that she summoned to her aid from the depth of her consciousness the figure of the guardian angel who, as a child, she had been convinced had sat all night at the end of her bed, and who, even now, had not in her belief entirely forsaken its guardianship of her slumbers. It was, as was to be expected, a Victorian angel, closely resembling the picture of the angel carrying a dying child to Heaven that hung above the mantelpiece in Isabella's bedroom - an angel with a sweetly insipid face, long curling hair, substantial wings and a white robe as decent as a nightgown. But though Isabella's angel would no doubt have appeared mawkish to modern eyes, it performed its duty with admirable efficiency. It caught and quieted Isabella's stampeding heart. Furthermore, it gave Isabella the courage to open her eyes and look at the accursed tree.

The bough stretched blamelessly across the path, its ghastly burden vanished as though it had never been.

Isabella turned and ran for home, stumbling on and tearing the hem of her skirt as she ran. Along the path she fled, across the bridge and lawn, never pausing till she had run through the conservatory into the boudoir.

It was empty, except for Aunt Lizzie who was dozing on the sofa where Isabella had settled her half an hour ago, her face imperious and discontented in sleep, her lace cap a little awry, her massive bosom, which looked as though it had been poured into her dark silk dress, heaving in comfortable regularity. The boudoir was the same too. Isabella's affrighted eyes took in the safe, familiar details; the fringed velvet curtains, the draped mantelpiece and its vases, the occasional tables with their rich tablecloths and burden of knick-knacks and photographs. All was substantial, seemly, accountable, as she had (till less than half an hour ago) believed the entire universe to be.

She ran upstairs, meeting no one on the way, for the first dinner gong had sounded, staggered into her bedroom and there, before the alarmed gaze of her sister Florence and of Agnes Allen, fell down in a faint.

They put her to bed and administered the usual remedies. By the morning she declared herself to be completely recovered.

That she had at any rate recovered sufficiently to carry out her bridesmaid's duties is shown by the photograph of the wedding group.

There is the bride, a mysterious figure veiled in clouds of white tulle, for it seems that even after the ceremony her virgin charms must be concealed from her lover's eyes. There is the bridegroom, a pleasing, rather waggish-looking young man (it is satisfactory to be able to record that Aunt Lizzie was wrong and that he did live to make old bones). And there, against a background of bonnets, tiny hats, shawls, dolmans,[6] beruffled and looped-up skirts, frock-coats, top hats, side-whiskers and beards, are the ten young bridesmaids in their festal dresses, and among them Isabella Skelton, looking a little wan. But that may be because she is sitting next to Miss Kathie Allen, whose saucy, roguish air beckons unmistakably to us across the gulf of seventy years.

One thing is certain: only Isabella's enjoyment on that festive day was overshadowed by the thought of the appalling vision that had assailed her. Amid all her terror and mental disarray she had resolved that no knowledge of this ill-omened thing should mar her dear Blanche's happiness and, intensely as she longed to unburden herself to some sympathetic listener, Nanny's dictum, 'Tell one, tell all', fortified her resolve to keep total silence. In answer to all the solicitous enquiries she only said (praying that the untruth might be forgiven her) that while out on her walk she had stumbled and fallen down, and that the shock had made her feel a little seedy, but that she would be quite set up after a rest.

Happily her secret dread that the appearance foreboded some evil to the bridal pair was unfounded. But having once determined to keep silence, Isabella thought it wisest to continue to do so. It had all been so horrible, not at all the kind of thing that one wished to connect with one's dear home, or, for that matter, with the universe. She wished that she could have consulted some really wise, experienced clergyman – someone like Dean Farrar[7] for instance – but unfortunately Mr Henderson, though a most worthy and earnest man and most helpful about Isabella's classes for young boys, was not at all the kind of person to whom you would go for enlightenment on so weird and unpleasant a matter.

So in the end, Isabella's journal remained her sole confidant.

To her account of her experience she added, rather unexpectedly, this quaintly worded prayer that is carved above the family crest over the fireplace in the Great Hall of Maryiot Cells:

'Therefore O Lord, in Thee is my full hope and trust that Thou wilt mee defend from sin, the world and deville, who goeth about to catch poor sinners in their snare and bring them to that place where grief and sorrow are.'

3

LADY SOPHIA MET HER MATCH

'Stubborn unlaid ghost.'[1]

IN ONE OF the attics of Maryiot Cells there was, till the recent fire which destroyed the house, a large, wooden antique chest, painted in the Dutch fashion with neat landscapes and bunches of spring flowers, and furnished with a massive double lock. In this chest there lay, among title deeds, letters, estate maps, and other family relics accumulated throughout several centuries, detailed plans for the complete rebuilding of Maryiot Cells. These plans were drawn out in 1781 by Mr Josias Wedgeworth, an architect of no little repute at that period.[2]

It is evident from the bundle of letters which accompany the plans that, though his patron was nominally Sir Charles Skelton, who had succeeded to his father's title and estates the previous year, it was in fact Sir Charles's wife, Lady Sophia Skelton, who was the prime instigator and director of this ambitious architectural scheme. 'Her ladyship desires me most particularly …' 'With regard to the Folly, her Ladyship is most earnest in her wish …' 'It is her Ladyship's intention ...' These and similar phrases appear frequently in the letters which Sir Charles addressed to the (doubtless) harassed architect.

The scheme may be fairly described as 'ambitious', for it embraced a reconstruction of the ancient manor house of Maryiot Cells so drastic as to entail, for all intents and purposes its demolition (though it seems that the beautiful Long Gallery was to be partially spared). In place of the irregular, rambling, venerable and inconvenient house with its twisting staircases and narrow passages, its clustering chimneys, stone obelisks, gables and mullioned windows, whose Tudor frame incorporated elements of its medieval origin, there was to arise a no less inconvenient but modern and hence classical mansion, with all the frigid magnificence of a portico designed in the Ionic order, supporting a pediment, colonnades, niches in the corridors for the reception of classical statues, lofty ceilings depicting mythological amours and so on.[3]

That Lady Sophia had the means to carry out this bold project is explained by the fact that she was the only child and heiress of the wealthy Earl of Terrall; that she had the energy and resolution necessary to surmount the inevitable difficulties and annoyances of such a scheme is evident from her portrait, and from the tales still told about her in the locality.

In her excellent portrait by an unknown artist (which happily was stored in London at the time of the fire) she wears a large hat of fashionably masculine shape with an upturned brim and an ostrich feather; her hair is powdered and drawn back from her face in curls; she has a narrow black velvet ribbon round her throat, and over her pale-coloured dress she wears a little black silk cape or mantelet fastened in front with a cameo brooch. Her face – that of a woman in her late thirties – is not beautiful but it is comely and arresting. There is something almost boyish about her wide forehead and rounded chin, but her dark lively eyes are very feminine. Though there is good humour in the firmly closed mouth, determination is the dominant expression of Lady Sophia's face. Here, you feel, is a woman who would have swum triumphantly through life in any class or any century. She has none of that air of overbred, swan-like helplessness which characterises many portraits of eighteenth-century women.

No wonder that her husband and her children (seven sons and four daughters) loved and deferred to her. No wonder that the villagers of Maiden Worthy accepted her beneficent if autocratic rule with due meekness.

She was a fine horsewoman and an enthusiastic rider to hounds, and the only woman to see the end of the Garston Gorze hunt, famed in local song and story. But there was more to Lady Sophia than physical dash and daring. When the neighbourhood was scourged by an epidemic of 'putrid fever', or typhus, Lady Sophia sent her children away to safety and settled down, with Sir Charles to keep her company, to help the over-worked apothecary Mr Browning fight the disease. Defying infection, she sailed into cottage after cottage bringing blankets, syllabubs, sage tea and courage to her husband's stricken tenants, and acting as Mr Browning's assistant – if the word 'assist' can be stretched sufficiently to cover the cheerful unconcern with which she pooh-poohed his suggestions and disobeyed his instructions.

Her ideas on hygiene were in advance of her times. Regardless of the outcries of her patients and the protests of the hapless Mr Browning, she tore open tiny casement windows, letting the fresh air into darkened, pestiferous cottages, ordered infected bedding to be burnt and, with her own hands, shaved the heads of her female patients, promising them each a gift of a close cap with blue ribbons if they submitted with patience to her ministrations.

On her own initiative she drew a quarantine cordon round the parish, forbidding its inhabitants, under pain of her severe displeasure, to leave it or to allow strangers to enter it. Her methods, high-handed though they were, were justified by the fact that there were fewer deaths in Maiden Worthy than in any of the surrounding parishes, and that it was the first village to be free of the epidemic.

It is no surprise after this to learn that, in later years, when England was faced by the threat of a Napoleonic invasion, Lady Sophia Skelton raised and, at her own cost, maintained a body of volunteers from among her husband's tenants.

Certainly a woman of character, and one not easily deflected from her purpose. Which makes it the stranger that of her vaunting architectural schemes there remains no trace except the Folly, or miniature Grecian temple, set down in desolate incongruity by the banks of the river, and those plans which were stored away for years, dusty and forgotten in the attic at Maryiot Cells; for the partial rebuilding of the west wing after the outbreak of fire in 1782 was obviously an emergency measure and in no way connected with Lady Sophia's original plan.

The solution of this teasing little mystery can however be pieced together from the bundle of letters, tied with faded red ribbon, which accompanies the plans. A solution?

Perhaps that is hardly the word for an explanation so unnatural, so contrary to reason and so strange.

The letters are written by Lady Sophia to Sir Charles who was over in Dublin at that time, engaged on business connected with property in that city which had been left to him by his great-uncle Lord Maynooth.

The plans for the reconstruction of Maryiot Cells had evidently reached completion, and demolition work was to begin in a matter of a few weeks, when Lady Sophia would remove herself and her family to Beechlands Grove, which fortunately or unfortunately (according to whether you consider it from Lady Sophia's or Mr Wedgeworth's point of view) was within driving distance of Maryiot Cells.

Probably Sir Charles was not altogether sorry to miss the final stages of the running battle between his lady and his architect. His long, handsome face, as depicted in his portrait, which is a pendant to that of his wife, is perfectly amiable but lacks her conquering air.

Lady Sophia was a devoted wife and mother, and she wrote often and affectionately to her absent lord. The first few letters, of which the following is a typical specimen, deal with the daily happenings at Maryiot Cells, trivial in themselves but important to this fond and united couple.

March 9th 1782.

'My dearest husband,

I give you a thousand thanks for your kind letter which

was vastly welcome. It vexed me to learn that you had such a bad crossing, but I rejoice to hear that, thanks to your cousin's claret and your own excellent constitution, you were totally recovered from the effects of it when you wrote to me. Anything that causes you uneasiness, however slight, must cause uneasiness to your wife who loves you better than herself. Pray, my dear Sir Charles, regard your health as my most precious possession and treat it accordingly.

Our sweet lambs are well and send their duty and kisses to dear Papa. Your daughter Elizabeth – the baggage! – desires me to remind Papa to bring her a pretty toy from Dublin. The new footman is a dolt. I thought 'twas not possible to find anyone stupider than Samuel, but events have proved me wrong. However he appears to take the utmost pains to please, poor creature, so I shall endeavour to bear with him.

Lady Roxley called this morning desiring to carry me with her to visit the "nouvelle mariée", but I resisted her solicitations, for to tell the truth, I dare not leave this place for a moment in case Mr Wedgeworth should profit by my absence to plan "quelque bêtise".[4]

I have made it tolerably clear to him, I believe, what I require of him, that is to say to carry out *my* ideas (and of course yours too, my love) not his own. I find that his opinion agrees with mine lately in a way that I would not have believed possible when we first entered into this building project. I must confess that I had a few words with him yesterday over the extra windows in the boudoir, Mr W. maintaining that he would risk his reputation extremely by consenting to any such thing, but upon my assuring him that I held my comfort far dearer than any man's reputation (and why, pray, should I mope in darkness during the winter months to please any man?) he hauled down his colours, as brother Jack* would say.

I believe it will not be long now before the work of pulling down this antique and incommodious building will begin. I am more in love with the idea of our fine new house than ever, am ready to endure every inconvenience to obtain it, and pray God that He will spare us and our children to enjoy many happy years together in it.

I will acquaint you when I shall move to Beechlands Grove. I shall stay here as long as I can to see what Mr Wedgeworth and his minions are about.

If you should bring me some muslin for the little girls' caps and fine linen damask for tablecloths I will not say nay to it, but pray do not trouble yourself if you are too much occupied with business.

Believe me, my dear Sir Charles, your faithful, affectionate and obedient wife,

S. Skelton.'

Her next letter strikes a less carefree note.

March 10th.

'You will be surprised, my dear Sir Charles, at receiving another letter written less than twenty-four hours after my last and, lest you should conclude that some illness of the children has occasioned it, I hasten to relieve your mind

---

* 'Brother Jack' was Sir Charles's younger brother, Captain John Skelton, R.N., later Sir John Skelton, K.C.B., Admiral of the Blue.

by assuring you that they are pure well (not excepting our sweet rogue Frederick, who is a little perverse and saucy by reason of toothing, but nothing to signify).

I am also in tolerable good health though in extreme ill humour, Mr Wedgeworth having come to me today to inform me – if you please – that he cannot get any workmen from the neighbourhood to work on the house. Recollecting that he was always for bringing a number of hands down from London, I rehearsed to him again our reasons for employing men from these parts, viz not only greater economy, but also our wish to give employment to the neighbourhood. I added that when he had completed the task of demolishing the old house and building up the new he might bring down what London craftsmen he chose for its embellishment. I was sensible that I must leave such matters to him, but I hoped that Buckinghamshire was not such a county of ninnies that it could not produce sufficient good labourers – stone masons, carpenters and so on – for his purpose.

When I was out of breath Mr W. said, "Indeed you quite mistake me. I by no means think myself capable of gainsaying any of your ladyship's wishes. In this case it is the workmen themselves who make so bold. If you do not believe me pray ask your steward," and with that he bounced out of the room. What ridiculous "canard"[5] or, more likely, misunderstanding is behind this business, I cannot guess though I shall soon find out (it was too late when he came to me for me to see Hunter). In any case you may depend upon it that I will soon clear it up.

Now, mon très cher, I must beg your forgiveness for venting my peevishness upon you. I fancy how you will laugh when you receive this letter and say, "There is Sophie *flaming* again!"

Never mind, you are at liberty to laugh at me as much as you please as long as you think of and love,

Your ever affectionate wife and partner, S.S.'

But the matter was not to be cleared up as easily as Lady Sophia anticipated. Her next letter reads:

March 13th.

'My dear husband,

I fear that I can by no means give you so good an account of affairs here as I would wish. I saw Hunter at the earliest opportunity after my conversation with Mr Wedgeworth and asked him to explain this nonsensical business about the workmen. Whereupon he assured me that it was indeed as Mr W. had said, that he could not for any money – nor he added for an even stronger consideration viz the esteem and respect that the people hereabouts have for the family and for us both – induce a soul to undertake the labour of pulling down this house.

This news struck me dumb, as you may imagine. If I did not know Hunter to be a man of integrity and honest character I would not have believed him. Upon my questioning him as to the reason for this extraordinary state of affairs, he became as close as an oyster, shifted from foot to foot, and mumbled that the country people here were prone to take notions and to listen to foolish old tales. You may guess that I am not satisfied with such lame excuses and will make it my chief purpose and business to sift this matter to the bottom.

Till then adieu, my dear love.

Your affectionate and entirely devoted wife,

Sophia Skelton.'

The next few days brought Lady Sophia some explanation but little satisfaction.

March 16th.

'I have but this moment returned, my dear Sir Charles, from visiting William Waite at his cottage, whither I went in my chaise, with the idea that if anyone could explain to me the reason for the insolence, indolence – I know not what to call it – in short the extraordinary conduct of these workmen, it would be this venerable and good old man, who may truly be termed the Father of the parish.*

He was as pleased to see me as ever, and not only I flatter myself for the sake of the pigeon pie that I brought with me. I acquainted him with my problem which he listened to with many head noddings and sage "Aye, aye, I had heard as much", and then gave me an explanation that I am sure would divert you were it not proof of the pitiable fears and superstitions to which the lower class of people are so prone.

In short, my dear Sir Charles, these foolish folk will not work on this house because they believe it to be haunted.

---

* William Waite was coachman to Sir Charles's father for forty years.

The spirit (I will not honour her with the name of lady!) who is so uncourteously interfering with my plans is, it would seem, your great great aunt of evil memory, Barbara Lady Skelton.

What could give clearer evidence, my dear husband, of the enduring influence of bad deeds, for while the virtues of your many honourable and discreet ancestresses have been forgotten, the crimes of a profligate woman, who has mouldered in her tomb these ninety odd years, are still so well remembered in the neighbourhood that grown men (in this age of reason) dare not lift a pickaxe against the house that she inhabited for fear of displeasing her shade!

Something of my feelings must have appeared in my face, for old William said, "I fancy my lady that you have not much notion of spirits?"

"None whatsoever," I assured him laughing. Upon which the old man said, "If I may make so bold as to ask, has your ladyship never been troubled with any disturbances since you and Sir Charles took up residence at the Great House?" I told him, "I will not deny that there has been idle talk among the maidservants, but for my part I have never heard nor seen anything during these last two years that could not have been caused by mortal agency. I know very well what the country people say about Maryiot Cells, but the notion of haunted houses is quite exploded except among those with weak and ignorant minds."

At which he shook his head doubtfully and said, "That may be, my lady, but she was an uncommonly wicked woman and came to a strange and violent end."

"She is dead and buried these ninety years and more," I reminded him. "That is a long time."

"To you, my lady, in the pride of your youth, it may seem a long time, but to me, who will be eighty-seven come Michaelmas, it does not seem so long after all."

"Long or not," I concluded the argument, "I would like to meet the woman alive or dead who could turn me from my purpose."

At this the good old man's countenance changed excessively, and he seemed so affrighted and shocked that I had pity on him and refrained from teasing him any longer.

I do not know, my dearest love, why I have treated you to all this nonsense, except to show you how these illiberal superstitions will gain a hold over the mind of even so sensible a man as William Waite where there is no superior education nor philosophy to combat them.

It seems now that Mr Wedgeworth will have his way after all and that we shall be obliged to hire hands from London. Peu m'importe,[6] provided that I get my new house in the end.

The children are vastly well and making a great riot in this very room. Little Fanny begs me to come with her to feed her chicks, so I must bid my dear love adieu.

Your obedient and ever loving wife,

Sophia Skelton.'

Sir Charles was detained in Dublin beyond his expectations by legal affairs. He had hoped to return home early in April; now he thought that he would be lucky if he had made an end of his business by the middle of May.

It would seem (judging by Lady Sophia's letters) that he was as eager to return to her as she could wish. She writes soothingly:

'I am indeed sorry that you chafe at your situation, but I assure you that your disappointment could not possibly exceed, though I will allow that it might equal, mine. We are both to blame for having forgotten that lawyers are persons naturally delighting in and thriving on delay who appear to ignore the fact that all things – including the time at their clients' disposal – are subject to the sway of "sad mortality".'

Lady Sophia's letters to her husband during the next six weeks are remarkable only for the even, humdrum tone in which she recounts everyday facts and events.

'Little Frederick bids me tell Papa that he has a fine new tooth.' 'Your son Charles is writing you a letter with his own hand.' 'The girls are improving daily in beauty.' 'Lady Sefton carries me on Monday se'ennight[7] to a drum[8] at Cranborough Park.' 'I have bespoke a pretty chintz for my new bedroom, rose pink with pale stripes. You will laugh at me for looking so far ahead but I thought 'twas wise to secure it while I could.' 'The sowing goes on as well as the weather permits... Daniel is sick of the smallpox.'

The workmen had evidently arrived from London. Lady Sophia writes that she 'must muster the brick carts', also have the Church lane repaired 'for it is so torn up by the brick carts that 'twill soon be impassable.'

It is easy to imagine how startled Sir Charles must have been when he received the following letter from his wife dated

May 6th.

'My dear husband,

The eight years that I have had the happiness and honour to be your wife have, I fondly believe, made you sufficiently acquainted with my disposition to know that falsehood is not one of my faults. More than once you have been pleased to tell me that I have a nice regard for truth and accuracy that you would expect to find in a man rather than in a woman. God forbid, my dearest husband, that I should ever fall short of your high opinion of me in this respect.

I remind myself and you of these things not to gratify my vanity, but to encourage myself to commit to writing a relation of events so extraordinary and so inexplicable that I would not dare expect anyone to believe them, unless they had that absolute faith in my veracity that I hereby claim from you.

The letters that you have received from me during the past six weeks have given you no hint that anything was amiss, and if I tell you now that hardly a night has passed during that time that I and my household have not been harassed by the most dire and horrid disturbances, you must not blame me, however fondly, for concealing these things from you. If it had been a case of ordinary domestic distresses how eagerly I would have confided them to my dearest partner and friend.

But this uneasiness that I and my family have endured has been something more than commonly horrible, because so full of surprise and wonder, that I could not bring myself to write of it, even to my dear Sir Charles, till assured that my senses were not deceived.

As you know, I have never been prone to superstitious fears, having in fact little interest in the unseen world beyond what our sacred religion teaches us is right and proper. Yet what we have experienced here at Maryiot Cells during the past six or seven weeks so passes the bounds of reason and credibility that, against all my previous beliefs, I am forced to attribute it to a supernatural cause.

But I will endeavour, my dear Sir Charles, to give you a sober account of events.

These disturbances commenced on the night of March 16th. I recollect the date for I had sate[9] up late writing to you an account of my conversation with William Waite. It was eleven o'clock when I retired to bed, as the sound of the clock striking in the hall apprised me. The house was perfectly quiet. As I ascended the great stairs, a lighted candlestick in my hand, I felt something grasp at my dress. I turned sharply but perceived nothing but shadows. At the time I believed that I had caught my dress on a nail or that the cat had passed me on the stairs, but now I think otherwise.

I was in my bedroom, undressed and preparing to get into bed, when I heard the sound of a door slapped to three times with great violence. I threw a wrapper over my shoulders, and ran along the passage and on to the landing to look down into the hall from where it seemed to me the noise had come, but there was absolute silence. Not satisfied with this, I descended into the hall and looked into all the principal rooms. All was snug and in place. I should mention that the night was still and windless. As you may conceive my first thought was housebreakers. Having reassured myself on this point I believed that one of the younger domestics had been up to some pranks, tho' I was loath to suspect any misdemeanours of this kind, for as you know I account myself singularly fortunate in my family. I returned to my room, puzzled but in no way concerned, not being aware of what greater disturbances this first slight alarm was the forerunner.

The following night I was in bed, but perfectly awake, when I heard three loud and violent knocks on the door of my room. In an instant I was out of bed and in the passage, but nothing was to be seen. I returned to my bed and fell asleep, to be woken an hour or two later by the sound of footsteps in the room overhead, and a heavy dragging noise as though someone pulled a large chest across the floor. I was in two minds whether to rise and investigate, but being drowsy (though perfectly in my senses) and the noise ceasing, I decided against leaving my bed and soon fell asleep again.

It was not till the next morning that I asked myself, more positively and with some astonishment, who could have been stirring overhead for, as you know, I have moved to the Chintz room during your absence and though, judging from the external appearance of the house, there is rafter space and to spare above this room, there is certainly no apartment.

By now I was convinced that there was some irregularity among my household, and summoning Robert Godwin* I acquainted him with my surmise. To my surprise he told me that he had also been aware of unusual noises the previous night, to wit doors opening and shutting and

* The butler.

a ponderous thud like (he said) a sack full of logs or coal thrown down with violence.

But though he had been on the alert for the best part of the night, he had been unable to discover any cause for it. He was as reluctant as I was to fasten the blame upon any of the domestics (and indeed I believe that we have never had a steadier and more honest set of servants than at present) but suggested that they should be locked into their rooms the next night, which precaution, he said, they would readily submit to if they were as innocent as he believed.

Accordingly that night all were secured in their rooms, not excluding the nurse and nursemaid, and my trusty Mary Willmot. Robert Godwin himself took up his position with firearms in the Hall, as being the most likely place to surprise the unknown intruder.

Several hours passed quietly after I had retired to bed, and I flattered myself that our precautions had solved the mystery (though grieved at supposing that one of our servants had been guilty of such a senseless and unworthy prank), when I heard the sound of footsteps coming down the passage. By the lightness of the step and the sweeping noise of a skirt I knew that it was a woman. As the footsteps approached my door they stopped and I heard the handle of my door move gently, as though someone tried it, but the door itself was not opened. In a flash I had sprung from my bed and seizing the rushlight ran out into the passage, but there was nothing to be seen, though there had been no sound of footsteps in retreat, and 'tis certain that no human being could have escaped my view in so very short a time.

I went downstairs to speak to Robert Godwin. He was in the Hall, leaning against the newel post of the staircase, and as I descended the stairs he looked up at me with a pale and sickly face. "Oh my lady, 'tis you," he breathed in tones of heartfelt relief. Then, recovering his composure, he told me that as he sate there with his pistols and two lighted candles on the table beside him, he had become aware of a sudden feeling of silence and cold, and then that a woman was coming down the staircase towards him. He heard with the utmost distinctness the stirring of a silken dress and the tap of heels, but though the staircase was plainly visible by the candlelight, he could perceive no form nor shadow. So he sate, unable to move for astonishment and alarm, till the footsteps reached the bottom of the stairs when, with a loud rustling as of skirts, they rushed past him.

While we stood there looking at one another, I being unwilling to credit his extraordinary tale, and yet unable absolutely to disbelieve him, on account of the earnestness of his manner and my trust in his veracity, there came from behind us the noise of a door opening and slamming with a vehemence that shook the house and made us both start like shot hares.

This roused me not to fear but to anger, and bidding Godwin examine the rooms to the right of the hall, I looked into the others (for we could not determine which door was the one to be clapped to) but all was silent, the windows fastened and nothing amiss.

'Twould be tedious and unnecessary, my dear husband, to give you exact particulars of the noises that disturbed the house during the following weeks. It is enough to say that though sometimes a night or two passed in tranquillity this was the limit of our respite. The noises which were of various kinds were heard by all the household (excepting Mrs Mudge, whose deafness has secured her a peace of mind which we all envy). There were footsteps, for the most part light and stealthy but occasionally followed by the plodding step of a man, rappings, loud thuds, as though someone beat urgently upon a door, a peculiar clatter or jingling like a horse's bridle, snatches of harmony (this was heard by me and Elizabeth Wilson only), also on several occasions in the dead of night a crash would resound through the house in so violent a manner as to awaken the household.

The men servants (of whose steadiness and resolution I cannot speak too highly) took it in turns to watch up, two at a time (for alone they would not stay) but never could catch sight of any thing or living creature to account for the disturbances.

I was still unwilling to believe that a supernatural agency was responsible, and so caused all the outside locks of the house to be altered, also, though I was reluctant to bruit our troubles abroad, let it be known in the village that a reward of £60 would be paid for information leading to the discovery of the evilly disposed persons who were making divers kinds of noises at Maryiot Cells. These measures led to no result whatever and the noises continued unabated.

By March 29th they had assumed a different and a more intolerable quality (I speak for myself, but I believe this was also the opinion of my poor harassed and affrighted household). It seemed now that they had become more *human,* if I may use the term. A murmur of urgent voices was heard (though the words themselves could not be distinguished), also a peculiar low moan or cry and a dismal groaning.

At first when this was reported to me I attributed it to the nerves of my household being much sunk by the constant state of affright and terror in which they now lived, till one night I myself was roused from sleep by the sound of shrill, furious, despairing crying, as of a woman in horrible suffering. Only a few nights later, I was again disturbed by plaintive cries, accompanied by a sobbing sound. I need hardly add that neither on these nor any other occasions did the strictest scrutiny on my part reveal any appearance of human or brute being.

On April 3rd (I remember the date on account of it being our little Fanny's birthday) I was woke at dawn by a sound of gasping and groaning as though someone lay dying in my very room. This last alarm, so more than commonly horrible, induced me to have Mary Willmot to lie in a truckle bed in my room, for though I believed my resolution equal to all that might befall, I will not deny that the thought of her company was comfortable to me.

Two nights passed in undisturbed quietness and when I retired to bed on the third night I rashly remarked to Mary Willmot that I believed the alarms were over and that we should at last enjoy repose. I slept very peacefully and soundly till the small hours of the morning, when I woke to hear someone stirring about the room. Believing it to be my woman I said, "What ails you Willmot? Lie still." There was no reply from her, only a rustling of the bedcurtains, as though someone touched them. Suddenly I was sensible that this person, whoever it might be, was not Mary Willmot. With this knowledge, my courage for the first time in my life utterly deserted me, and I knew that I dared not open the bedcurtains and see who stood without.

As I lay there in a kind of stupor these words, spoken in a low threatening tone, seemed to sing through my head, "I am the spirit of Barbara Skelton and bespeak your attention." (But for the certainty of this I cannot vouch, for I was much disordered.) I heard a stifled groan, and then footsteps retiring to the door and the door softly opening.

In that moment my faculties returned to me, and I leapt from my bed, to find my woman lying with her head under the bedclothes, almost deprived of sense and motion from fright, and the door not opened as I had supposed (since there had been no sound of it closing) but bolted as when we had gone to bed.

When Mary Willmot had recovered herself sufficiently, she told me that as she lay there in her bed, she heard someone enter the room. Being thrown into the greatest possible terror by this alone (for she herself had bolted the door when we retired to rest) she durst not raise her head to see who had entered, but lay quite still and sweating extremely. Presently hearing no sound she ventured to open her eyes, but was so appalled by what she saw that she shut them immediately, for by the light of the rushlight she perceived on the wall and ceiling the shadow, very great and dark, of a woman, stooping towards my bed, and holding a cup or goblet in her hand. It was at this moment that I spoke to her, but terror had bereft her of speech.

This night was the prelude it would seem to the third phase of the haunting, for I know not what better name to give it. For now, it appeared as though the evil thing that disturbed our peace had gathered strength and was striving to make itself not only audible but visible.

On April 6th, in the evening, but in a sufficiently clear light, Robert Godwin having occasion to go to the print room, caught sight of the sweep of a woman's dress round the passage corner. Hastening after it in amazement, for he had been alone a moment before, he was still more confounded to find that part of the passage silent and empty, though there was nowhere for a rat, far less a human being to hide itself.

I will now relate to you the experience which befell me, and which I think you would find it hard to believe did you not know that my nerve is firm and my veracity beyond reproach.

On the Sunday following I went up to my dressing-room after supper to fetch down my French brocade gown, it being my intention to use the embroidery on it as a pattern for my needlework (not having the heart to oblige one of the maids to venture through the house at that late hour). As I came up to the wardrobe, with a lighted candle in my hand, I saw a woman's face reflected in the polished surface. Heaven be my witness, the face was not my own. 'Twas the face of a young woman and had the ghastly look of death, but the eyes were alive and fixed wide upon me, and I pray God that I never see the like of that gaze again. You will excuse me from giving you further particulars of this at present, for I care not to think of it.

I uttered a cry and immediately the apparition faded. Turning round I found the room quiet and empty.

You will, I believe, be surprised that I have not yet mentioned our dear children during this narrative of events. I need not assure you that my chief anxiety has been lest they should be frightened by any of these nasty doings, and my best support during these very trying weeks was that they were in no ways alarmed or disturbed (for which much merit must be taken by their nurse and nursemaid and the other servants for their prudent and discreet behaviour, but may also be accounted for by the fact that the disturbances occurred mostly in the other part of the house).

You can imagine then my consternation, when little Charles ran up to me the other day crying that as he and Elizabeth played at some game on the nursery staircase they saw a white face looking down at them from above, and saw it "hop away". (I give you his exact words which will no doubt sound as strange to you as they did to me.)

I questioned him lightly, as though attaching no great importance to the matter. I asked him which of the servants was it. No, it was none of the servants, he said. It was a lady, "and oh Mama, we did not like her face and so we ran away."

The very next night little Fanny woke up shrieking and, Nurse running in to her, she screamed out in terror that someone had come to her bed to fetch her away, nor could she be quieted for over half an hour.

I had taken the resolution, my love, not to acquaint you till your return from Dublin with all this uneasiness that we have endured during your absence and to have rubbed on till then, not wishing to bring you posting back while your business was still unconcluded, and perhaps not being willing either, through the obstinacy of my disposition, to admit myself worsted. But now that this thing whatever or whoever it may be, threatens our children's peace of mind I dare no longer keep the matter in my breast.

'Twas unavoidable that rumours of these disturbances should spread among the workmen before they had been down here twenty-four hours, and not a day passes without a report being brought to me of some dire thing which they have heard or seen; one day they are nearly ridden down by an invisible rider and horse, another evening 'tis a woman hanging from a tree, but I will not trouble you with particulars of what I take for the most part to be idle tales, for though your great-great aunt richly deserved hanging, 'twas not, as you know, the manner of her death.

Nevertheless all this has added greatly to my embarrassment and anxiety. Though you need not have the least uneasiness about my health (which remains good in spite of wakeful nights and some agitation to my nerves and spirits) I will confess that your presence and advice would be a vast comfort to me.

I must bring this long letter to a close. Heaven send us after all these troubles an agreeable meeting.

Your affectionate and ever loving friend and wife,

Sophia Skelton.'

But the next morning between husband and wife narrowly escaped being a tragic one. On receiving Lady Sophia's letter, Sir Charles set out immediately from Dublin.

The night before he arrived home a fire broke out in the west wing of Maryiot Cells, where the nurseries were situated. Thanks to the courage of their nurse the children escaped unharmed. The west wing was destroyed, but prompt action on the part of the indoor servants and the estate labourers prevented the fire from spreading to the rest of the house.

The cause of the fire was never discovered. Local gossip naturally attributed it to the same malevolent influence that had been disturbing the peace of the Great House for the past two months. That the unseen entity who apparently resented the prospect of Maryiot Cells being rebuilt should itself attempt to destroy the house seems to indicate that logic is as rare a quality in the spirit as in the material world.

But of course it was the *nursery* wing. This ugly thought may have occurred to Lady Sophia. We know her to be a passionately devoted mother, and where her children were concerned she may have been influenced by superstitious fears to which she would have scorned to have yielded on her own account. Maternal solicitude was perhaps the chink in the armour of her singularly resolute personality. Or perhaps Sir Charles, who it may be suspected had never taken enthusiastically to the notion of having his ancestral home pulled down and reconstructed at vast expense, seized the opportunity to dissuade his wife from the scheme.

Whatever the reason the fine new house, of which Lady Sophia had dreamed, remained stillborn – an architect's plan. The rebuilding of the west wing, and some minor alterations to other parts of the house were the only changes that were made at this time to the structure of Maryiot Cells.

Among the bundles of papers connected with these events is a curious little memorandum in Sir Charles's handwriting.

Dated, 'August 9th 1782', it reads:

'This day the workmen who are engaged in altering the kitchen and domestic offices came upon a narrow staircase bricked up behind the wall in the passage outside the kitchen. They acquainted me at once with their discovery and, as during the recent unexplained disturbances at Maryiot Cells there was much talk among the domestics of the sound of footsteps and stumbling, dismal groans, sighing and inhuman furious cries proceeding from this part of the house, I determined at once to investigate, taking Lady Sophia and Godwin with me as witnesses.

The staircase, which was narrow and steep, appeared not to have been used for many years judging by the dust and the rats' droppings underfoot. We followed it up and found ourselves in a small chamber or garret which, as far as we could judge, must be situated directly above the Chintz room. The room was bare except for a wooden chest painted in the Dutch fashion. The chest was secured by a lock, but this was easily opened and we looked inside hoping to find there some object or document that would explain the recent disturbances.

But there was nothing within except a silvered buckled riding belt (the silver being much tarnished) and a withered flower which in Lady Sophia's estimation might once have been a white rose, but of this we could not be sure of, as she held it up, it fell into dust...'

PART II

THE STORY OF BARBARA SKELTON

'Read but take heed that you such actions shun.
For honesty is best when all is done.'

The English Rogue, 1688[1]

1

THE WEDDING

'Take heed of inning at the fairest signs,
The Swan hath black flesh under white feathers.'[1]

February 1678

HER FACE LOOKED back at her from the mirror. She gazed at it intently, almost greedily, as though in its eyes and contours she would read the secret of her future and her fate. It was the face of a girl of sixteen who would one day be a lovely woman. It was the face of a bride on her wedding morning. Most important of all it was the face of Barbara Worth, soon to become Barbara Skelton.

It was such a young face, changing, unfinished, the mere sketch of the adult face into which it would gradually mature. But already, as she noticed tenderly, passing by its imperfections unheeded, it was a face that fascinated and arrested. The skin, pale and smooth as thick cream, was set off by the bronzen darkness of the hair; the heavy-lidded eyes under the fine eyebrows had a slumberous air, but, when the long lashes lifted, they gleamed with a cat's-eye green; the nose was prettily shaped without distinction except that afforded to it by the nostrils. These were curious. Delicately cut away, they gave an eager and ardent look to the indolent face. 'Winged nostrils', a Court poet was later to describe them. All the emphasis of the face lay in the fine eyes and the interesting nostrils. The mouth expressed little but rosy youthfulness and incipient discontent.

Aunt Dorothy Worth, Nurse, and the bridesmaids, cousin Ursula Worth, Arabella Crosbie, Bess Speke, Penelope Carew, and Anne and Moll Kirby, fluttered round her, excited, foolishly elated, each putting little finishing touches to her toilet that spoilt someone else's finishing touches and so merely added to the delay: rearranging the chaplet of pearls on her hair, tweaking an errant ringlet on her forehead, twisting round their fingers the curl that hung down her long slender throat; patting the white satin, silver-embroidered gown and the lemon-coloured petticoat, smoothing out the fall of fine lace that cunningly concealed the girlish angularity of her elbows; and fidgeting with the bride's favours of peach-coloured, silver and carnation ribbons, which must be attached firmly enough to her gown to remain in place during the marriage service and loosely enough for them to come away easily, without tearing the gown, when the guests scrambled for them after the wedding feast.[2]

Their remarks were as excited and inconsequent as their gestures.

'Sure, when the bridegroom sees all this bravery he will be right out of his senses for love,' giggled Bess Speke.

'I believe we would have done better to have dressed her hair in the French fashion. But I suppose it would be too late now to pull it down and start afresh?' fretted Penelope Carew.

'Provided Barbara makes an obedient wife and a proper housekeeper it will not matter how her hair is dressed on her wedding day.' So Aunt Dorothy improved the solemn hour with a note of asperity.

'Oh! to think that my pretty Precious is being taken from me,' moaned Nurse.

The young girl who was the centre of this attention accepted it as her due. This group of chattering women regarded her with intense if transitory interest because she was a bride, the only and virgin daughter of the house whom they were decking for the hymeneal rite, but Barbara Worth herself could not remember a day, or even an hour when her own personality and appearance had not seemed to her of paramount importance.

At last the point was reached where the bustle and solicitude of her attendants could do no more. Aunt Doll, Nurse and the bridesmaids agreed that the bride's appearance was perfectly handsome and genteel.

Time pressed. A creaking, a rumbling of wheels, jingling of bits, and the sound of horses' hooves from below the window announced that the coaches which were to carry the bridal party to church were gathering in the courtyard.

Aunt Doll said, 'Come now, we must be going.' She pressed a valedictory kiss on her niece's forehead. Her faded eyes were moist. Old Nurse was sniffing loudly. The bridesmaids, suddenly concerned about their own looks, peeped in the mirror, straightened the chaplets of snowdrops and violets on their heads. Snatching up their sprigs of rosemary tied with silver lace,[3] they waved their hands perfunctorily to the bride and hurried from the room, all but Ursula Worth and Arabella Crosbie, who as chief bridesmaids were to remain in attendance.

A little silence fell on the room and on the three girls. Barbara sat staring at herself in the mirror.

Then Arabella Crosbie said in low inquisitive tones, 'What are you thinking about, Barbara? Are you happy? Are you glad to be marrying Sir Ralph?'

Barbara dropped her eyelids. She said guardedly, 'Of course. We are the most convenient matches in England one to another. Had I matched to another family I might have found myself living in some deep dirty county like Lincolnshire or Devon, among people who knew nothing of me, and with no hope of going to London above once a year.'

'Yes, but Sir Ralph?' Arabella persisted. Boldly, she pressed the point. 'You love him, don't you?'

Barbara shot her a glance from beneath her lashes. She said demurely but with an air of worldly wisdom, 'I have always resolved to marry where I might hope to live happy. I believe that Sir Ralph is a man I may live very comfortably with in time.'

This was showing off, and she knew it. The match had been arranged between the respective parents when Barbara was six years old. But she had never been one for girlish confidences, being of a naturally secretive nature. She was certainly not going to betray herself to these silly girls at this late hour.

Arabella, disappointed, said flatly, 'Well I am sure I wish you all happiness in the enjoyment of each other.'

'And so do I, dear Bab,' gushed plain, kindly Ursula Worth. Barbara made no acknowledgement of these good wishes. She continued to gaze at her pensive reflection.

She was not sure what she hoped or expected of marriage. Aunt Doll, Nurse, all the older women of the household seemed to regard her to some degree as the victim of a sacred sacrifice to be decked out with jewels and flowers and tears. Her bridesmaids envied her her new importance, yet (she sensed with annoyance) hoped for some keener felicity, some younger more gallant lover themselves.

But this did not matter. Barbara was accustomed to consider everything from the point of view of her own pleasure and convenience. Marriage, as she regarded it, was a means of escape from the trammels of maidenhood – the only means open to a young woman of quality. For this she had been educated since childhood, in good manners, an elegant carriage and all the accomplishments, such as dancing, music, French and card playing, that would make her considerable and lovely in the eyes of some eligible man. She was making an exceptional match. Sir Ralph Skelton was her father's neighbour; their estates joined. He was wealthy, a man of weight and influence in the county. As Lady Skelton, mistress of Maryiot Cells and a town house in Lincoln's Inn Fields, she would live in style, even in some degree of magnificence. Who could say what delights and pleasures she would not experience? Marriage for other girls might mean tedious household cares and the rearing of a brood of infants. Her face – especially those eager nostrils – surely promised her some rarer and more delectable fate.

Thus she was musing vaguely, when there was a knock at the door. Her father's steward, staff in hand, announced in much the same tones that he would have used at a funeral:

'Mistress Barbara, your honoured father bids me say that he awaits you below.'

Barbara Worth rose to her feet with a swish of skirts. She was a swift and vivid mover. 'I am ready,' she said composedly.

She threw one last glance over her shoulder at the maiden face in the mirror and walked out of the room.

Her father was waiting for her at the foot of the great staircase. Relations, guests and members of the household, all wearing bride's favours, crowded the hall, and watched with curiosity and emotion the kiss that the grave man gave his only surviving child. He hung a thin gold chain, with a pendant in the shape of a fine ruby heart encircled with diamonds, round Barbara's neck. 'Daughter, your mother, who is now doubtless a blessed saint in heaven, required me on her death-bed to give you this jewel on your wedding morning. Wear it, child, and strive to emulate her in fidelity, modesty and obedience.'

Barbara's face twitched. She looked like a child who is going to weep. Her mother had adored and indulged her, and Barbara had reciprocated her love with a passion and possessiveness that she had felt for no other living being except herself. Her mother's death from smallpox when her daughter was fourteen had left Barbara furiously if silently resentful. She had not forgiven God for this untimely removal.

She regarded the ruby with pride as it glowed on her breast. How red it looked, like a huge drop of blood on her creamy skin. She trusted that marriage would develop her bosom. She was tall for her age, small-waisted, and long-legged, but as yet too thin.

She only half listened to her father's admonition. He was saying in a low voice, 'He is a gentleman and will soon be your husband. It will be your duty to study his wishes and your honour to conceal his faults.'

She thought with a spurt of rebellious contempt, 'And my faults? Ah! I will conceal them myself!' But she nodded her head dutifully.

Nurse, now sobbing openly, wrapped her nursling in a white velvet cloak and hood edged with fur. Her father took her by the hand and led her to the door. The family coach had been refurbished for the occasion. It was black with silver standards and adornments. The coachman and footmen were in new green serge livery. The stolid coach-horses of the shire breed (capable of taking their turn at the plough when necessary) had new green reins, and red ribbons in their manes. The other coaches which were to take the rest of the wedding party were equally fine. And so Barbara Worth drove away from her home.

Inside the coach Barbara and her father jolted along together in a solemn and stuffy silence. Her father regarded her with a new, almost respectful interest. He had been greatly saddened and disappointed at the death of Barbara's two elder brothers, one in infancy, the other as a promising young student at Oxford University. A daughter, even a pretty one, was a poor substitute, to his mind, for two sons. Moreover Barbara's looks, so different from his wife's placid comeliness, gave him a feeling of slight unease. But now that she was to become the wife of a man of Sir Ralph Skelton's worth and consequence she seemed to him safer and more accountable, a daughter of whom any man might be proud. He remembered that she had always acted dutifully, whatever she might have looked, that she was motherless. He wished, with an odd fleeting feeling of compunction, that propriety and custom had enabled him to give her some practical advice about his own sex to help her on her way. But of course the girl must learn by experience as every young wife before her had had to learn.

It was a fine morning for a wedding. The sky was full of light, and dove-coloured clouds. In the east the rising sun, hidden behind a smoke-grey cloud, poured down the benediction of its rays upon the waking earth. The horizon was the colour of a peach, the western sky a tender, elusive blue. Sunlight gleamed on the muddy puddles in the road, the pools in the fields, the bare branches of the trees; the shadows lay light as veils on the shining grass. Bird song and clumps of snowdrops proclaimed the spring.

As the coach passed through the gates of the park a crowd of villagers and tenants waved their hats and wished the young lady of the manor joy in her marriage. All the short way to Bishops Worthy church was lined with gaping, cheering country folk.

Their squire accepted the homage as a due and natural tribute to his God-ordained status in the county. Barbara inclined her head graciously to them through the new-fangled glass windows, lowered for the occasion.

A stylish equipage, consisting of a coach with a silver body and gilt standards, and six outriders, rumbled past them. The armorial bearings showed that it belonged to Lord Hogarth, Barbara's maternal uncle, down from London for the wedding, and in a hurry to reach the church before the bride.

There was such a press of coaches, riders, guests, servants and beggars round the lych gate of the little church that it was several minutes before the bridal procession could be sorted out and set in motion. Musicians led the way with fiddles and flutes, followed by a bride-page carrying a bride cup of silver gilt in which was stuck a gilded sprig of rosemary. Now came the bride, young, immature yet seductive in her finery, two little bride-pages in satin suits and lace (nephews of Sir Ralph) leading her by the ribbons on her gown, thus symbolising the modest reluctance of the virgin to enter the married state. Behind came the bridesmaids walking two by two, each with their sprig of rosemary in their hand, their chaplet of snowdrops and violets on their heads. And behind again the principal kinsfolk and guests, in all the bravery of periwigs and curls, velvets, silks and satins, laces and ribbons, muffs and fans, cravats and buckles, velvet shoes and embroidered stockings, as brilliant in the rustic churchyard as a flock of exotic birds.

The bridegroom and his groomsmen were waiting at the church. As Barbara was led up to Sir Ralph Skelton she thought with a sudden physical shrinking, 'This is my fate!'

She raised her strange green eyes and looked dispassionately at the man she was to wed. He was thirty-six, fresh enough looking even to the arrogant eyes of sixteen, well set up enough with an air that his friends would call dignified, his detractors consequential. His periwig of light brown hair suited his florid complexion. His eyes were blue and prominent, and he had sandy lashes. There was nothing distasteful about his appearance nor anything to stir the senses. He was richly dressed in a long-skirted coat of carnation velvet with a vest tunic of silver cloth and black velvet breeches. He wore knots of peach-coloured carnation and silver ribbon on his shoulders in compliment to his bride, and red heels to his shoes. He drew himself up as he met his bride's gaze, smiled at her complacently and reassuringly.

Something wild and innocent in Barbara cried out in panic, 'No, this can never be my fate! Escape before it is too late!' But she knew that it was too late, and with downcast eyes and a demure smile gave her bridegroom her hand.

The ring was on her finger. A gold ring with a posy of Sir Ralph's own choosing engraved inside, 'God make me prolific, obedient and sedulous.'

Barbara Skelton twisted the unaccustomed ornament round her slender fourth finger while, with eyes fixed in apparent devotion on the clergyman, she mused on all that she would do now that she was a married woman and Lady Skelton.

Old Mr Belcher was in his element. Wedding sermons were his speciality. Many a newly joined couple had knelt before him to receive his advice and admonition, and if their unions had not always turned out satisfactory it was certainly not Mr Belcher's fault, for he made a point of stressing the perils and trials as well as the blessings of matrimony, urging young couples to honour one another and bear with one another's foibles, also to practise those innocent arts that increase and stimulate love. What these arts were Mr Belcher did not specify, leaving this to his hearers' imaginations.

The bride, being the weaker vessel, naturally came in for the larger slice of Mr Belcher's advice. Barbara, through her day-dreams, heard herself being admonished to be good-tempered, obedient, and modest. She must eschew gossip and be a right housekeeper, preferring her home to all other places, and not decking herself up like Jezebel to attract the attention of strangers. She must not ask if her lord was wise or simple, but must honour and obey him in all things.

But Sir Ralph too came in for his smaller share of the homily. Husbands who were choleric and testy with their wives were justly to be censured, while Mr Belcher deplored the masculine habit of speaking slightingly of women's constancy, comparing them to clouds in the sky, motes in the sun, snuffs in the candle and the like.

Carried away by his own eloquence Mr Belcher soared into less prosaic regions. The husband and wife should illuminate each other's lives like two candles; like two flowers the sweet perfume of their godly lives should mingle; their voices should join in harmony like two well-tuned instruments. It really seemed as if there would be no end either to his similes or his sermon, but at last Sir Ralph and his bride emerged from the dim church into the pale February sunshine. The bell-ringers, inspired by a draught of ale and ten shillings distributed among them by order of the bride's father, rang out a lusty peal, the crowd cheered, and sweet rushes and snowdrops strewed the path down which Sir Ralph Skelton and his lady walked smilingly arm in arm.

The first part of the wedding-day festivities – the feast given by the bride's father at his house – was over. The long, rich and highly indigestible meal had been consumed, toast upon toast had been drunk, the guests dipping their sprigs of rosemary into their tankards, the bride bowing prettily in response over her glass; the bride's cakes, enclosed in iced sugar to form one large cake, had been broken, with laughter and jest, over the bride's head. Her gifts had been admired – the fine jewels which were now to be hers, the green velvet riding saddle with silver fringes and lace, the money-chest painted with landscapes and nosegays in the Dutch fashion, as well as such dainty trifles as a diamond bodkin and a silver fork. Scarves, gloves and rings had been distributed among the guests.

Custom decreed that the newly wedded bride should remain for three weeks among her own people but, at her future mother-in-law's request, the motherless Barbara was to go at once to her new family. Now, as the short afternoon faded, Sir Ralph carried his lady off to Maryiot Cells, and all the relations and friends (many of them flushed and unsteady on their feet) followed in their coaches or on horseback exclaiming, not for the first time that day, on the conveniency of a match between two such close neighbours, which thus enabled them to enjoy the friendly rivalry of both Sir Ralph and his father-in-law's hospitality.

The Great Hall at Maryiot Cells was festooned with ropes of evergreens, fashioned by the industrious fingers of the bridesmaids. Scores of wax candles, set in silver sconces, put to shame the twilight that crept in through the leaded lights of the casement windows.

The Dowager Lady Skelton stood with her family grouped around her to receive her guests. She was a dumpy little woman with a flurried expression who might or might not have been pretty once. The best proof that she must have possessed some attractions lay in the person of her married daughter Lady Kingsclere, a large opulent blonde who, though somewhat handicapped by the prominent blue eyes of the family, had a brilliant pink and white skin and an abundance of yellow hair that entitled her to consider herself a beauty. The death recently of an older married daughter in childbirth, and the death long ago of two young daughters and a son from smallpox, had left large gaps in the Dowager Lady Skelton's family. Henrietta Kingsclere was only twenty-four years old. Secure in the possession of a fine white bosom, a handsome if dull husband and two sons, she displayed a patronising affability towards her young sister-in-law.

Her younger brother, Roger Skelton, a slight, pale, pink-eyed youth, was twenty-one. He had just returned from a tour of Europe during which he had acquired some bad statuary and a passion for gaming.

The youngest member of the family, Paulina Skelton, was a silent, self-contained girl of twelve. Unlike the rest of her family she had clear-cut features and an intelligent expression. She eyed her new sister-in-law distrustingly, thinking that she would not buy a horse that had such uneasy nostrils and eyes.

As the guests poured into the house, the damask curtains were drawn, candle after candle broke into its little flower of flame, the musicians in the gallery struck up the strains of a coranto.[4] Lord Kingsclere, as the highest-born gallant in the room, led out the new Lady Skelton. Behind them flowed the bright train of the dancers, making the gay music visible with their gaily clad bodies. The colours, orange-tawny, grass-green, yellow, peacock-blue, flame, carnation, violet, scarlet, black and white, mingled and shifted, as though the dancers were gaudy threads being shuttled to and fro by an invisible hand.

Before feet had had time to grow too weary or foreheads too sweaty beneath heavy periwigs, supper was announced. Maryiot Cells, always renowned for its hospitality, lived up to its highest standards that wedding night. There were the wines of France, Spain, the Rhineland and the Orient, as well as homely ale, for the thirsty, and for the hungry a bewildering display of eatables, from the solid toothsomeness of collared pig and stewed carps, to the more refined tastiness of marchpanes, pistaches and chocolate amandes. Yet all but the elderly, the stout and the gouty were ready to dance again when the repast was over, to dance the spirited galliard as well as the stately pavane.[5]

To claim a dance and a kiss from the bride was the privilege of each male wedding guest, and young Lady Skelton declared laughingly that she needed a hundred mouths and as many pairs of feet to fulfil her obligations. As it was, a wild and buoyant gaiety upheld her, a gaiety without root or reason, born of the moment, of her youth, of the wine and music and bright colours, the flattery, the kisses and the laughter. An unwonted flush stained her cheeks to a pale carnation, her lips were moist and red, her eyes gleamed between the long lashes, her dark burnished curls hung loose. So debonair and heedless she seemed that more than one of the older ladies regarded her curiously, hardly knowing whether to pity or disapprove, for after all marriage was a serious thing, as the poor, giddy young creature would soon find out, and no cause for wanton jollity.

But Barbara neither noticed their pursed lips nor would have cared had she done so. This was her hour, brimful of the excitement, the sharp edge of delight for which she craved. All time was gathered up in this room of shimmering candlelight and quivering music, and laid at Barbara Skelton's feet as a wedding gift.

But Sir Ralph had other notions. He was showing signs of restlessness, as his friends noticed with sly amusement. It was past midnight and time for him to claim his bride.

They were dancing a cushion dance, which entailed more kissing than ever.[6]

'She must come to and she shall come to and she must come whether she will or no,' went the refrain, and then: 'She must go fro and she shall go fro and she must go whether she will or no.'

As Barbara frolicked her way through the dance her bridesmaids, at a nod from the Dowager Lady Skelton, came forward to escort her to the nuptial chamber. Instantly the dancers swarmed round her, scrambling with shouts and laughter to snatch the lucky love-favours from her gown. Flushed and dishevelled, her low-cut bodice slipping from her shoulders, Barbara made her escape and ran up the Great Stairs.

From above she could hear that the dancing had begun again. She leant for a moment against the balustrade listening to the muted sound of music and tripping feet and voices from below.

'She must go fro and she shall go fro and she shall go whether she will or no.'

The words, unaccompanied by the candlelight and smiling faces had a sinister sound as though some obscure threat lay behind their apparent inconsequence. Standing there in the shadows in her pale gown Barbara felt like a forlorn and resentful ghost. To be out of the bright centre of things, to be forgotten, even for this brief space, was to taste something of the anonymity of death. Why could she not stay where she belonged among those riotous young people below, instead of being undressed and put to bed with a man whom she did not love?

But to her bridesmaids this was the crowning moment of the day. A vicarious excitement was apparent in their gestures and voices. 'As though they prepared me for my execution,' thought Barbara sulkily. Before undressing her they urged her to partake of beer and plum buns swimming in a bowl of spiced ale. 'To keep away timorous thoughts, dear cousin,' murmured Ursula Worth kindly. Penelope Carew laughed boldly, 'Oh never you fear! She will cheer up quick enough when her bedfellow comes.'

Arabella Crosbie worried, 'I hope we have remembered to put everything in the benediction possett – milk, wine, yolk of eggs, sugar, cinnamon, nutmeg ... Moll, did we remember the nutmeg?'

But Moll Kirby and her sister were admiring the bridal bed. It was richly upholstered with olive green, rose and silver brocade hangings and curtains, and topped with plumes of ostrich feathers. Ann Kirby fingered the head valances. 'Lord! this is the finest bed I have ever seen. Why,

Her Majesty couldn't wish for better. You ought to beget some pretty little children in it.'

Barbara said complacently, 'Sir Ralph is wondrously free and kind in his behaviour to me. He will deny me nothing.' Arabella recalled her companions to their duty. 'Come now, girls, or the groomsmen will have undressed Sir Ralph before we have Barbara ready.'

They crowded round her, lifting the chaplet of pearls off her hair, taking care to leave no pins in her curls, for that would have portended the direst ill luck. They had her in her satin bed gown, her hair combed and perfumed, and had bundled her into bed, when the noise of footsteps and masculine voices outside announced the arrival of the bridegroom.

Into the bridal chamber burst the groomsmen, all very jocular and all more or less drunk, and in their midst Sir Ralph in his embroidered night-shirt, steady enough on his feet but flushed and sweating profusely. Clapping him on the back they urged him with all the bawdy jokes proper to the occasion to get into bed with his bride.

Now was the moment for the time-honoured game of throwing the stocking. The best man and groomsmen seated themselves with their backs to the bridegroom's side of the bed, the bridesmaids seated themselves in like manner on the bride's side. Each groomsman held one of the bridegroom's stockings, each girl one of the bride's. At a word from the bride they tossed the stockings backwards over their shoulders. Those who scored a hit on the bride or bridegroom might expect to be married themselves within the year. The room was filled with guests who had crowded in to see the fun. There was a gust of laughter, shouts, giggles, and girlish shrieks as the silken hose flew wildly across the wedding bed. Everyone talked at once, argued, accused each other of cheating, vowed that they must have another chance, scuffled about on the floor to retrieve their stockings, ended by pelting each other with them, snatching them from one another, chasing each other round the bed, kissing each other, excited, tipsy and hilarious. The married pair sat up in bed and laughed politely, Sir Ralph concealing his impatience and Barbara her yawns, for she had been up since half-past four that morning and was sleepy.

Arabella Crosbie brought in the benediction possett at last, and handed it to the bride and bridegroom, who toasted one another as they drank from the silver cup. The guests, in spite of this hint, would have gone on rollicking in the bridal chambers for hours, but Arabella with a firmness beyond her years took the situation in hand. Assisted by her fellow bridesmaids and the more staid onlookers, she pushed and urged the revellers out of the room, warning them that if they lingered much longer it would be dawn, and time for the bride to be roused with music and a sack possett. It was obvious, even to the most inebriated, that this would not be a very satisfactory state of affairs for the bridegroom, and so the room was emptied. Footsteps and loud voices and laughter died away down the passages.

Arabella Crosbie drew the curtains of the bridal bed, saying with an arch smile, 'I wish you joy of one another,' extinguished all the candles but one and tiptoed from the room.

Her good wishes were not fulfilled as far as Barbara was concerned. She submitted to Sir Ralph but did not enjoy him.

2

MIDDAY AT MARYIOT CELLS

'Like rich men that take pleasure
In hiding more than handling treasure.'[1]

March 1683

THE LADIES OF Maryiot Cells were sitting at their needlework in one of the bay windows of the Long Gallery – young Lady Skelton, the Dowager Lady Skelton, Paulina Skelton, Aunt Dorothy Worth (who had come to live with her niece since the death of Barbara's father), Mistress Agatha Trimble (a widow and a relation of old Lady Skelton's), as well as a waiting gentlewoman who was some kind of an ignored and impoverished cousin of the Skelton family.

As they stitched away at their crewel work, their rosemary stitch and needle-point, they chatted about this and that, all, that is to say, but young Lady Skelton, who was embroidering tiny silken nosegays on a flowered taffeta gown, with a patience that by no means expressed her inner feelings, and her sister-in-law Paulina who was always of a silent habit.

The Dowager, as usual, was preoccupied with the subject of health – her own and other people's. Now that the March winds had come round again she must expect to find herself very out of order and troubled with her cough. As a girl her mother had always given her, at this time of year, a chest preservative made of the dried lung of a fox ground to a powder and mixed with a little almond milk or broth. There was nothing like these tried remedies, when all was said and done, but Dr Henley would have none of it, and ordained for her syrup of roses and asses' milk, which she did not believe to be by any means so efficacious. This reminded her how feeble Cousin Jonathan had grown since his last apoplectic fit.

'He should wear oiled cloth between his socks and the soles of his feet if he does not wish to go to his earthly mansion within the year,' said old Agatha Trimble, in a tone which conveyed that only Christian charity of the highest order, overcoming her dislike of Cousin Jonathan, had prompted her to make the suggestion.

Aunt Doll was telling how a beggar – a distracted woman – had stopped her at the bakehouse door that morning and asked for alms. On being given a piece of bread and cheese instead, the pretended madwoman had recovered her wits sufficiently to say such things to poor Aunt Doll as flesh and blood never heard before.

'Which will teach you, I trust, not to encourage these filthy, barbarous folk, my dear Dorothy,' commented Agatha Trimble incisively.

Aunt Doll's hands trembled. The only way to endure Agatha Trimble was to regard her as a joke. Her late husband had evidently been deficient in the necessary sense of humour, for he had died within three months of their marriage, leaving his large and unalluring widow just sufficiently badly off to make it obligatory for her richer relations to offer her a home, and with sufficiently independent means to enable her to be insufferably rude.

Aunt Doll was no match for Agatha. But now, emboldened by the presence of her niece, who was bound by ties of kinship and affection to support her, she said:

'Barbara dear I must recommend you to lock up your silver dragée box. I peeked into it today to see if I should make you some more sugar-plums and I found only one solitary sugar-plum left. I believe you have not sat in the little wainscoat room this last week, so I fear one of the serving-maids has been dipping her fingers into it.'

Aunt Doll was as well aware as everyone else in the household of Agatha Trimble's inordinate greed for sweetmeats, and her total lack of scruple and delicacy in helping herself to any that she found unguarded, and she rejoiced now to see the dull flush that suffused her enemy's heavily jowled cheeks.

Barbara said in her smooth low voice, 'Thank you, Aunt Doll. I will speak to Housekeeper about it.'

She rose with one of her swift, unexpected movements and went to the ebony cabinet, ostensibly to select another strand of silk, in reality to prevent herself from betraying in some violent manner the extreme exasperation that seethed within her.

These women with their puerile chatter of physics and ailments, of housekeeping and servants' misdemeanours, of local births and funerals – was it possible that she had lived five years among them and preserved her reason? For five years their trivialities had buzzed in her ears ... 'A black velvet tippet. Every gentlewoman who wishes to make a show in the world has one ...' 'He is a servant fit in all respects to serve a gentleman ...' 'Seville oranges and Malaga lemons at the present price are too dear for my purse …' 'The poor lady was brought to her bed a month before her time … ' 'They gave the old gentleman a very worthy funeral with scutcheons and burnt wine and biscuits in plenty.'

There was no end of their supply of small talk; it flowed on as incessant and as senseless as the river below the house, bearing away on its surface, so Barbara had sometimes felt in a spasm of helpless fury, little fragments of her own youth and vitality.

If she could have felt a hearty dislike for one of them (such as she had felt almost from her wedding day for her sister-in-law Henrietta Kingsclere) their company would have been more endurable, but not one of them was worthy of her mettle. Even bullying old Agatha deferred to her as the mistress of the manor, dispenser of comforts and hospitality. Aunt Doll was her sometimes peevish but on the whole willing slave. Her sister-in-law Paulina would not serve Barbara as either confidante or rival. She had grown into a handsome enough girl, with her regular features, clear colouring and level brows, but, Barbara thought impatiently, she seemed to belong to an outmoded generation. She would have been at home during the heroic and strenuous days of the Civil War. She wore her brown hair more plainly than was consistent with fashion, preferred a riding habit to any other attire, and led a silent, reserved life of her own in the library and stables.

As for the Dowager Lady Skelton, she accepted her daughter-in-law's graceful manners and dutiful ways at their face value. Undistinguished in appearance herself, she was not a little bedazzled by the beauty of her son's wife.

Even the fact that Barbara had so far presented Sir Ralph with nothing more substantial than two early miscarriages, had not shaken her pride in her daughter-in-law. She was confident that before long her 'dear children' would be blessed with a sweet brave babe, to their own and the family's infinite content. Next time, dear Barbara must make much of her dear self, and not hazard herself in the least degree either by riding or dancing. She was collecting a formidable array of nauseating prescriptions in readiness for that auspicious moment.

Barbara herself did not know if she regretted her childlessness or not. Childbirth might have impaired her supple and elegant figure, nor could she share her mother-in-law's enthusiasm for the prospect of a child of Sir Ralph's begetting. On the other hand she resented being denied anything that might have added to her consequence, any cause for triumphing over the blonde complacency of Henrietta Kingsclere. And, in the prevailing tedium of her life, she would almost have welcomed childbirth's exciting, elemental pain. As it was, the carved cradle that had rocked generations of infant Skeltons to sleep remained as empty and cold as Barbara Skelton's heart.

It astonished, outraged, Barbara to look back over the five years that had passed since her wedding day, that day which she had naïvely believed to be the gateway to a dazzling future. How aimlessly they had crawled by, sluggard as an earthworm.

Her first experience of her husband's caresses had been almost ludicrously disappointing. Habit had not made his marital attentions more agreeable to her. She regarded them as a tedious necessity to be endured with as good a grace as possible.

There had been some satisfaction at first in the new importance of her married state and in her position as lady of the manor. But this had soon staled. Barbara had intended and expected since childhood to make a good match. What then? For what end and to what purpose had her body flowered to its present perfection, her face achieved its present curious loveliness? To preside at Sir Ralph's table, sit through the solemn stately meals, to entertain his worthy, usually dull guests, listening with smiling lips and stupefied mind to talk of Quarter and Petty Sessions,[2] of vagrants and recusants, of poachers and tenants, crops, the importation of Irish cattle, the Popish Plot and Exclusion Bill;[3] to hear the family chaplain droning the same prayers morning after morning; to sit in the family pew in Maiden Worthy church Sunday after Sunday, submerged beneath a stream of turgid piety; to distribute alms to the deserving poor, to supervise the making of the Christmas plum pies and plum porridge, the work of the stillroom and brewery and the spring-cleaning of the house with soap, ashes and fuller's earth,[4] to embroider, to play the lute and harpsichord, to stroll between the parterres of the formal garden and in the shade of the yew rides – was it for this tame existence that Barbara Skelton had been endowed with this graceful body, smooth creamy skin, this wealth of bronzen curls, these sleepy beckoning eyes and mettlesome nostrils?

Expectation had died hard. Like someone in a maze, she had been constantly on the alert to find the hoped-for outlet. Each fresh day might bring the thrilling sensation, the vivid emotion which her youth and temperament demanded. And like someone in a maze, she had been continually baffled, trapped in a narrow, shut-in place, tantalised by the laughter and singing of the libertine world without.

It was not that she lacked company. Maryiot Cells was always full of people. Every relation of the family, however distant or unwanted, had the right to claim its hospitality, and could descend uninvited with a retinue of children, chaplains, maids, servants, horses and coaches. Or worse still, poor relations would arrive, dingy widows who hoped that Barbara would find husbands for their plain daughters, ne'er-do-weels in hiding from their creditors, or old dodderers like Cousin Jonathan, who had had an apoplectic fit while on a two days' visit to Maryiot Cells four years ago, and had remained there ever since, grumbling and drinking Sir Ralph's sack and port.

Moreover Sir Ralph prided himself on keeping open house, and the neighbouring families were frequently entertained at Maryiot Cells, as well as any visitors of distinction who were passing that way. But Barbara had not found a friend among the women or a lover among the men. Friendship she did not desire. It seemed to her at once too tepid and too exacting a relationship to repay attention. But she would have welcomed the distraction of a lover.

The atmosphere of Maryiot Cells, however, was not conducive to amorous intrigue. Clerics and elderly folk never wearied of deploring the vicious frivolity of Court and society. Life at Maryiot Cells was as seemly and decorous as though His Merry Majesty had never been restored. Prying relations and servants were in every corner and cranny. It would take a venturesome and ingenious gallant to cuckold Sir Ralph, and no such gallant had come young Lady Skelton's way.

She had entertained vivid hopes that her existence might be enlivened by visits to London. But she had only been three times to the capital since her marriage. Her first visit had been agreeable enough. Sir Ralph had taken his young bride to town in a new chariot; he had bought her some pretty jewels and several pieces of walnut furniture; taken her to Court and to the playhouse, the New Gardens at Vauxhall, the New Exchange and other fashionable resorts.[5] It was all fresh to the country-bred Barbara. She was content to see the sights and fashions, enjoy the bustle of the town, and bask in the admiring looks evoked by her immature but already provocative charms.

After this, ill-luck had dogged her London expeditions. The second one had been a family affair, with the Dowager and Paulina of the party, and the family coach laden with portmanteaux, pet dogs and provisions. Once in London, Paulina had promptly fallen sick of the smallpox, so that no one had ventured near the Skelton house in Lincoln's Inn Fields, nor had the family been invited to visit their friends. Paulina had been (most unfairly in Barbara's opinion) the centre of attention, as if there was some merit in being a nuisance and spoiling everyone else's enjoyment, thought Barbara moodily, as she sat embroidering in the parlour or helped to mix some apothecary's concoction for the invalid. All had been anxiety and solicitude. Old Lady Skelton lamented that her daughter had not been taken ill in the country, where they could have laid a sheep in her bed, as had been done when she had measles, it being well known that this animal was so prone to infection that it drew the venom from a sick person to itself. Everyone exclaimed on the singular mercy of Heaven in bringing the young girl safely through the illness, and with an unblemished complexion. Barbara, brooding over her lost opportunities and pleasures, cared little for Paulina's complexion.

Her last visit to London had been cut short by Sir Ralph himself who, hearing that his friend the Clarenceux King of Arms[6] was passing through Buckinghamshire to attend the funeral of one of the local nobility, had insisted on returning to Maryiot Cells to entertain the distinguished traveller. Since then he had obstinately resisted his wife's pleas for a season in London. The harvest – the sheep shearing – the Quarter Sessions – there had always been something to claim his attention. He could not conceive why his wife should wish to leave the clean wholesome air of Maryiot Cells for that ugly noisy London.

He could not conceive, in fact had no inkling, of the brooding resentment, rising at times to a kind of sullen fury, that was taking possession of Barbara's soul. Other women might have sulked, stormed or nagged, but this was not Barbara Skelton's way. She was of a deeply secretive nature, delighting in concealment. To outward seeming she remained smooth-mannered, gracious, docile. Inside herself she led an intense impatient life, all her thoughts concentrated on her own personality, and always watchful to seize the opportunity for self-expression that must surely come to her before long.

But meanwhile some form of outlet was essential to her, and she found this for a time in the fashionable pursuit of gaming. Even the staid Sir Ralph could not discourage his guests from playing cards – young and old they were crazy about it – and whenever young Lady Skelton had the opportunity she played deep. She had very fair luck as a gamester, being both bold and wary, and by her success escaped the reproofs which her cautious husband would certainly have administered to her had she fallen into debt. The money she won meant little to her – as her late father's only surviving child and heir she was well-endowed, and Sir Ralph was not ungenerous – but the sense of power that she experienced as, sweetly smiling, she stretched out her hand for her gains, observing her opponent's mortified or downcast face, gave her a curious satisfaction.

It is doubtful if this partial outlet would have satisfied her indefinitely, appealing as it did only to her brain and not to her starved emotions (while, for that matter, her country environment gave her neither unlimited opportunities for indulging in it, nor the background of febrile excitement which is the gamester's natural element). But before the enjoyment of gaming had begun to pall, another prospect, far more alluring and uncommon, had very strangely opened before her.

It had come about through her card-playing and through her intense dislike of her sister-in-law, Henrietta Kingsclere. This had been the soil from which her project had sprung, but the idea had been her own, bursting like a fantastic and poisonous plant from the seed of her frustration.

It happened like this:

The previous autumn Lord and Lady Kingsclere came on a visit to Maryiot Cells. These visits were odious to Barbara. Henrietta Kingsclere's careless patronage of her young sister-in-law had sharpened to jealous distrust as she had seen Barbara develop into a woman of unusual attractions. Accustomed to being the beauty of the family, Barbara's looks, so different from her own, affronted her. Though in many ways a stupid woman, she sensed that something vital, even violent, throbbed behind Barbara's composed manner. She lost no opportunity to assert her superiority over Barbara: her handsome husband, her two pretty young sons, above all her gay and fashionable life at Court – these were all weapons with which to daunt the younger woman. It would have flattered her to feel that Barbara envied her – on this basis they could have become friends – but Barbara's green eyes were insolent.

Henrietta was as enthusiastic a gambler as Barbara, and at the card table their rivalry found fevered expression. More often than not Barbara was the winner, but fortune was against her this visit. With silent chagrin she saw her sister-in-law win night after night. Her own losses mounted to an alarming degree, but pride absolutely forbade her either to abstain from play or to play for lesser stakes.

It was the last evening of the Kingscleres' stay. The family party gathered in the withdrawing-room, where tea was served with some solemnity in delicate China dishes. (Sir Ralph considered it a base unworthy Indian practice and unbecoming to a Christian family, but the ladies insisted.)

Then they settled down for their usual parlour game. This evening it was 'I love my love with an A',[7] the ladies sitting on a carpet in the centre of the room. Henrietta Kingsclere's supercilious yawns indicated her boredom at this tepid domestic version of a game that, played in fashionable circles, was made the excuse for the most bawdy wit and daring impropriety. Needlework and music filled up the interval till supper, after which the servants came with torches to light the older ladies to their rooms. (Paulina had disappeared long since into the library.) Sir Ralph, who had been snoring in his velvet-covered chair, followed their example. Lord Kingsclere, after strumming on a cittern,[8] declared that he was also for bed.

Sunset was the accustomed hour for the Skelton household to retire to rest, but for Barbara, Henrietta and her younger brother, Roger Skelton, who was also down from London, the real business of the day – their game of ombre[9] – had yet to begin.

Cards, wine and candles were brought, the gilded leather curtains drawn, a table set by the fire which crackled in the vast, elaborately carved stone fireplace (for it was late September and growing chill). Except for this pool of mingled fire and candlelight the withdrawing-room was in shadow; the richly panelled walls with their tapestry hangings and the ceiling with its pendant plaster work seemed, in the dim light, to have a life of their own as mysterious and luxuriant as a forest.

The firelight shone rosily on Barbara's pearl-coloured satin gown, drew an answering glow from the beautiful ruby heart which she wore round her neck. The fashionable game of ombre was her favourite. To play it skilfully required a great deal of application, and this was where she scored over Henrietta who, for all her expertness, was easily distracted, joining in overheard snatches of conversation or picking up her pet spaniel to coo over it. It pleased Barbara particularly when it fell to her lot to be ombre – the solo player against whom the other two players combined. To think only of her own concerns and strive for herself alone suited her disposition exactly. She felt confident that this evening she would recuperate herself for her recent losses. It was indeed imperative that she should win, if she was to avoid the mortification of having to confess to Sir Ralph and beg him to settle her debts. She knew him well enough to know that he would do so, but only on condition that she abstained from deep play in future. Intolerable thought. The feeling that much depended on her success tonight, added to her animosity towards Henrietta, made her tingle with a nervous and not unpleasurable excitement. Roger Skelton, eager as a ferret himself, gave his sister-in-law a shrewd look.

For the first hour or so it seemed as though her luck had indeed turned. The pile of counters before her increased slowly but steadily. Growing confident and impatient, Barbara proposed that they should double the stakes. Roger Skelton agreed with a shrug of his shoulders; Henrietta, who was looking flushed, with a curt nod.

And as though the suggestion had snapped the tenuous glittering thread of her good fortune Barbara, from that moment, began to lose. And losing, she felt her concentration slipping from her. Strive as she might she could not thrust the thought of tomorrow's reckoning out of her mind. Already she owed her sister-in-law more than she could easily afford. This night's doing, unless she could retrieve herself, would land her in serious money difficulties for the first time in her gaming career. To confess her predicament to Henrietta, and to ask for a few months' grace on the grounds of their relationship was unthinkable. There was not a woman in the kingdom to whom she could bear less to be beholden than Henrietta Kingsclere.

With an air of graceful unconcern, which was the exact antithesis of the hot perturbation within her, she said, 'I do very ill tonight. You must give me the opportunity to recover myself a little, Henrietta, or I shall have to go very meanly – if not barefoot! – for the rest of the year!'

'All the opportunity you wish, dear Bab. It is only midnight, and in London that is when we begin to wake up. Lord! if I were in town tonight I suppose I should be at Whitehall, and dancing like mad till six or seven in the morning.'

Barbara rose, fetched fresh candles from a side table, and replenished the wine glasses. These candles had burnt low, the untended fire had smouldered into embers, before Barbara, with a little gesture of defeat, admitted herself at the end of her resources. Her face was pale, the dark ringlets lay damp on her forehead, but her hands were steady and her mouth firm. Roger Skelton, glancing at her, thought, 'She bears her losses with a pretty indifference, the jade!' He had tried to fondle his brother's wife soon after her marriage, and had been repulsed, but he could admire an undaunted gamester.

It was now that Henrietta made the remark that was to prove her – and in a far wider sense, Barbara's – undoing. In a tone of sneering jocularity she said, 'I declare, Roger, that it was cruel of seasoned gamesters like ourselves to get poor Barbara into this lamentable pickle. But no doubt our worthy brother will thank us for it, if it gives her a disgust of gaming and teaches her to be content with her housekeeping and her needle.' The colour sprang into Barbara's cheeks. She opened her eyes wide and fixed them on her sister-in-law with a look of undisguised spite. Then she pulled the gold chain with its ruby pendant over her head and threw it down on the table.

'I will play you for this. It is a jewel of the greatest brilliance and rarity – worth all your paltry gains put together.'

Henrietta bit her lips. She said, 'Well, Roger, it seems that Barbara has not learnt her lesson yet. Shall we take her on?'

Roger's eyes glistened. 'As you wish.'

Henrietta said, 'Very well, Barbara. We accept the challenge. How many games shall we play?'

Barbara said fiercely, 'I will stake it on a single game.'

Better to know quickly what was in store for her. As Roger dealt the cards Barbara, her hands clenched on her lap, prayed, 'God, if you make me win I shall forgive You for my mother's death.'

She was ombre and she played as though her life depended on it. She lost.

There was a moment's silence. Roger, shuffling the cards nervously, glanced at Barbara. Her heavily-lidded eyes gleamed green between their long lashes, her delicate nostrils quivered. The curious, rather feline proportions of her face were more than ever noticeable. He thought inconsequently, 'She has a dangerous look.'

The ruby heart lay like a gout of blood on the table. Henrietta Kingsclere put out her plump hand and took it.

'Yes, it is a pretty jewel. I shall wear it when next I go to Court. And if you ever have a daughter, Barbara, I might leave it to her in my will, provided that she is a dutiful niece to me and that I have no girl of my own. It was your mother's jewel, was it not?'

Barbara nodded. She could not speak. She was suffocating with remorse and rage. She cried wildly to herself, 'Mother! never mind. I swear I will get it back!'

Henrietta yawned, showing a large amount of teeth and pink mouth. 'Thank heaven, I can lie abed tomorrow. My lord leaves for town early in the coach, for he has business with the Privy Council, but I shall not set out to the Forresters' till the afternoon. I shall lie at Ischam for two days and then return to London after sunset on Friday, for they have a supper party for me that evening. I shall be their most considerable guest, and I would not disappoint the good folk for the world.'

Henrietta was the kind of person who thought that all her arrangements, however trivial, must be of as much interest to other people as they were to herself.

Barbara said softly, 'Take heed that St Nicholas's clerks[10] do not take my – your ruby from you. The Fenny Stratford road is famed for highwaymen.'

And as she made the casual remark the thought flamed up in her mind, 'Why not?'

Why not? It was being done most days and most nights on all the roads of England. Nothing was needed but a horse, a pistol and a bold heart. And in this case, a suit of man's attire. But in this large household that would be easy to procure. She was tall for a woman, slender but well-built. Her hands? They could be hidden in gloves. Her voice? It was naturally low-pitched. She could disguise it sufficiently. Her thoughts raced on, wildly elated. At the best it would be a novel experience, a delicious, secret triumph – would that pink and white jelly scream, weep or faint in a crisis? At the worst it could be passed off as a prank. But there would be no worst. She felt an extraordinary sense of confidence and pleasure surge through her. She felt capable of everything – mad to put her crazy, beautiful idea into execution.

She rose, smoothed out her satin skirt, and going to the window pulled the heavy curtains apart.

She said gaily. 'Why, it is dawn.'

Now, on this March day, as she drew the brightly coloured skeins of silk from the cabinet drawer, she recalled with a sharp amusement and satisfaction the night when she had robbed Henrietta Kingsclere.

How she had smiled at her own unfamiliar reflection as she dressed herself behind locked doors for the night's adventure, telling herself that she made a very pretty young man, in the long skirted coat and breeches of dark cloth that she had purloined from the big chest where Hogarth the steward kept the men-servants' spare suits. Beneath the large, flat-brimmed beaver hat her face was provocatively feminine. But a mask would remedy that. The high, spurred boots, the heavy gauntlet gloves, the leather belt and pistol holster – what a piquant change from muffs, lace caps and painted fans!

She drew the loaded pistol from the holster and examined it carefully. Her elder brother – dead now these seven years – had amused himself one holiday, by teaching her something of the use of firearms. How he would have stared – laughed too, for poor Charles was of a reckless and merry humour – if he could have foreseen to what use his pretty little sister would put his tuition!

She had set out after dark, riding her own bay horse, her Fleury. The night was windy, chill, full of restless noise and the movement of swaying branches. The moon shone clear and high then, like a masked desperado, hid itself behind the scudding clouds. Barbara had known this countryside since childhood. As she trotted along the narrow, deeply rutted lanes, she passed familiar landmarks, a farmhouse with its thatched roof and barns, filled now with the summer's yield of grain, crouching snugly among the trees like an old farm dog asleep, a willow-fringed pond by the roadside, then the tall wrought-iron gates of a neighbouring domain, and now she had ridden quickly through a sleeping village. The little huddled cottages with their overhanging eaves had ignored her passing. In one tiny window only a rushlight shone – some sick person or woman in labour no doubt – a dog had broken out barking. She had met no one – neither watch nor beggar – and indeed she had not far to go.

The countryside had seemed so forsaken that, as she waited in the little coppice that she had selected as her hiding place, it seemed to her impossible that any human being should come that way. She had small fear of intercepting the wrong vehicle. This road was little used, being nothing more than a side lane, but the most convenient way from Ischam Park and village to the main St Albans road. But supposing Henrietta had decided to lie at Ischam for another night? Supposing something had gone wrong with her chariot – a wheel off or a horse lamed – and she had been obliged to turn back? The mere idea of being outwitted, however unconsciously, by her enemy, made Barbara clench her teeth.

She had shivered a little with excitement and the chill night air as she sat there on her restive horse, murmuring to it as though it were a human being, a childish habit that she had never outgrown. 'Quiet, Fleury. She will come, I promise you. Wait! you will see. We will have good sport tonight.'

And sure enough her attentive ears caught at last the sounds for which she waited so impatiently, the steady clip-clop of horses' hooves, the rumble of wheels. She edged her horse to the side of the road. Peering out cautiously she could see in the moonlight the dark but unmistakable shape of Lady Kingsclere's smart new chariot. Fool! she was travelling unescorted, except for the coachman and two footmen, one on the box, one behind in the boot.

As the chariot approached, Barbara experienced a stab of trepidation. Supposing the men-servants showed fight? Supposing she or her horse were recognised? What kind of a figure would Lady Skelton of Maryiot Cells cut if she was discovered in this perilous foolery? Then she thought of the ruby heart, heard Henrietta Kingsclere drawl, 'It was your mother's jewel, was it not?'

She drew a deep breath, spurred her horse forward and with pistol levelled at the coachman's head called on him to 'Halt!'

After that it had been amazingly simple. The cowardice of the Kingsclere retainers had to be seen to be believed. The fat old coachman had dropped the reins with a wheezing groan, the footmen had sat as huddled up and unresisting as half empty sacks of flour. The window of the chariot was lowered. The face of Henrietta Kingsclere, large and pallid between the folds of her hood, was thrust out.

'Good sir, have pity on a defenceless woman,' she implored.

Barbara felt her stomach contract with a violent spasm of laughter. It was all she could do to shout in a hoarse, strange voice, 'Your jewels!'

Lady Kingsclere clasped her hands together and protested in extreme agitation, 'No! No! I am travelling in great simplicity. I have not a jewel with me,' the moonlight glittering on her diamond rings as she spoke.

Her cloak had fallen apart, and Barbara's keen eyes had seen something dark lying on her wide expanse of bosom. So she had come away in full dress from the supper party, where she had been flaunting her newly-won jewel for all to see. Frantic to retrieve her treasure and to be away, Barbara wrenched open the chariot door and tore the pendant from off the screaming woman's neck. But a flash of caution warned her that a real highwayman would not be content with a single jewel, and so she dragged the big diamond brooch from Henrietta's corsage, ripping off a piece of lace with it, and seizing her limp hand stripped it of its rings. For all her wild excitement part of her brain remained cool and watchful, and her fingers in their riding gloves worked nimbly without a fumble.

She thrust her booty into her deep pocket, covered with her pistol one of the footmen who, shamed by his lady's squeals, was attempting to scramble out of the boot, wheeled round her plunging horse and galloped off down the lane. She could hear Henrietta's voice screaming hysterical directions, the servants shouting, the coachman trying to turn the chariot; but, mounted on her swift Fleury and knowing every short cut in the district, she could afford to laugh out loud in her triumph and relief.

When she was sure that she had evaded pursuit – if indeed those white-livered menials had any real intention of pursuing her – she drew rein; then, waiting till the clouds had passed, she pulled the pendant from her pocket and, with face uplifted to the moon and the restless night wind, pressed the ruby heart ecstatically to her lips.

Yes, it had been a delightful night, and the best of it had been when the news of poor Sister Kingsclere's misadventure had come to Maryiot Cells. How sedulously she had joined in the exclamations of dismay and sympathy, declaring herself as shocked beyond measure, enquiring solicitously if Henrietta had been very frightened and hurt and what jewels she had lost, crying, 'What, my ruby heart too! I will own that I grudged losing it even to her, but when all is said and done she is one of the family and had promised to leave it to my daughter in her will. But to think of my mother's sweet jewel in the hands of a knavish highwayman – oh, that is ill beyond expression!' This in such a pitiable voice that she had felt quite deceived by her own self!

It had been enjoyable in the extreme to hoodwink these stupid, complacent folk. As if any person of sense could care what happened to Henrietta Kingsclere! (To do Paulina justice she had been the only one who had said tartly, 'People who travel these roads at night decked in all their jewellery deserve to lose it.') Barbara herself had felt very much better since she had committed this violence, mild as it was, against her sister-in-law. She felt that she would be able to bear Henrietta's patronage in future with Christian patience and exemplary equanimity!

She would not be able to wear the ruby heart in public – perhaps never again – but it would be there, locked up in her jewel case, her secret treasure, to be taken out, fondled and gloated over when the tedium of life became unbearable.

This source of private satisfaction had enlivened and sufficed her for about a week. Then an odd restlessness had crept over her. There had certainly been a vast amount of personal gratification in robbing Henrietta Kingsclere but, looking back on it, what a tame affair the robbery itself had been. It would have been more enjoyable had there been some element of danger attached to it. It had gone off far too easily. The abject cowardice of Henrietta's attendants had not enabled Barbara to do justice to her own courage and resource. It flattered her to remember how nimbly she had worked. She believed that she could attempt a more difficult robbery with success. No doubt she had much to learn, but she had all the qualifications for a successful highwayman, daring, good horsemanship, a quick eye and hand, coolness, and a firm disregard of other people's feelings.

So she mused, thinking it no wonder that so many spendthrift sons of good family, so many people of all classes, in fact, from disbanded soldiers to scholars, took to the Road. It would be a new thing, she thought, her nostrils quivering a little, if a lady of quality joined the fraternity, not so much for love of gain, but because life was so cruelly dull and grey and empty…

And so it came about that the neighbourhood was scared that autumn by talk of the highwayman whose depredations were said to equal in daring any committed in recent years. He worked alone, always after sunset or at dawn, seldom spake, and seemed by his figure to be young, perhaps little more than a youth. Mr Riggs, riding home from a visit to his father-in-law, with his wife pillion behind him, had been waylaid in Carter's Lane and obliged to hand over his purse and his wife's pearl necklace. A coach containing Squire Mainwaring and his daughters, travelling home from the waters at Bath, had been attacked near Woburn by this same rascal (it was believed). The servants had fired on and missed the robber who, in return, had shot one of the servants in the arm and, in the confusion, had gone off with a small iron box containing valuables which one of them was holding.

The extraordinary quickness and dexterity with which this fellow worked was commented upon. It seemed that he could wrench an earring from a lady's ear (no considerations of chivalry apparently deterring him) before she could let out a shriek, and it was seldom that he made his escape without bearing some trophy with him.

And in the dawn Barbara Skelton would trot quietly up the dark yew glades of Maryiot Cells, her lovely face uplifted to the cool air and the paling sky, her slender body sweating beneath her man's coat from her recent exertions, her mind strangely relaxed and satisfied.

Young Lady Skelton sometimes lay very late abed those autumn mornings, her languor raising great hopes in her mother-in-law's breast. And when she got up on these occasions she would go out, wearing her little black velvet coat edged with white fur, and a hood, her skirts tucked up to display her pretty silver-laced petticoat, pattens on her feet, and go for a long stroll down by the river. This too her mother-in-law approved of, for gentle walking exercise could not harm a breeding woman.

The good lady would have been less approving and considerably startled could she have seen her daughter-in-law digging vigorously at the roots of the oak tree whose bough overstretched the path between the Abbots Pool and Purgatory. It was here that Barbara made the caches in which to conceal the jewellery and money that she had wrested the previous night from their lawful owners.

She had no very clear idea what she intended to do eventually with these valuables. Perhaps one day she would be able to dispose of them – money in abundance was never to be despised, as Sir Ralph's frequent lectures since the Kingsclere's' visit on the subject of her gambling debts, and his insistence that in future she should confine her card playing to gleak[11] and cribbage, reminded her.

Meanwhile it pleased her as she dug away at the moist, good-smelling earth with a little trowel and, slipping on a pair of gloves so that she should not stain her shapely white fingers, thrust the wrapped-up jewels and coins into safety, to recall the exploit of which they were the trophy; the restless wait in hiding, the breathless moment as the sound of hooves or wheels announced the victim's approach, the plunge into the road, the shouts, the startled faces, the brutal joy of seizing this man's purse, that woman's brooch, the swift homeward flight across country by devious ways and tracks.

Winter came with its heavy rains, turning roads and ditches into a uniform quagmire of mud, and flooding them so badly that in places it was hard to see where streams ended and roads began. One night Barbara sank up to her saddle girths in mire. Few people travelled at night as the winter closed in, except those who were obliged to it by extreme urgency. Barbara settled down sulkily to months of inaction.

The winter had never before seemed so interminable; never before had she waited so impatiently for the spring. Of what use to her were sickly snowdrops and dangling catkins, when the lanes were still of the consistency of mud porridge? Only when several weeks of dry weather succeeded each other did her spirits revive.

The last few mornings had been frosty; in the wan March sunshine the daffodils shone strangely bright and golden in the milky grass. Old Lady Skelton trusted that this untimely frost would not harm her seedlings. Young Lady

Skelton, walking out in her velvet cloak and hood, rejoiced to see how path and track had hardened up.

She closed the drawer of the cabinet now and, strolling to the window, stared out across lawn and river. Outside the breeze would be sharp, but here indoors, with a fire still burning and the sunshine pouring through the leaded casement windows, it was easy to cherish the illusion that spring had come with warm finality. In the clear blue sky the pearly clouds sailed by.

The Dowager Lady Skelton said, 'I believe that we may consider winter at an end at last. Do you mean to venture out, Barbara dear?'

Barbara laughed softly. 'Yes, I shall venture out.'

3

MIDNIGHT ON WATLING STREET

'One night's good fortune under the stars.'[1]

The house was asleep at last. No, not the house but its inhabitants. Sir Ralph snored alone in his bed with the mulberry-coloured hangings; Barbara was a light sleeper, and her restless tossing and turnings (for it was at night that the futility of her existence gnawed at her most keenly) had so disturbed Sir Ralph that he had agreed, if somewhat grudgingly, to her suggestion that they should occupy separate bedrooms. Old Lady Skelton, having taken her nightly syrup of gilly-flower cordial, would be lying with folded hands, her face fretful but innocent under its nightcap, her dumpy, sturdy little body endeavouring in sleep to recover from the effects of all the strange potions with which she dosed it during the daytime. Agatha Trimble most likely would have sucked herself to sleep with a sweetmeat tucked in the corner of her large, ugly mouth. Cousin Jonathan would be a mountainous, snuffling lump of flesh under the bedclothes. Paulina might well have her smooth cheek pillowed on a book. In every attic and closet servants would be drowsing, except where some couples indulged their furtive amours.

The household was at rest, but the old house itself never slumbered. In the deep silence of the night there were strange little creaks and crepitations, as though Maryiot Cells stirred like an old rheumatic hound.

Barbara had no particular love for Maryiot Cells. She was its mistress, and so it had considerable importance in her eyes, but it was too old-fashioned for her taste, the symbol of her cramped and confined life. She would have fancied a handsome and symmetrical mansion in the fashionable style, but Sir Ralph, though he had allowed her in moderation to redecorate the house and had given her even greater liberty in the garden (provided that he had his hunting, hawking and bowling, he cared not how much his lady adorned the pleasure garden with orange and lemon trees in tubs, sundials, or yew clipped into fantastical shapes), would not allow her to alter the house itself in the slightest degree. The present structure had been built 140 years ago on the foundations of the dissolved monastery by his great-great grandfather. What was good enough for his forebears was good enough for him.

Barbara never speculated on the personalities of these past tenants of Maryiot Cells, whose portraits in stiff, ungainly Tudor costume, or in the still more ridiculous though less remote fashions of the Martyr King's reign, decorated the walls of the Long Gallery. There was only one person dead or alive connected with Maryiot Cells who interested her, and that person was Barbara Skelton.

Nevertheless, she felt a certain hostility towards the house because she was vaguely aware that other personalities than her own, with their emotions, hopes and fears, had left their mysterious impress on its atmosphere.

She was not fanciful, but tonight it seemed to her that Maryiot Cells was more than ever watchful, as though it were aware of her secret purpose. She stood by the fireplace in her bedroom and, stirring the logs with her foot, provoked them into a flame that threw a faint warmth on to the silk Indian gown which she had thrown over her night-shift.

She was ready for bed, her hair brushed and combed into a wreath of shining bronzen curls; even her hands – those hands that would soon be holding pistol butt and reins – had been rubbed with scented paste to keep them white and delicate. She had submitted to her waiting-maid's ministrations with the same languid patience that she showed every other night, had bid her 'good night' in agreeable if absent tones.

Now she roused herself suddenly from her reverie, darted to the door and locked it, drew the rose-coloured curtains round the empty bed. She stood for a moment in the middle of the room, not so much listening, for she knew that the house was still, but savouring the intense secrecy of the moment. In all this great house, the tapestried figures on the walls, Venus, Mars and the other embroidered deities who stared at her stupidly, were her only witnesses.

She took a bunch of keys from a silver box and, carrying a lighted candle in her hand, went into the closet that adjoined her bedroom. Slipping her hands over the panelling she opened a little door in the wall. Perhaps this door had been originally intended as a secret mode of egress; if so its purpose had long been forgotten. Its existence was known to, but ignored by, the present occupants of Maryiot Cells. It led to a very narrow staircase in the thickness of the wall which wound up from the lower regions to a disused room above.

Young Lady Skelton slipped through the little door and, lifting her Indian gown to save its hem from the dust, went lightly up the narrow staircase. She unlocked the door at the top with one of the keys she was carrying and let herself into the room. It was small, a mere attic with sloping walls and ceiling. It was bare except for a table with a gilt mirror on it, a silk covered stool and a chest painted in the Dutch fashion with sprigs of spring flowers.

Barbara set the candlestick down on the table, and opening the chest pulled from it a suit of men's riding clothes, boots, hat, belt, pistols, all the cherished accoutrements that she had laid away reluctantly for the winter. She handled them with a caressing eagerness that, fond as she was of the bravery of fine clothes, she had never accorded to lace mantua or embroidered sultane,[2] for these things were the symbol of her partial emancipation from the dragging reality of life.

With the impatient but deft movements characteristic of her, she stripped off her Indian gown and silk nightrail, smiling down at her beautiful naked body, before clothing herself in her man's attire. When she was ready, the long heavy boots pulled on, the over-large belt girded round her elegant waist, her wide-brimmed hat set jauntily on her head, she sat down at the table and gazed at herself in the mirror.

She loved her face in all its moods, but never better than in this strange, bizarre aspect; the green eyes wide and wild with excitement, the curious nostrils poised – you might almost say! – for flight. Her face looked back at her, daring her to bold and dangerous deeds, and it was then that she resolved to try her luck on Watling Street.[3]

Up till now she had avoided the important highway which led from London through St Albans, Dunstable and Stony Stratford to the North, keeping to the by-roads where she might hope to pounce on unwary and solitary travellers who believed themselves safer on these less frequented ways. On Watling Street she would be exposed to greater risk of detection and pursuit, but she could hope for a more certain prize. Nothing galled her more than to wait – as she had done on more than one occasion – hidden in thicket or ditch for several empty hours without reward. This thwarting of her talents, as she had grown to consider her aptitude for highway robbery, plunged her into an irritated and melancholy humour that was scarcely to be borne.

Carrying her saddle over her arm – not her crimson velvet one with a matching fringe, that she used when she rode abroad on her lawful occasions, but a serviceable leather one – she made her way down the staircase. It ended in a little cubbyhole or cupboard. With infinite caution she let herself out of this into a narrow stone passage. She was now in the lower regions of the house, and must take care lest a noisy movement roused one of the scullions sleeping by the fire in the great vault-like kitchen near at hand. The passage was very dark, but she slipped along it till she came to a low door, used mostly for bringing wood into the house. She unbolted this and was out in the cold starlit night.

The stars glittered with a brilliance that showed that there was frost in the air. Barbara, taking a deep breath, regarded the coruscating worlds above and thought what a fine and fit night it was for her purpose. She was standing among bushes. The dark irregular shape of Maryiot Cells rose behind her, ominous against the spangled sky. Below her, across the sloping grass, she could hear the river singing.

Fleury was out at grass. When she reached the meadow where he grazed she had only to call his name softly. He came to her at once, whinnying with delight. She shared his pleasure. To stroke his velvet nose, to saddle him, to spring on to his back, to trot gently across the stone bridge and down the dark gallery of the yew glades, to canter across the sleeping countryside – all this gave her infinite content.

She rode west, then crossing a river before reaching Fenny Stratford struck north, and passing Eaton and its church and Bletchley, reached the shelter of Rickley wood.

And so she came to Watling Street. The highway lay empty and silent under the twinkling sky. Hard to believe that it was the channel for a vigorous and multifarious stream of human life. Its surface was as deeply rutted as a side lane; patches of loose stones, gravel and bundles of furze testified to the unwilling labours of the parishioners, the 'King's highwaymen' (the 'King's loiterers', they were jeeringly nicknamed) who had been recruited to repair it. In parts, trees and scrub threatened to overgrow the road. But Barbara regarded it with the eye of a marauder, not a traveller. Its very deficiencies might lend themselves to her advantage. The difference in outlook between the prey and the one who preys was a lesson that she was learning with ease and satisfaction.

Yet she chafed at her inexperience, as she rode along, half deciding on, then discarding, this or that lurking-place. There must be some art in all this; highway robbery surely had its rules as much as any other science. She wished to perfect herself in her chosen career. To match daring with a nice kill was her aim. She could only acquire this exact knowledge by practice. Meanwhile she must rely on her intuitions.

Finally she selected a spot that she believed would suit her purpose. The road, thickly wooded here, dipped into a little hollow; on either side a rough track wound away aimlessly, to all appearance, under the trees. In one of these, screened by the bushes and the bare but overhanging branches, Barbara took up her position and awaited her luck.

This period of waiting never failed to exacerbate her nerves and depress her spirits. Her wide-opened eyes strained into the shadows, as though by their intense staring they could conjure something out of nothing.

The sound of hoofs approaching roused her expectations, but her hopes drooped again as the plodding tempo announced a string of pack horses. Unmolested they passed her with their no doubt mean and commonplace burdens. Barbara sneered inside herself to think how their driver, shambling along unsuspectingly beside them, would stiffen into terrified attention if he knew what lurked in the bushes a few yards from him.

Another wait. The frosty sky sparkled unconcernedly above the shadowy, ill-defined world beneath. Barbara's hands inside her riding gloves were stiffening with cold, her mind stiffening with tedium. She gnawed at her lower lip in chagrin. Must she go home unfulfilled and empty-handed? And on this, her first outing of the new year. Oh cruel!

And as she fretted through the vacuous moments, there came the sweet rumble of a coach's wheels. Expectation flowed into her body, warming it with a physical glow. Whatever was coming along the highway, however well guarded, she was resolved to attack it. With a gentle pressure of her knees she edged her horse forward. A cumbrous shape was advancing along the road. It had not the appearance of a private equipage. Could this be the stage coach, delayed beyond its usual hour and lumbering now with clumsy haste to safety? Barbara blessed her good fortune. This was novelty and the certainty of booty. Her body tingled with the familiar sense of excitement and power. Fleury pricked his ears; fidgeted with a rustle of twigs and withered bracken. Barbara breathed deeply once or twice to steady herself. Then as the coach approached in a surge of hoof-beats and rumbling wheels, she drew her pistol from its holster and urged Fleury forward. And as she swept down athwart the coach, shouting 'Stand and Deliver!' a masked horseman broke cover from the opposite side of the road and seized the horses' heads.

This unexpected sight disconcerted Barbara, but only for a moment. The passengers of the stage, rudely jolted out of their drowsy security, were poking their heads out of the window, fumbling to hide their valuables, cursing or squealing, as their sex inclined them. Their confusion and alarm invited robbery. Barbara set about her business with her usual briskness. Forcing each passenger at the pistol muzzle to descend into the road so that she could the better see what she was about, she neatly collected purses and loose coins, pitilessly stripped jewellery off the ladies, removing as well from one woman a modish fur tippet that took her fancy.

To speak more than a few words in an assumed masculine voice was a strain, so she left unanswered her victims' indignant protests. 'You'll hang for this, you rascal!' 'Fie on you, you wicked brute, to treat a poor helpless woman so.' Her unnatural silence, accompanied by her business-like actions, produced an uncanny and alarming effect upon her victims and helped to paralyse their already feeble powers of resistance.

Meanwhile the strange horseman kept the plunging horses from bolting, covering the coachman and guard with his pistol as though it were the most natural thing in the world that he and Barbara should work together in unison.

Only when Barbara had robbed the last passenger did he forsake his passive role. With a cool deliberation that surprised Barbara, he shot the leading coach horse, shouted, 'After me!' and, dashing across the road, galloped away down the track where Barbara had been hiding. As she followed him the coachman, stung into courage by the wanton slaughter of his beast, fired at the retreating riders. But the shot fell short of Fleury's flying hoofs. Soon Barbara and her unknown companion were deep among the trees.

Barbara neither knew where she was going nor with whom she was going. But she resolved recklessly to see this adventure through to its end. The track widened up into a rough lane, and after cantering along this for a while the highwayman drew rein, wheeled his horse round and faced Barbara.

She waited in wary but agreeable anticipation for the congratulations which she felt were her due. She had done a pretty piece of work. This man – whoever he was – could not fail to acknowledge that.

He seized her by the throat and said, 'Now, you son of a bitch, perhaps you'll kindly tell me who gave you leave to trespass on Jerry Jackson's preserves?'

To reply was impossible – his hands held her neck in a cruel grip. But as she struggled, gasping horribly for breath, her hat fell off. Even by starlight the contour of her head and hair, the soft line of her brow and chin, proclaimed her masquerade.

He dropped his hands abruptly. As she put her hands pitifully to her throat he ordered, 'Unmask!' She obeyed him. There could be no refusal in the face of his brute force. But already she intended to exploit her weakness to the utmost. Though her throat ached painfully from his throttle-hold, she was not displeased with the resonant masculine note of his voice.

The crepe mask slipped off from her face and she turned her strange heavy-lidded eyes towards him. He stared with intense curiosity for a moment, then burst out laughing. 'Be poxed to it! So now our wild ladies are turning bridle-cull!' Barbara said in her low soft voice, 'You seem surprised, sir, at my sex. I am surprised at your behaviour. Since when has dog taken to eating dog? The world has come to a sad pass when rogues must prey on each other.'

The man chuckled. 'You're saucy, aren't you? Never mind. I like it. I never could endure a melancholy fusty humour in a woman. Well, remember this the stretch of Watling Street between Fenny Stratford and Nether Weald is sacred to Captain Jerry Jackson at present, and those who poach there do so at their peril.'

He spoke in a braggart tone, but Barbara knew that he was impressed to find by her voice that she was not a common adventuress but a woman of good condition.

He added, sweeping of his hat in a flamboyantly gallant gesture, 'But that is not meant for you, my pretty lamb. *You* may poach where you will.'

Barbara acknowledged this with a slight inclination of her head. She said, 'You were hiding there before me? You saw me come?'

'Why, to be sure. I had a blow set me that the stage was late and would be passing Dolly's Dell at midnight. You don't suppose that Gentleman Jerry waits about these chill nights without some chance of profit. I took you, from your figure, to be a sprig of a university lad who was making his first purse on the highway.'

'But when you saw me at work, you knew then that I had been out on the highway before?' Barbara asked quickly, jealous for her professional reputation.

Captain Jackson smiled. 'Yes. You handled that coach very nicely. I saw that you weren't altogether fresh to the Road. I thought myself in luck, I can tell you. Nothing to do but hold the horses while you collected the gold-finches for me.'

He eyed her capacious pockets as he spoke. Barbara stiffened with mortification and apprehension, but she said casually,

'Why did you kill that horse? I would rather kill a man than a horse any day.'

'You won't, my lady, when you have been as near wearing a Tyburn tippet[4] as I have. Only a fool shoots to kill on the Road, except in a case of dire necessity. You may say, isn't highway robbery a hanging matter anyhow? True, but you have a fairer chance of buying an acquittal if you are not a killer. As for horses,' he slapped his horse's neck genially, 'no one is fonder of a prancer than I am, nor looks after his mounts better, but your first aim on the Road should be to elude pursuit, and for that reason you should always either tie up the traveller, or if there are too many for that – as there were tonight – shoot one of the horses.'

Barbara listened with interest. This man could teach her something of Road lore. Meanwhile there was the delicate matter of the booty to be considered. She took a sudden resolution and said boldly:

'Before we ride along any further together, Captain Jackson, would it not be well to settle up the matter of tonight's gains? As I took most of the risk and did all the work I consider myself, not unnaturally, entitled to a share. But as you are a man and a strong man' (she gave a sidelong glance at his tall, well set-up figure and powerful shoulders) 'and I am but a weak woman my opinion scarcely counts. Unless your own generosity and chivalry plead to you on my behalf, there is nothing for me to do but to hand everything over to you with as good a grace as possible, resolving to avoid Captain Jackson's stretch of road in future.'

She ended lightly, but there was a threat behind her words, for she knew that already he desired her.

He said quickly. 'This is not a matter that can be settled in a moment – or with dry mouths! A drink or two would help us to come to some arrangement. I know of an inn near here whose hostess is a good friend of mine, and one of the best cooks in Buckinghamshire. I don't know how it is with you, but my appetite is pretty sharp set by this cold night air. Will you do me the favour, Madam, of supping with me?'

'Willingly,' said young Lady Skelton, and putting their horses to the trot they rode together in a guarded but affable silence.

They came to an inn, set back among the trees and near the sound of running water. Jackson avoided the main entrance, and riding round to the side knocked three times in a peculiar fashion on a door set in a wall. He murmured to Barbara, 'Mask yourself, my dear. The hostess here can be trusted, but she is only a woman when all is said and done!'

The door was opened cautiously by an ostler with a lantern in his hand. 'Ah, it's you Captain. Good night. Come in, sir.'

In the cobbled courtyard Jackson dismounted, threw his reins to the ostler, stretched himself and said in the complacent but self-conscious tones of one who wishes to show that he is an honoured guest, 'Can your mistress give me and my friend here a bite of something?'

'Why surely, sir! I'll go and tell her directly I've put the horses up, or maybe you'll see her yourself, if you go through, for there is a party of gentlemen still drinking in there.'

Captain Jackson motioned to Barbara to follow him and led the way through the obscurity of the back premises to the tap-room door, behind which could be heard a buzz of voices and rowdy laughter.

Captain Jackson opened the door a crack and whistled. The hostess came out, a tankard of ale in her hand. She was a full-blown woman in her middle thirties, with a bright, high colour, thick black curly hair, too much chin, and brown eyes as hard as pebbles.

She greeted Jackson effusively. 'Ah, Captain, you're welcome! And this gentleman too.' She eyed Barbara speculatively, twisting a ringlet round her plump finger.

'Who is in there?'

'Just Will Lemon and his sparks, making themselves merry after their evening's work.'

'Well, this gentleman and I wish to be quiet and talk business. Can you give us a bite in the parlour? I have told my friend that you are the best cook in Buckinghamshire, so see you don't disappoint me.' He put his arm round her voluminous waist and tickled her ribs. She simpered, vowed that he was a pestilent wretch and bustled off to prepare supper.

This was brought into the little parlour without undue delay – stewed carps, a pigeon pie and a dish of neat's tongues[5] and cheese. Candles were placed on the table, a log of wood thrown on the dying embers of the fire. Captain Jackson and Lady Skelton were alone.

He poured her out some wine and said, 'This is very snug, but I should enjoy my food more if I had an uninterrupted view of your charming face.'

Barbara raised her hands to her mask, then hesitated. 'I have some curiosity to see *your* face, good sir.'

Jerry Jackson laughed and pulled off his mask and hat. 'At your service, Madam!'

He was a man of about twenty-eight, fresh-complexioned, large-featured, with uneasy hazel eyes and a full mouth and chin. In middle age his face would coarsen, but at present he was, as Barbara noted with satisfaction, a handsome enough, likely-looking man. His teeth were noticeably white and even.

He wore his own hair, which was abundant and of a beautiful auburn colour. His dress was rich – a suit of green cloth with a flowered tabby vest and gold lace at the wrists. His hat was edged with ostrich feathers. As Barbara looked at him he glanced down at his lace cravat, flicking away an imaginary crumb, all the self-complacency of the fine male animal in his expression.

He urged her, 'Now for your share of the bargain.' She slipped off her mask, sat with downcast eyelids and widened nostrils as he regarded her.

He said enthusiastically, 'Lovely! 'Tis a damned shame to cover it with a mask.'

'My face is tolerably good, I believe,' Barbara said coolly, 'but I fancy that you are more interested at present in the contents of my pockets.'

He laughed this aside. 'Not at all. I never talk business at meals.' He filled up her tankard. 'No, what interests me at the moment is to know whom I have the honour of talking to, and why a fine and noble lady like yourself has turned Road Collector.'

Barbara looked at him from under her lashes. She said with a little smile, 'As to my name, sir, you can not expect me to tell you that.'

'Why not? I have told you mine.'

'Your name is your own – presumably. Mine belongs to a very worthy gentleman.'

'So you are married?'

'Why yes. Married these five long years.' She sighed faintly.

Jerry Jackson gave a satisfied smile. 'Your husband, madam, if you'll forgive me saying so, should know his business better than to drive you to find your pleasure on the highway. For I take it that it is not lack of money that set you on this course?'

'No. I do not rob for gain, though I confess that I should find little enjoyment in robbery if there was no gain attached to it.'

Jackson laughed loudly. 'Why so say we all! No, if I am to dance in a rope at Tyburn at the end I must have my pocket full of guineas meanwhile. So you won't tell me your name?'

'Does my name really concern or interest you? Does it make any difference to you what I am called?' He shook his head. 'I thought not. Priscilla – Dorothy – Barbara. Any of these names would suit me as well as another. You may call me Barbara if you like.' This was risky, but her own name meant much to her, and seemed to her the only possible one.

'Why that will do famously. The name suits you as well as if you had been christened with it. And so, Mistress Barbara, you do not go out on the Road to make money.

What for, then? For it is a dangerous life and often a short one, as you must know very well.'

'What for? To delude the tedium of my life, I suppose.'

He leant across the table and took her hand in his. She noticed how hard and strong his hand was and how it had little fine reddish hairs across the back.

He said in a low urgent voice, 'For a beautiful woman there are better ways of deluding the tedium of life than trotting the highways. If you would admit me to your favour I could teach you a soft love lesson that you might find as agreeable to learn as I would to impart.'

Barbara gave him a little wanton look. 'You go very fast, Captain Jackson. You seem to take me for a common jilt. I am not a glove for everyone's drawing on. I have never yet been false to my husband's bed.'

'Then it is high time you began. The fellow deserves all he gets, to let you wander about unattended on Watling Street for any rogue in a laced coat to pick up.'

His impudence made Barbara laugh. She had already decided to give herself to him. This was better than gambling, better than highway robbery, to yield recklessly, impudently, in an impulse of sheer animal passion to this handsome scoundrel. But even in this headlong moment when her hungry senses clamoured to surrender, she was mindful of Barbara Skelton's interests.

She mocked him. 'Sir, it is as hard to trust you as to deny you. What of the jewels and the money?' She thrust her hands defiantly into her deep pockets as she spoke.

He said hoarsely, 'Keep them. Keep them all. So long as I get the delicious prize of your body, the devil may take all the rest.'

She lay back unresisting as he took her in his arms and, tearing open her man's coat, revealed her lovely woman's body to his ravished gaze.

4

FIRST KILL

'Guilty thou art of murder and of theft.'[1]

So BEGAN A curious partnership between Barbara Lady Skelton and Captain Jerry Jackson – a partnership of business as well as pleasure. For though Captain Jackson was inclined at first to treat Barbara's partiality for the highway with derision, taking it to be the whimsical fancy of a spoilt and idle woman, it was not long before he changed his tune, accepting her first as an able assistant and then as a valued partner in his nocturnal prowls.

He was – to tell the truth – somewhat astonished at his good fortune in having secured at one stroke, and in one person, such a useful accomplice and so rare and delectable a bedfellow.

The eagerness of ladies of fashion to pay visits of condolence to condemned highwaymen at Newgate was well known. But how many gentlemen thieves (for so he described himself) could boast of actually having a woman of quality as their doxy?

Being of a naturally exuberant and talkative nature, Jerry Jackson disliked working on his own. He had had several partnerships with other highwaymen, all of which had been dissolved abruptly – either by a violent quarrel over booty or a woman, or by his partner meeting with some accident. On more than one occasion Jackson – most regretfully – had had to gallop off at high speed, leaving a wounded comrade to his fate, for the rather spasmodic displays of chivalry which had earned him, among his brothers of the blade, the soubriquet of 'Gentleman Jerry', and the reputation of being 'a civil obliging robber', were reserved for the fair sex, and did not extend to male friends in distress.

Certainly the disadvantages of working with a partner outweighed the advantages. Chief among them was the danger of the trusty comrade turning informer and 'making a discovery'. Now he was safe. As long as Barbara was content to lie, convulsed with passion, in his arms, he need fear no betrayal.

But Barbara's merits as a partner were not merely negative. Jackson had soon discovered with surprise and admiration what courage, briskness and mettle lodged in that slender and elegant frame. Her fault was that she was too impetuous. Anxious, in the way of women, to excel and to go one better than the man, she was all for attacking without prudence or delay. Jackson had to teach her the business side of highway robbery; how without cunning and caution no highwayman could hope to survive for more than a few months.

He told her, 'Damn my soul, Barbara, you don't want to be like the country lad who, when the sheriff asked him why he was laughing to himself at Tyburn, said, "I came to town but last Monday, on Tuesday I had a whore, on Wednesday I lost my money at dice, on Thursday I made a purse on the highway, on Friday I was condemned for it, and now on Saturday I am to be hanged, so I think I have made a pretty week's work on't".'

Captain Jackson, Barbara found, prided himself on his duplicity as much as on his daring. He delighted to tell how he had cozened wayfarers – making friends with a traveller at an inn, and riding along with him next morning till they reached a solitary spot where he relieved him of his saddle-bag and thirty pounds in gold. Another time he had 'protected' a country squire against a feigned attack by his own gang, had been invited by the grateful gentleman to spend the night at his country house, and had decamped in the early hours of the morning with a haul of silver plate and jewellery.

He acquainted her with many of the finer points of the profession: It was advisable to cut the traveller's girths and bridle. By muddying his boots a highwayman could give the appearance of having ridden a long way, though actually he might be drinking a mug of ale within a few miles of the robbery. If the traveller was attended by servants they must be ordered to ride ahead after the robbery, to enable the highwayman to make his escape. It was worth remembering that travellers were under the impression that by travelling at night or on by-roads they would escape the attention of the 'Road Collectors'. You could not always judge a victim's potential yield by his or her outward appearance. A lady riding in a fine gilded coach might have nothing more than twenty shillings and a few paltry jewels about her, while a scrubby-looking grazier, returning from a fair, might 'bleed' to the tune of several hundred guineas.

Then there were different methods of approach, to be suited to the different types of travellers. A courteous, 'May I beg the favour of your purse,' might have such an emollient effect on an agitated female that, in her relief at not being raped or murdered, she might give not only her purse but her concealed jewellery. On the other hand, it might be necessary to scare a more truculent male with a volley of oaths and a 'Deliver or die!'

Barbara must remember that the most simple-looking travellers were often full of subtle crafts. To make a traveller take off his boots – 'shelling the peas' as it was called – was routine work. There were dozens of other ways in which experienced travellers might attempt to defraud the gentlemen of the road.

A highwayman should make a rule of exchanging horses with the traveller if he were better mounted than himself. Coats, too, could often be exchanged to advantage, as long as the misadventure of Dick Adams was borne in mind who, having robbed a gentleman of gold watch, silver snuff-box and money, cast a covetous eye on his fine laced coat and saying, 'Sir, you have a very good coat on. I must make so bold as to change with you,' stripped him of it, only to discover too late, to his unspeakable rage and mortification, that he had left his booty in his own coat.

Barbara learnt that behind the activities of the highway fraternity was an elaborate organisation of confederate innkeepers, ostlers, tapsters, chamberlains and chambermaids, besides the actual *fencing cullys* or receivers of stolen goods with their headquarters in London. Captain Jackson could give the names of inns in most districts in England where a gentleman of the Road could be sure of a welcome, and where there were privy hiding places for stolen goods or for the highwayman himself. But for Barbara and Captain Jackson's present purposes the 'Leaping Stag', where he had taken her that first evening, was a sufficiently convenient rendezvous, near enough to Watling Street yet in a retired and wooded spot, with a hostess who was a good friend to the brotherhood in general and to Captain Jackson in particular, who was not afraid to see pistols loaded in her kitchen, and who boasted that in a sudden alarm she could convey a fugitive 'from chamber to chamber to the backside of the house and so away.'

Barbara listened attentively. She was ready to learn all that this man could teach her. It had not taken her long to gauge his character. Boastful, braggart, childishly vain and talkative, outwardly daring and bold, inwardly ill at ease and longing for reassurance, a mixture of insensitive brutality and careless good humour – she saw him with a clarity that her sensual thraldom to him in no way dimmed. When she told him, with a docility that delighted him, 'I am content to be ruled and ordered by you in all things,' she was not being so very deceitful. For it was true that she needed him, needed him for his fine vigorous body as well as for his professional experience.

He had an endless store of tales, mostly relating to his own exploits, and to these Barbara gave doubtful credence. They were illustrative of his wit, his ruthlessness or his gallantry, according to the mood that he was in when he related them. Was it true that he had stopped Lady Castlemaine[2] and, relieving her of her jewels, informed the haughty favourite that it was his trade to rob one whore to maintain another? Had he really agreed to throw a main for £150[3] with another of his distinguished victims, the Duchess of Mazarin,[4] and, having lost, gallantly allowed her to keep her winnings? Had he, as he related, had a swearing match with a well-known judge, a boxing match with an earl, and obliged a Bishop to preach an extempore sermon? And what of his tale that he had stopped a gentleman and his wife on the Bath Road and, on the man refusing to pay up, had taken his wife into a nearby thicket and 'acted a man's part by her', informing the husband, as he collected fifteen guineas off him, that this was no more than was his due for he was not obliged to do his drudgery for nothing?

How many of these stories, growing more incredible as he helped himself to the wine, could be believed? Or which were borrowed from the experience of some other highwayman? Barbara neither knew nor cared, but when he told her that he had robbed on nearly every road in England she believed him, for when in action he displayed a skill and assurance that could only have been gained by long experience.

In fact he had been on the Road since the age of seventeen. In a burst of naïve confidence he had confessed to her that 'Captain' was a self-bestowed or, as he put it, an 'honorary' title. The son of a Shropshire butcher, he had run away from home at the age of fourteen, taking his father's savings with him. He had worked, or perhaps idled would have been a more accurate description, as a stable boy in various London inns. Then his upstanding appearance had got him the job of groom to a nobleman. In this capacity he had learnt to ride, to gamble and to imitate the vices and to some degree the deportment of his betters. But this situation came to an abrupt end when he seduced her ladyship's favourite waiting-maid. He was dismissed, and left with some of his master's jewellery and gold plate. He joined the army as a trooper, was flogged for insubordination, deserted, and, for his part in a drunken riot, was consigned to the Poultry Compter.[5] Here he fell into the company of highwaymen, learnt what a profitable and gentlemanly trade highway robbery was and, in his release, took to the Road.

Such was his history, not precisely as he related it to Barbara, but as she shrewdly took it to be when stripped of the embellishments provided by his vivid imagination. Yet it did not hurt her pride to know that her lover was a man of base birth and rascally character. On the contrary, she derived a perverse satisfaction from feeling that in breaking thus, secretly and violently, from the traditions of her class and upbringing, she was revenging herself on Sir Ralph, on her in-laws, on fate itself for these five long, never-to-be-recalled years of her frustrated youth.

It seemed strange as a dream to Barbara, and with a dream's uneasy fascination, that she, Lady Skelton of Maryiot Cells, should ride out thus night after night with this graceless scamp, on robbery bent. Side by side they prowled through the sleeping, unsuspecting countryside – through the milky refulgence of the moonlight, under the glitter of the stars, through the sighing wind and sharp, malicious lashes of rain. They could see each other's dimly-outlined masked faces and cloaked figures, hear each other's quick breathings and whispers, the jingle of bits, creak of saddle or stirrup and thud of hoofs as their horses paced together neck by neck and flank by flank. They were bound together in a partnership closer even than that of their bodily embraces, the partnership of a common business and danger.

Sometimes as they rode to their hiding place they talked, or rather Jerry Jackson talked for the most part, for while he was eager to chat and boast about himself, Barbara maintained a resolute silence, which he had endeavoured in vain to penetrate, about her identity and her day-time life. Sometimes they were silent in instinctive enjoyment of their proximity and the hushed yet watchful mystery of the night, or revelling like birds of prey in expectation of the approaching swoop. Or less happily, when their path took them past a roadside gibbet where a gruesome object, horribly blackened and tattered by weather and decay, hung in chains. Then Barbara would see by the way that Captain Jackson threw back his head and squared his shoulders and looked to the other side that, however light he might make of 'half an hour's pastime', as he called hanging, he was haunted by the dreadful thought that one day his handsome body might also rot in chains by the wayside.

Barbara was aware that there was a part of Jackson's life that she could not share. She was, unhappily, precluded from joining in his daytime robberies. She was a night bird, her coups must be swiftly executed and at no great distance from her home. Daylight must find her sleeping quietly behind the rose-coloured curtains of her great bed at Maryiot Cells. (Her lie-abed habits were a matter of some concern to her mother-in-law. As Barbara's figure remained disconcertingly slim, old Lady Skelton concluded that her daughter-in-law was in a decline and fussed over her with asses' milk and sugar of roses.)

Then, after a particularly good haul, Jackson would go to London to spend his share of the proceeds at the gambling table, on wine, fine clothes and (Barbara knew by his sleek air and the assiduousness of his attentions to her when they were reunited) on women. It riled Barbara that while he was gallivanting in town she must relapse into the unrelieved role of a country lady, full of domesticity and good works.

Nor, from Jackson's accounts, was his revelry confined to low taverns, to the unlicensed theatre at Sadlers Wells, or to the bawdy houses of Mother Temple and Madam Bennet's in Drury Lane or Moorfields. No, Captain Jackson boldly displayed his new finery and that of his frail and rapacious lady friends at the fashionable French eating-house in Covent Garden, at the Opera House, the old Spring Gardens and other modish resorts. It puzzled Barbara how he was able to show himself in public like this without being apprehended, till he explained to her that the longer his career of highway robbery continued unchecked, the higher would be the reward offered for him, and the more valuable he would become from an informer's point of view. Therefore it paid those persons who were, without doubt, watching his movements with the calculating interest of a sportsman watching the form of a certain horse, to allow him to remain at liberty as long as possible. A murder committed by him on the highway would, of course, double his value, and this was one reason, he explained to Barbara, why he continued to kill horses instead of men.

One night, after several weeks of bad weather, when travellers had been scarce and takings poor, Jackson said to Lady Skelton:

'Barbara, you seem to me a person who would not baulk at an adventure because dangerous. I have had a blow set me that there is a farmer near here by the name of Cotterell, who has two hundred guineas laid by in his money chest. I intend to relieve him of them on Friday night. This is something different from the highway lay, but the goldfinches will be none the less good for that and, as it is so convenient for you, I would not care to leave you out of the affair if you have a mind to join me.'

Barbara was startled. The Cotterells were tenants of Sir Ralph's, prosperous and worthy folk. She knew them well. Many a time she had ridden by their farm-house and had accepted a syllabub from beaming, curtseying Mrs Cotterell, had chatted graciously with her about her rheumatism or the weather or her latest grandchild. She had even honoured their house with her presence on the occasion of their eldest daughter's wedding to one of Sir Ralph's coachmen. To break into that peaceful home under cover of dark, in company with this desperate man, was a different matter to robbing strangers on the open road.

Yet she was flattered that Jackson should want her help on this venture. And how curious it would be to allow her two lives, her tame, open, day life and her wild, secret, night life to impinge thus on each other! Her thirst for new sensations, assuaged but by no means quenched, urged her to accept.

And so on that June evening, young Lady Skelton, as she paced between the roses in her formal garden, cast impatient glances towards the sunset sky. It had been raining during the day but now it had cleared, and a great bank of cloud, creamy yet flushed a little angrily with rose, was floating across the blue expanse. Here, even in the enclosed garden, there was a restless little wind, but above, in the evening sky where the clouds sailed by slowly and triumphantly, there was a serenity that seemed full of purpose. To the north there were long slithers of cloud softly grey as a pigeon's wing; southward the trees were backed by a violet darkness.

It seemed to her – her restless mind busy with thoughts of tonight's project – a long time before the sky and garden were drained of colour. The summer's day was so long adying. In the dusk the roses had faded to poignant ghosts of their glowing selves; only their perfume grew more insistent with the approach of night.

It was not quite dark when Barbara set out – a bird still sang, the trees were like sombre lace against the colourless sky – but luckily Sir Ralph's rule of early hours for his household held good for summer as well as winter. Those who wished to stroll out or hold tryst after sunset must do so by stealth. Barbara knew how to avoid porter and watchman, and make her way unobserved to the dark yew glades. Here she could relax her caution, give Fleury his head and gallop away to her lover and her other life.

Jerry Jackson was waiting for her in the parlour of the 'Leaping Stag'. The hostess brought in a tankard of mulled port as Barbara arrived. 'To give you heart for your night's business,' she said, ogling Jackson and ignoring Barbara as was her wont.

When she had left the room Barbara said, 'I do not trust that woman.' 'Molly? Why she is a good friend to me.' 'All the more reason why she should not be my good friend. She knows that I am a woman. Though I have never unmasked in her presence she may guess by your attention to me that I am neither the worst favoured nor the most unkind of my sex. She has been your mistress. (Pray do not trouble to deny it. She must have been quite personable before her chin and bosom got out of bounds.) There is nothing here to make her dote on me!'

Captain Jackson laughed uncomfortably. 'Believe me, it's a long time now since I gave Molly a green gown. She was a saucy enough baggage in those days, but she has given up tight-lacing and jealousy long since, like a sensible woman.' He drew Barbara into his arms. 'I'll tell you this, sweetheart. Since I've had the enjoyment of your person there is not a town miss that can satisfy me. If I take them out when I am in London, why truly, it is more from duty than pleasure!'

Barbara laughed at him. 'What you do with your Bridewell beauties in London does not concern me, but if you are ever false to me here, then our knot is broken for ever.' 'Never fear that happening,' he assured her. 'You are likely to be made a hempen widow long before I tire of you.'

She smiled to herself. How typical of him, she thought, never to imagine that she might be the first to tire!

As they rode towards Cotterell's farm he said, 'You are not feeling timorous, my pretty lamb?' Then, as she shook her head scornfully, 'I should have known better than to ask you. The old fellow should give us no trouble. There is a great lubberly coward of a man-servant – he should be easy to dispose of – and one son at home. He may show more fight, but they will be asleep and easily surprised.'

A rough cart-track led through the trees to the hollow where the farm-house lay snugly with its outhouses round it, like a cat nursing its kittens. It was on the bank of a mill-stream and, as the two riders crossed a narrow bridge, their ears were stunned with the noise and rushing water. When they had passed over the bridge and speech became possible again, Jackson whispered to Barbara, 'We will leave the horses here under this tree. My information is that there is a window at the back that is carelessly fastened and will let us into the kitchen. We will avoid the front door which is always strongly bolted. It is round there on our left.'

Barbara nodded. (Mrs Cotterell curtseying in the porch. 'You're welcome, my lady. Will your ladyship take a sip of my elderberry wine?')

They dismounted. Jackson whispered, 'Pistols ready?' They walked stealthily towards the house. There was a growl at their feet, and a large black dog sprang out barking from a kennel against the wall of the house.

'A pox on it! I was not told of the dog,' muttered Jackson, and drawing his pistol made to strike at it with the butt.

Barbara ran forward, 'Prince! Hush, good dog. Good Prince. You know me. Quiet, good Prince!'

The dog, reassured by the sound of its name and the soft, vaguely familiar woman's voice, jumped up on her, paws on her stomach, licked up at her face, allowed himself to be fondled, subsided into his kennel with a rumble of half-hearted growls.

Jackson said, 'What! so you know this house?'

Barbara nodded, enjoying his astonishment. 'Tolerably well. Follow me and I will show you the way to the Cotterells' bedroom.'

The window, its rickety latch easily raised with a knife's point, let them into a little outhouse or scullery and from there into a big stone-flagged kitchen. The fire was still alight; by its glow they could see the copper saucepans above the fireplace, rows of hams hanging from the rafters, a big wooden churn in a corner and, lying on a heap of rushes before the fire, the sleeping man-servant.

With a cat-like swiftness Jackson leapt upon the recumbent figure, clapped a hand across his mouth, one on his throat and, before he could do more than give a half-strangled grunt, had, with Barbara's assistance, securely gagged and bound him.

Barbara beckoned to Jerry Jackson to follow her. They stood side by side at the foot of the wide shallow staircase. The last time that Barbara had been here the staircase had been thronged with jovial wedding guests. Barbara had stood a little apart in her gown of amber satin with the flowered petticoat and her plumed hat, her gratified host and hostess flanking her on either side. Her beauty and her rich attire had drawn many respectful and admiring glances. Her gracious smiles had masked the boredom that she had felt at having to watch the revelry of these 'base bumpkins'. Very prettily she had accepted a bride's favour from comely, blushing Deb Cotterell, had dropped her sprig of rosemary in the sack possett as she drank the young couple's health. The staircase and the hall had been adorned with wreaths of summer flowers; the sun had poured through the casement windows, there had been much merriment and chatter and laughter...

Now all was dark and silent, except for the squeaks and tripping of mice behind the wainscoting. And she, the gracious lady of the manor, was standing here in man's attire, hand on pistol butt, eyes straining upwards into the darkness of the house, a robber in robber's company.

What, she asked herself in a moment of utter bewilderment, had brought her to this rash and crazy act? A ruby heart lying like a drop of blood on a card table? Her own heart, frustrated, unfulfilled, beating like a wild bird in a cage?

From the woods outside came the menacing hoot of an owl. Barbara shivered. She whispered to Jackson, 'Come with me. I will show you their room.'

They crept up the staircase, every creak sounding loud as a pistol-shot in their guilty ears, and along the passage. Barbara remembered perfectly where the bridal couple had been put to bed amid jests and laughter, and Mrs Cotterell saying, 'We have given them our own bed-chamber, your ladyship. As I said to my good man, "Let them have the best chamber and the best bed. A girl's wedding night comes but once in a lifetime".'

Barbara paused before the door, raised the latch with a gentle hand. The room within was dimly illuminated by a rushlight. From behind the curtains of the big oak bed a mild snoring proclaimed that the Cotterells were enjoying their well-earned sleep. Barbara drew the curtains apart. Husband and wife lay there, placid and rosy as two grown-up children. Jackson drew his pistol, whispered 'Keep an eye on the door,' and rapped sharply on the farmer's shoulder.

Cotterell gave a snort, stirred, sat up, rubbing his eyes. 'That you, lad? Buttercup calved yet, eh?' Then as he saw the masked figure at his side, 'Mercy on me! What are you? What do you want?'

Rough and to the point came 'Gentleman Jerry's' reply,

'What do we want? What the devil do you think we want, you old bastard, you. To ask after your health or to know the time of night? No, we want your money.'

Mrs Cotterell had woken up and was clinging to her husband, her plump, good-humoured face all crumpled up with terror. He put his arm round her. 'Steady now Martha, lass. Leave this to me.' He said stoutly to Jackson, 'You've come to the wrong house, sir. We are not gentry to keep money and jewels in our house. We are simple country folk. All our wealth, such as it is, is out in our byres and fields.'

Jackson sneered, 'Indeed! And what about the bay mare and the drove of cattle you sold at Stony Stratford fair, and the two hundred guineas you brought back in their stead? None of your tricks, you lying old son of a whore. Show me where the money is or I'll blow your brains out.'

Cotterell raised himself defiantly in bed. 'Then, you'll hang at Tyburn sooner than you expected, you scoundrel.

You seem to be well-informed about my affairs, but I believe you are a stranger to the neighbourhood all the same if you think that Tom Cotterell is a man likely to be scared by your knavish threats.'

Barbara smiled maliciously to herself. She knew Jackson's reluctance to shed blood and was interested to see how he would react to the sturdy farmer's defiance.

Mrs Cotterell, her eyes attracted to Barbara by some movement on her part, gasped, 'Sir, you seem quite a young lad. For God's sake think of your own parents and persuade your friend here to have pity on us.'

Jackson laughed contemptuously. 'Your crocodile snivellings won't have any effect on my friend. He may be young but he is a flash cull and a lad of the most undaunted courage. Come now, we haven't time to wait on you all night. My information is that you have a pretty young daughter. You wouldn't like me to pay a visit to her bedside, I suppose, while my friend keeps guard over you?'

Mrs Cotterell, in a panic, broke out, 'For God's sake, Tom, let them have the money – anything so long as they leave the house. No! they mustn't harm our Joan.'

'I came here for your guineas not your Joan, you old fool, but if I can't have your money I'll have your daughter, I tell you plain.'

Cotterell said fiercely, 'Take the money then, you villain, and may it help to speed you to the gallows and damnation. It is up above there.' He pointed to the tester of the bed.

'Thanks for your good wishes,' said Jackson, his good humour restored now that he had achieved his object and, climbing on to the bed, he threw the moneybags down to Barbara, who kept the husband and wife covered with her pistol.

Carrying their booty they backed to the door, ran down the stairs, through the kitchen, out of the window and to the tree where their horses were tethered.

They had been quick but not quick enough. As if their departure had released the despoiled house from a spell, lights flickered in the windows, there was the sound of voices.

Jackson, cursing violently, packed the money into their saddle-bags, scrambled on to his horse and held Fleury's bridle while Barbara mounted. 'Look sharp, Barbara. We may be pursued.'

They galloped between the trees, across the rushing millstream, the wooden bridge thundering under their horses' hooves, and down the cart track on to the road. But, glancing back over their shoulders, they saw in the half darkness of the summer night a horseman galloping after them.

'The son for a certainty. Damn his soul, he hasn't wasted time,' said Jackson.

Yes, it would be young Ned Cotterell, Barbara thought, a fine horseman, and an active, spirited lad. He would not let thieves get away with his father's gold if he could help it. The Cotterells kept good horses. Ned Cotterell's mount would be fresh, unhampered by saddle-bags full of stolen gold.

He was in close pursuit, shouting something at them, calling them to halt. He was gaining on them. To Barbara, bent forward over Fleury's neck, urging him forward, it was not Ned Cotterell alone who was pursuing her but her hated real life, ignominious exposure, scandal, utter ruin. He must not come up with her and recognise her, or even Fleury. At all costs she must stop him. Deaf to Jackson's shouts she wheeled her horse round, waited till Ned Cotterell was close, raised her pistol, took careful aim and fired. His horse reared, he fell forward on to its neck, then slumped from his saddle on to the ground.

Barbara sat still for a moment in her saddle, staring at the smoking weapon in her hand. Then she dismounted and kneeling beside the dead youth peered into his face.

Yes, it was Ned Cotterell, eighteen years old, his parents' darling and youngest son. Ned Cotterell, with the flaxen hair and sunburnt face and bright blue eyes, who had been foremost in all the parish sports and merrymakings, who had whistled loudly as he worked with the haymakers in his father's fields, who had had a friendly word for man, woman, child and dog, who had looked at young Lady Skelton with bashful admiration as he doffed his cap to her at the church porch.

When she had come to Maryiot Cells five years ago as a bride he had been little more than a child. She had seen him grow from a boy to a fine young man. And now she had killed him. He would never dance again round the Maypole, work at the harvest, stroll arm-in-arm in the dusk with his sweetheart, kneel down in his Sunday clothes in the church at Maiden Worthy, because he lay here in the muddy road a senseless lump of flesh and it was she who had robbed him of life.

Jackson stood beside her. He said in a low voice, 'What have you done? Is he dead?'

Barbara did not hear him. She knew that she must make her choice now and for ever. If she admitted remorse into her heart she must renounce the dark, secret pleasure of her highway life, the night maraudings, the savage rapture of the attack, the hot embraces of her rogue lover. She must return for ever to the dragging tedium of life as Lady Skelton, wife of Sir Ralph Skelton of Maryiot Cells. God had no right to ask this of her, she thought with fury.

She said to Jerry Jackson, 'How much money did we carry off tonight?'

He said, surprised, 'Why, I can't say for certain till I count it, but I am sure it can't be far short of two hundred guineas.' Barbara rose to her feet. She said in even tones, 'Two hundred guineas. 'Tis a price worth killing a man for anytime!'

5

THE LADY AND THE STEWARD

'False face must hide what the false heart doth know.'[1]

THE NEIGHBOURHOOD WAS greatly disturbed by the outrage which the Cotterells had suffered. Highway robbery was a commonplace – it was said that 'in Bucks if you beat a bush it's odds you start a thief'. But this breaking into a peaceable homestead, this wanton murder of a promising and popular lad, was shocking beyond common experience.

Everyone joined with the bereaved parents in mourning the dead boy. Sir Ralph was sincerely moved to pity and indignation. The Cotterells had been tenants of the Skeltons for a hundred and forty years; they were bound to them by many ties of service and devotion. That such a crime should have been committed on his property, and within the bounds of his jurisdiction, hurt his dignity both as a landlord and a Justice of the Peace. He made the usually somnolent lives of the constable and the watch well-nigh unbearable with his demands for immediate and effective action. He declared, not once but ten times a day, that if the malefactors were caught he would see to it that their executed bodies were hung in chains on a spot conveniently near the scene of the crime.

As a token of his sympathy and esteem for the sorrowing parents, he even lent them a mourning bed, not of course the best one, a massive and practically immovable affair which housed the corpses of the immediate family during their lying in state, but the second best bed which was used for lesser members of the family, and lent round the countryside for the obsequies of distant relations.

Furthermore, Sir Ralph paid a visit of condolence to the Cotterells the day before the funeral, and insisted on Barbara accompanying him. It was noticed how young Lady Skelton, very pale in her black gown and veil, shrank back as the weeping mother clung to her hands, as though the sight of the poor woman's grief was too much for her, also that she leant on Sir Ralph's arm on the threshold of the mourning chamber – signs of sensibility that were considered very much to her credit.

But once inside the room she had controlled herself, as befitted a lady of her quality and, standing by the sable draped bed, had gazed sadly and steadily on the fair boy who lay there in the strange, sculptural pallor of death. Only her nostrils had quivered a little, a sign of her inner agitation. And indeed, who would not have been moved at the sight of this youth struck down on the threshold of his hopeful manhood?

She had not knelt in prayer as the others had done, but had covered her eyes with her black-gloved fingers. Then she had laid a red rose near the dead boy's hand.

Barbara had killed her man, and this stark fact had subtly altered her relationship with Jerry Jackson. He regarded her with a new respect, even, she suspected, with a touch of fear. No longer could he treat her with playful condescension. She had proved herself to be the more ruthless man of the two. He had reproached her at first, on the grounds of security, for her rash act, but she had refused to excuse herself. It had been essential for her, she explained to him, to stop their pursuer. She had done it. And that was all. If he was afraid to associate himself with her he was at liberty to break the connexion.

'No fear of that,' he assured her hastily. 'I love you to distraction, my lady of iniquity.'

And indeed her beauty now held an added and perverse fascination for him. As she lay in his arms, he gazed in a kind of wonderment at her face, the smooth white forehead, the somnolent, long-lashed green eyes, the eager nostrils and the cat-like elegance of her not very significant mouth and chin. Who would have supposed that this charming face masked the spirit of a woman who could kill a man at point-blank range? He no longer felt at his ease with her. He felt her to be unaccountable, sinister, but his passion for her was stronger than ever.

Yet the present situation could not last. His vanity – his dominant trait – could not tolerate that his prestige as a highwayman should be in any way inferior to that of his mistress. That her crime had placed him in this humiliating position was made abundantly clear by the advertisement published after the robbery in the *London Gazette*. It read as follows:

'On June 10th 1683 at midnight was committed by two men a great robbery in the house of Mr Thomas Cotterell of Waterbrook Farm, three miles from Maiden

Worthy in the county of Buckinghamshire, to the value of two hundred guineas taken by force from the aforesaid Mr Cotterell. Likewise the said robbers afterwards murdered Edward Cotterell, the said Mr Cotterell's son, on the road by Stony Gap. Of the said robbers one was a long, lusty man about twenty-nine or thirty years of age, fresh coloured, his own hair, inclinable to red. He was wearing a cloth coloured riding coat with silver buttons, riding sprig-tailed sorrel mare. His companion is a lad of eighteen or nineteen, middle stature, slight form, thin favoured, with curled dark brown hair, in a green coat and buff belt with silver buckles. Whoever can discover the persons aforesaid to Sir Ralph Skelton Bart of Maryiot Cells, Maiden Worthy in the County of Buckinghamshire or to Mr Cotterell shall have their charges and £30 reward, with a further £20 to be paid on the conviction of one of the robbers for the murder of Edward Cotterell.'

There it was in print for everyone to read – and Barbara read it with a sarcastic little smile. The slayer of Ned Cotterell was worth £20 more than the companion who had stood by and merely watched the slaying. No one but Barbara might be aware of this mortification, but it was enough. From the night of the Cotterell robbery she began, with a feline sureness and lightness of touch, to taunt Jackson about his squeamishness.

He had been rough and brutal enough in all conscience when out of humour, but if he happened to be in a better mood, fancying himself as a gallant knight of the road, he was not impervious to such softer influences as the tears of a pretty woman. Barbara herself, totally lacking in sentiment, watched him with irritation while, after robbing a coach, he bent down to give a kiss to a curly-headed child or, with a generous flourish, handed a fashionable lady back a guinea for her travelling expenses.

This was not Barbara Skelton's way. When she robbed she stripped her victims bare of valuables, leaving them neither their favourite trinket, nor a groat with which to bless themselves. She took snuff boxes from venerable old gentlemen, watches from dashing young noblemen, earrings from pretty girls, even lockets from cherub-faced children. All was grist that came to her mill. They could plead, curse, scream, sob – nothing moved her small cruel heart.

Jackson's wide experience, ability and daring entitled him to use his own methods. But now, with that murderous pistol shot, Barbara had placed herself in a more desperate and hence, by highwaymen's standards, a more eminent category.

For a man of Jackson's touchy vanity and lack of inner ease there could only be one solution. The next time that they met with a traveller who showed fight, Jackson fired not only to wound but to kill, and the man fell lifeless from his horse to the ground. And having once killed it seemed easy and convenient to kill again. Now, with several murders to his credit, Jackson could lord it again over his mistress as befitted his superb masculinity. Now they were bound together not only by the ties of passion and of robbery but of blood.

Barbara congratulated herself on the adroitness with which she had managed to keep her two lives apart. It was an understood thing in the household that young Lady Skelton – who was a very light and uneasy sleeper – was never to be disturbed at night except in the case of the gravest emergency. Once she was behind the locked door of her bedchamber her privacy and repose must be considered sacred.

The distance from the little back door, which she used for her nocturnal exits, and the field where Fleury or her other horse grazed, was short and sheltered with trees and bushes. She had never been pryed upon, to her knowledge, and felt a growing confidence in her security.

So when one sultry July day, Hogarth, the house steward, that glum-faced, trusty and pious man, asked for the favour of an interview with young Lady Skelton, she anticipated nothing more tiresome than the revelation of some household peccadillo, the seduction of one of the serving girls by a footman, or some other of the petty annoyances which the management of a large household entailed.

She received him in the summer parlour. Bowls of deep red roses glowed against the dark wainscoting and filled the room with their delicious perfume. The casement windows were wide open, but the day was overcast and close, and no breeze stirred the tapestry hangings on the walls. Lady Skelton sat in a carved, high-backed chair; the panel of white satin which she was embroidering with a picture of Susanna and the Elders[2] lay on the lap of her yellow satin gown. On the table beside her, with its covering of a Turkey carpet, lay scissors, stiletto, and an embroidered casket full of multi-coloured silks.

She said graciously, 'Well, Hogarth?'

The man standing respectfully in front of her stared at her with a fixed and solemn gaze. He was middle-aged, gaunt in his black suit, with greying hair and a long, ugly, reliable-looking face. His earnest scrutiny annoyed her. She said again with a touch of impatience, 'Well, Hogarth?'

In answer he pulled from his pocket a little purse of crimson knotted silk, embroidered with silver and, holding it out to her, said, 'This is your purse, isn't it, my lady?' He added heavily, 'I know it to be, for I bought it for Sir Ralph, along with other trifles at the New Exchange for the Christmas junketings, and my master charged me to see that it went to your ladyship, being scented with jasmine, your ladyship's favourite perfume. So I know it to be yours.'

Lady Skelton said carelessly, 'Well, what of it? The usual tale, I suppose, of pilfering on the part of one of the wenches?'

'No. It was found in Thomas Cotterell's house.' She said, in her quiet low voice, 'Ah, so it was there that I dropped it, the day that I went with Sir Ralph to comfort those poor people. I missed it, but to tell the truth I have not given it another thought. Thank you, Hogarth.' And she stretched out her hand for it.

But he did not give it to her. He said, 'It was found in the bedchamber of Thomas Cotterell and his wife the night of the robbery.'

Lady Skelton shrank back in her chair as though he had lashed her with a whip. But instantly she recovered herself and said, a little breathlessly, 'Indeed! And what do you make of that?'

Hogarth said, 'My lady, I'll not torment you, for God knows, if you have a shred of conscience left you must be suffering torment enough. I know all. Yes, I have made a full discovery of your foul work on the highway, the damned company you keep, all your scandalous, impious and wicked life. It was this little purse that first led me to the truth. Aye, by such trifles does the all-powerful God bring wicked deeds to light. I am Tom Cotterell's closest friend, as you may know. I was the first of their neighbours to visit the afflicted parents the morning after the robbery, and after I had prayed awhile with them, and the first violence of their grief had abated, they told me all that had happened that awful night. Then Mistress Cotterell showed me this little purse which she had found by the bedside after the robbers had left the room, saying, Was it not strange that desperate and bloody men should carry such a dainty trifle on them? I knew the purse at once and the sight of it was like the stab of a knife. But I said, no doubt it belonged to some trull that they went with, and took the purse into my charge. Now, they had told me that one of the robbers was a young lad, slightly made with dark curling hair, and this, and the finding of the purse, worked together most ghastfully in my mind, so that I was for several days in a great disquietness of spirit, thinking myself half crazy for my suspicions, and yet unable to banish them. And so, my lady, I began to observe your habits and your movements. Never, I believe, was a woman more subtle in crafts or secret in affairs than you are, but the Lord cannot be deceived, and first one thing and then another was revealed to me – your secret chamber and man's gear, your departures at night on horseback. I followed you to the "Leaping Stag" inn. I made discreet enquiries. I learnt that this was your meeting place with a notorious robber on the highway, known as Captain Jackson. The meanest scullion in the inn knew that you were a woman and his paramour but, mercifully, none guessed at your name and station. I watched you as you rode off together on your evil errands, watched you return with your booty, marked your sly gliding into the small back door of this house, and knew beyond a shadow of doubt that the highway robber who has troubled the roads in this neighbourhood last autumn and again this spring and summer is none other than the wife of my good master.'

He ended on a groan.

Barbara had listened to him with lowered eyelids, her face white but perfectly composed, except for a slight twitching of her nostrils. But when he had finished she opened her green eyes wide, and almost hissed at him: 'You must have been very busy, Hogarth, you must have been hard put to it, to combine your duties as house steward with your self-imposed duties as a spy. Ah, forgive me! – You call it having things revealed to you by God, don't you? And now that you have acquired this knowledge, what do you intend to do with it?'

Hogarth said sternly, 'My lady, I have wrestled night after night with my conscience, asking myself that self-same question. Is it my duty to hand you over to justice, without regard for your rank and my esteem for my kind master and the Skelton family? Sometimes I have believed so, and then the thought of the filthy dust that the public knowledge of this thing would raise, the shame and wretchedness that it would bring on Sir Ralph and all his family, has made me doubt the rightness of my resolution. Or may I, under Heaven's providence, be the means of calling you to repentance, giving you the chance of renouncing these irregular and soul-destroying courses and saving your sin-sick soul from the eternal fire? Whether you are guilty of the murder of young Ned Cotterell, I know not. My soul vomits at the thought of it. You shake your head. I *must* believe you. It is unthinkable that a delicately nurtured lady, and one who knew the poor lad from boyhood, could have committed such a foul crime. This means, then, that you are guilty of adultery and robbery. Terrible enough in all conscience, but Scripture teaches us that even adulteresses and robbers may find mercy through repentance.'

Lady Skelton sat upright in her chair; the white satin needlework had slipped unheeded off her lap. Her hands clutched the arms of her chair so hard that her knuckles shone through the flesh. But when he paused she gave a wild little laugh and said:

'You should have been a clergyman, Hogarth. A post as Ordinary at Newgate Prison would have suited you admirably. You would have been in your element riding in the cart with condemned criminals and exhorting them to repentance. So you think that Sir Ralph would believe your word against mine?'

'He would have no choice but to do so. I have abundant proof of your crimes.'

'You think that he would even listen to you? That he would allow his steward – his servant – to raise such a barbarous scandal on me?'

Hogarth said proudly, 'I have been Sir Ralph's house steward for fifteen years. He knows me as well as one man may know another. He knows that whatever my faults I have never told him a lie, nor defrauded him of as much as a tallow dip, nor borne false witness against any one of my fellow servants. And so I know that – however great his horror and amazement – he would let me say my say.'

Barbara lowered her head. She said very bitterly and spitefully, 'Yes. He *is* that kind of man.'

There was a long silence. Then she said, 'I see that I am at your mercy. You make me your scorn. You can do with me what you will.'

She sprang to her feet suddenly, her fists clenched and shrieked, 'You canting devil! What do you mean to do?'

He gave her a look that was pitying and yet unflinching, and motioned her to seat herself again, which she did, leaning back in her chair in an attitude of utter exhaustion and despair.

He said, 'For my good master's sake, for the honour of the family I serve, yea, for your own sake – for though your sin is abhorrent to me, as a Christian I must care for your soul – I wish to save you from this hideous way of life. If you renounce it absolutely, promising, as you hope for salvation, never to ride out again secretly at night, neither to meet nor to communicate with your lover Jackson, and to lead a new and blameless life, then I, for my part, swear that no living soul but James Hogarth shall know of your shameful secret. It shall die with me on my death bed. What is more, I shall never allude to it again, treating you with all the respect due to an honoured mistress. But,' he added grimly, 'do not think to deceive me. I am not a fool, and if you take this oath I shall see that you keep your word.'

Barbara rose and paced to and fro, her fingers twisting together. Her thoughts thrashed about furiously like trapped animals. Could she hoodwink this man, assuring him that her sport on the highway was harmless enough? Neither she nor Jackson had had any part in Ned Cotterell's death – no doubt he had been set upon by a skulking footpad.… He had wronged her by listening to the slanderous talk of scullions.… She had never had any unseemly dealings with Jackson or any other man.… True, she and Jackson took money from certain unworthy persons, gamblers, usurers, wealthy bawds and the like, but gave it all away to the deserving poor… No! Hogarth was not a fool. Such talk would not deceive him for an instant.

Should she try to bribe him? Offer him money, jewels.… She gritted her teeth as she acknowledged to herself his unassailable integrity.

What could she do, then? Gain time. Lull his suspicions. Woo him with soft and penitent words.

She turned to him, and said gently, 'I have said harsh things to you Hogarth, but I know in my heart that you are a good and just man. I am not so far gone in my soul-sickness that I cannot recognise goodness when I see it.' She fell on her knees and burying her head in the chair sobbed, 'Oh Hogarth, help me! Save me! I am not as lost to shame as you think. I was drawn into it by a foolish prank. You guessed, I daresay, that it was I who robbed Lady Kingsclere? And since then I have suffered the pangs of hell – but that evil, vicious man will not let me go. He swears that if I break away from him he will never be at rest till he has washed his hands in my blood, and so my errors and indiscretions will follow me to my ignominious end. My memory will stink in the nostrils of my good husband and my family and to all eternity.'

She broke into terrible, gulping sobs. And indeed she felt very sorry for herself.

Hogarth raised her to her feet, and though his words were stern, his hands were gentle.

'I heartily wish you better in conduct and more wholesome in your soul, my lady, before death seizes you, and if you truly wish to renounce your wicked life, you may count on me to help you. I will see to it that the man Jackson never troubles you again.'

Barbara raised her wet green eyes to him imploringly.

'And if I am good and truly penitent, you promise that my ugly secret will die with you?'

He promised solemnly, 'Yes, it will die with me.'

Lady Skelton told Hogarth, with a piteous meekness that was very touching to hear from so proud and captious a lady, 'I desire to be ruled by you in all things.' She had however one suggestion of her own to make. She was in great terror, she said, lest Jackson, either through desire for her company or fear of her betraying him, should try to seek her out. She therefore asked Hogarth to allow her to have one more interview with the highwayman, during which, she said, it was her intention to tell him that she was in very poor health and had been warned by the physicians that if she did not lead a quiet and easy life she might fall into a decline. She believed that she could persuade Jackson of the truth of this, especially if she promised to rejoin him as soon as her health was mended. In this way (for he would soon forget her) she would sever the connection between them without fear of some violent action on his part, and would be free to attend to her soul without the haunting fear of her past sins finding her out.

Hogarth did not altogether like the plan. He would have preferred her to have broken at once with her accomplice without ever seeing him again. He did not care for the falsehood that it entailed (though, as Lady Skelton pointed out to him, her *soul* was indeed sick almost unto death). But he had to admit that it would be a safe and convenient way of freeing Lady Skelton from this evil and dangerous connection. So at last he agreed to it, accompanying her to within a quarter of a mile of the 'Leaping Stag' inn, and there let her ride on alone, after exhorting her with many powerful texts and prayers to stand firm and not to slide back into perdition.

'Have no fear,' she assured him. 'My heart feels a kind of horror at the thought of my past misdeeds. Wait here, good Hogarth, and I will soon be with you again.'

And indeed her interview with Jerry Jackson was tolerably short, not lasting above three-quarters of an hour. But a great deal may be done and said in three-quarters of an hour. That whatever passed between them was satisfactory to both parties might have been guessed by Barbara's sleek smile as she kissed her lover good-bye, and by his chuckle as he held her in his arms and said:

'You're a subtle baggage, Barbara – a cunning, tricking baggage. Farewell then, my pretty, till the next merry meeting!'

6

AT THE SIGN OF THE GOLDEN GLOVE

'For her house inclineth unto death.'[1]

MISTRESS NAN MUNCE was a comely and comfortable-looking widow who owned a prosperous mercer and haberdasher's shop in the town of Buckingham. Her goods were justly renowned for miles around among the county ladies, who declared that, for stylishness and good quality, Mrs Munce's fringes, laces, ribbons, cambric sleeves, gloves, mouchoirs and the like could not be surpassed by those of any mercer of New Exchange or Paternoster Row.

In fact it was considered rather remarkable that the good lady did not ply her trade in the metropolis itself, but when questioned about this, Mrs Munce would smile and say, 'Oh mercy me, my lady! I couldn't live for three days in the foul air and stinks of London.'

'Well, Mistress Nan, I'm sure it's a blessing for us poor country folk that you are content to stay here,' her client would say condescendingly as she fingered Mrs Munce's new collection of lace caps. Mrs Munce's remark was more accurate than her customers might suppose. It was true that London would be a most unwholesome place for Nan Munce, though not for reasons of health.

Mrs Munce's career had been as varied as the names that she had borne during it. She had started life as Catherine

Getting, daughter of a poor and honest labourer in Essex, had run away from home at the age of fifteen and bound herself as apprentice to a seamstress in the Strand. But this was too much like drudgery for pretty Kitty's taste, and before she had been in London six months she had run away from her mistress, taking £10 in gold and three yards of white sarcenet[2] with her, and had set up house with a notorious highwayman called Nick Barton, who had maintained her in comfort and jollity till his sudden death at a rope's end.

Kitty Getting, or Barton, as she now called herself, being left a hempen widow, supported herself by picking pockets by day and by even less reputable means by night. But she was a girl of considerable resources, and before long she was earning a good living at the Question Lay.[3] Dressed up as a milliner's girl from the Exchange, and carrying a band-box, she would call at the house of some lady of quality and tell the maid that she had brought the gloves, fans, or what not, that her mistress had bespoken the day before. While the maid went upstairs to see if her lady was awake, Kitty would fill her band-box with the silver plate on the sideboard, or any other valuables within reach, and hurry away.

Growing more ambitious she took lodgings in Great Russell Street, hired a female vagabond to play the part of her woman, and sent her to a jeweller in Cheapside to order jewellery for her mistress, whom she represented as an heiress, lately come to town. When the jeweller arrived with his goods, Kitty sent a message to say that she was too indisposed to come down herself but would make her choice if the jewels were brought up to her by her maid. The jeweller, impressed by the luxurious appearance of the house, fell into the trap, allowed the maid to take the casket up to her ailing mistress, and that was the last he saw of his jewels, the two women having slipped out by a back door of the house.

Kitty Bellingham, as she now called herself, carried out a series of successful cheats and robberies of this kind, till at last she was apprehended, sent to Bridewell, flogged, and transported to Jamaica.

Here her good looks and sauciness attracted the attention of a well-to-do merchant named Rumbold. He procured her freedom, brought her back with him to London and, as the result of much cozenage on her part, actually married her. But he was too portly and middle-aged to please the lively Kitty and, after robbing him of all she could lay hands upon, she deserted him for a handsome young ensign. The young man married her, but his parents, learning something of her history, had her arrested for bigamy. The evidence against her being insufficient (her discomfited husband having retired to Jamaica) she was acquitted, and later took a third husband, a worthy and prosperous stay-maker. She lived with him very quietly for a year, after which time Mr Price, who had been ailing for some time, was seized by violent pains in his stomach and died in a few hours. This greatly distressed his widow, especially as she had with her own hands prepared the broth which was his last earthly meal.

The substantial sum of money which she inherited from him was, however, some consolation to her, both as a proof of his esteem and as a means of enabling her to leave London, where her neighbours and in-laws were spreading the most malicious rumours about her.

She was next heard of in Portsmouth, where she set up as the landlady of an inn. What she did in Portsmouth besides innkeeping would be best left to the imagination. Sufficient to say that, after a particularly barbarous highway robbery and murder on the Portsmouth road, she packed up and disappeared from the neighbourhood.

Her next recorded appearance was in Buckingham, and here Mrs Nan Munce, alias Kitty Price, alias Aubrey, alias Rumbold, alias Bellingham, alias Barton, alias Getting, settled down to her mercer's trade and to a life of, apparently, impeccable respectability. She was no longer young and had lost her pretty figure. She had certainly had an adventurous and risky career. It was little short of a miracle that she had escaped wearing a Tyburn tippet. It might easily be believed that she was content to deal in such innocuous wares as point d'Espagne[4] and scented gloves for the rest of her life.

True, her more favoured clients were aware that she also supplied on request rare perfumes and unguents for the complexion and the hands; moreover it was whispered that sometimes, after much persuasion, and in consideration of a handsome present, she would provide love-potions or aphrodisiacs for ladies who were plagued with a backward husband or lover, as well as other drugs for ladies who were expecting an unwelcome addition to their families.

Young Lady Skelton knew all this and, thanks to her association with Captain Jackson, who had been a crony of Mrs Munce's, she knew more besides.

And so one gusty day towards the middle of July, Lady Skelton drove over to Buckingham in her chariot, attended by her waiting gentlewoman, a page and two footmen. Her ostensible reason for this visit to the county town was to replenish her wardrobe, and though Hogarth might secretly grieve that his mistress – over whose newborn soul he watched with the anxious care of a nurse – should still be concerned for the adornment of her perishable body, he was sensible enough to realise that she could only be weaned to a better way of life by gradual stages. Better by far that she should be choosing fripperies at Mrs Munce's shop than committing robbery-under-arms on the King's highway.

Lady Skelton's yellow and black chariot clattered noisily over the cobblestones of the town, crossed the Market Place and entered a narrow street where the eaves of the houses nearly met overhead, and drew up before the small bow windows of Mrs Munce's shop. An elegant gilded sign over the door, depicting a Golden Glove, indicated her wares.

Lady Skelton gave her waiting gentlewoman an ivory tablet on which was written a list of groceries which she was to purchase for her – raisins, blue currants, cloves, prunes, mace, almonds, lemons (she was not to pay more than three shillings a dozen for them), candy sugar and nutmegs – ordered her coachman to wait for her at the inn, and went unattended into the shop.

Mrs Nan Munce, who was embroidering a white satin waistcoat with silk honeysuckle and carnations, rose and curtseyed respectfully at the sight of her distinguished client. She considered Lady Skelton to be one of the most elegant-looking ladies in the county, nay, in Mrs Munce's opinion, she would cut a very modish figure even at Whitehall.

Mrs Munce was stylishly but soberly dressed in black taffety with very fine lace at her bosom and elbows. She wore a black lace cap on her head, and jet earrings and bracelets. She was a small woman; her figure had spread, but her prettily turned arms and ankles testified to the seductive daintiness that had once made her so dangerously attractive. Her blonde hair was tarnished, but her skin still had the softness of a faded roseleaf. Her eyes were grey. She had a small mouth. At first sight she looked rather a sweet little woman.

'Good day, milady. It is a long time since I had the honour of your ladyship's custom.'

'Yes, Mrs Munce. I have been busy.' Lady Skelton seated herself, loosened her hood and placed her satin and beribboned muff on the counter.

Mrs Munce looked heavenwards. 'Ah, yes, milady, indeed. The cares and responsibilities of a country mansion – 'You would have thought that Mistress Nan Munce had lived the best part of her life in the stillroom and the herb garden.

'And pray what can I show you your ladyship? I have the sweetest collection of lace and frilled pinners here, as worn in Paris, that I would especially commend to your ladyship's attention. A settee or double pinner[5] is in the very last degree modish for dressing the head and would suit your ladyship to perfection. I am trespassing on a milliner's preserves, of course, but I cannot remain indifferent to my customers' heads. Heads are of prime importance in a woman of fashion, as your ladyship will agree, and your ladyship has such a *beautiful* shade of hair. What a delight it must be for your ladyship's maid to dress it! Or if your ladyship is interested in new materials, here is a length of incarnadine satin that was surely made for your ladyship.

Imagine it trimmed with a silver parchment lace and worn with a cloth of silver waistcoat! Oh, milady, that would be sweetly pretty!'

She babbled on in professional ecstasy.

Lady Skelton fingered the incarnadine satin casually. She said, 'Yes, I will have the satin and the cloth of silver for a waistcoat too. But I did not come here to buy stuffs.'

'No, milady? Gloves, perhaps? I have a collection of scented gloves that could not be surpassed by any merchant on the Exchange.'

Lady Skelton smiled gently. She said, 'No, nor gloves neither. Mrs Munce, it is the secret whisper of some that you keep even more interesting wares than these in your back parlour.'

Mrs Munce folded the satin with expert neatness. She put her head archly on one side.

'You have been hearing of my complexion milk?'

'Yes – and other things.'

There was a silence. Mrs Munce regarded Lady Skelton narrowly. Then she said in matter-of-fact tones, 'Will your ladyship do me the favour of coming to the other room?'

'Certainly.'

Mrs Munce led the way into a small back parlour. The room itself was dark and pokey, but it looked out into a very pleasant little walled garden with a chestnut tree in it. The greenness and flowery brightness of the closed plot was almost startling in contrast to the sombre little room.

Mrs Munce excused herself for a few minutes, and returned presently with a silver tray and a dish of chocolate which she offered to Lady Skelton.

'Now, milady, what can I do for you?'

'I want your help.'

Mrs Munce smiled deprecatingly. 'My poor services are your ladyship's to command. But is there really anything that I can do for your ladyship? A lady of your exquisite beauty will never make me believe that she is in need of one of my little love-potions!' She scanned Barbara's slender, untroubled figure knowingly.

Lady Skelton rose with a swift and graceful movement and went to a gilt mirror that hung on the wall. Leaning forward, she adjusted the black patch, in the shape of a tiny heart, that she wore near her left nostril. Behind her own reflection she could see that of Mrs Munce.

She said slowly and very deliberately, as she stretched her long neck backwards and tilted up her face, the better to see the patch:

'No, I do not want anything to draw a man to me, Mrs Munce. I want something to send a man away, *Mrs Price.'*

The face behind her in the mirror was the colour of cheese. She heard a rustling sound and turned round in a flash. Mrs Munce's hands were plucking at her taffety skirt, her mouth was working.

She said in a choking voice, 'I don't understand you.'

Lady Skelton gave a little laugh. 'Oh yes, I think you do. I want a little powder that would impart a *heavenly* flavour to a possett – or let us say, a *broth*. Do you understand me better now?'

7

DARK DESIGNMENTS

'...Murder though it hath no tongue, will speak with most miraculous organ.'[1]

AFTER THAT LITTLE jaunt to Buckingham, young Lady Skelton led as blameless, dutiful and dull a life as even Hogarth (or for that matter her most spiteful female friend) could wish. She had always been an indifferent if fairly competent housewife, performing her duties as lady of the manor with a languor that betrayed her boredom, leaving as much as could decently be left to the charge of her capable housekeeper, Mrs Sampson.

Now a transformation had come over her. No more lie-abed habits. She rose at five or six in the morning, and nearly every hour of her day was profitably employed. With a lace apron tied over her gown, her chatelaine of keys jingling from her waist, she spent many hours in the stillroom, distilling fragrant perfumes and essences – elder flower water for sunburn, rosemary to wash the hair, pastes for whitening the hands, red rose-water for medicinal purposes, and the more homely wines, ginger, elderberry, currant and cowslip. She supervised more actively than heretofore the work of the buttery, dairy, laundry, poultry-yard, flower and herb garden. A housemaid or laundrymaid, engaged in her morning's work, would be aware of a shadow falling across the threshold of the room and, looking up, would be startled to see young Lady Skelton standing there, watching her with her strange green eyes. At the time this had seemed no more momentous than a spur to a flurried display of industry, but in years to come it was something to tell their grandchildren by the winter fireside.

On fine days, with a lace veil over her face to keep off the flies, Lady Skelton stood patiently with her maids among the currant bushes, gathering the bead-like fruit. On wet days she entered in a vellum bound book a number of prescriptions that she had collected or that had been thrust upon her by elderly relations. For a quinsy – 'Take a silk thread dipped in the blood of a mouse, and let the party swallow it down...' Against bubonic plague – 'Take half of a handful of rew, likewise of madragories, featherfew, sorrel, burnet and a quantity of the crops and roots of dragons, and wash them clean and seethe them with a soft fire in running water...'[2]

And needlework. Her fingers were seldom idle. Even on sunny days she strolled no farther than the pleasure ground or paradise, as it was called, where, seated in an arbour, her nimble fingers made the piece of satin or canvas on her lap blossom into a mimic garden of silken flowers.

Apart from these housewifely preoccupations she showed, to Hogarth's gratification, active signs of her changed heart. She became assiduous in her devotions, attending church twice a day as well as family prayers. As she knelt on her dark red velvet cushion, hardly more conscious of the chaplain's prayers than she would have been of the droning of bees on a summer's day, she was aware that her sister-in-law Paulina, that silent, self-contained girl, was watching her with a quizzical, perhaps cynical curiosity. Barbara did not care. She had no wish to win Paulina's affection or esteem. She seldom thought of Paulina, except to wonder how soon she would marry (for her presence in the house, unobtrusive though it was, somehow irked her) and was indifferent to Paulina's opinion of her. But when Hogarth gave her a commending glance from beneath his shaggy eyebrows she experienced a real glow of satisfaction.

To Hogarth, Lady Skelton's very appearance testified to the improved health of her soul. Since she had given up her evil way of life she had acquired a new bloom, a glossiness and an air of soft youthfulness that even the austere Hogarth could not help but find appealing. Indeed, after the strain, feverish excitement and late hours of the last few months, Barbara did not find this period of enforced repose unwelcome.

It happened that this was the time of year when, with Hogarth's aid, she was accustomed to look into the household accounts, or rather that part of them that came into her province, a long and tedious business. Accordingly she summoned him to the little wainscot room and, seated at a gate-legged table, allowed him to lead her, docile and bewildered as a child, through a maze of figures (for her early education had been concerned more with lute playing, needlework and Italian sonnets than with mathematics) – the wages of the female servants, from the majestic Mrs Salmon and Lady Skelton's own waiting-maid, to such lowly figures as Joan-about-the-house or Mag-in-the-kitchen; the money spent on groceries, tea, coffee, and sweetmeats, on yards of holland for sheets, on aprons and tippets for the maidservants and frieze for their cloaks, on 'women's triflings', combs, pins, laces, thimbles and the like, bought from itinerant pedlars, and on silk for a quilted carpet for the table in the withdrawing-room, pintado printed with oriental scenes for the bedchambers, and green leather gilded hangings for the winter parlour.[3]

After a while Lady Skelton would say, 'Enough, good Hogarth. Enough for today. My head is wonderfully heavy, yes, and my heart is heavy too. Hogarth, I feel myself much sunk at present under the hand of Providence. Sometimes I wonder if Heaven will indeed overlook my past sins and keep me from the sad end that I deserve.'

Hogarth was not immune from the besetting foible of his sex – vanity. In his case it took the not ignoble form of believing that it was his special gift and mission to save errant souls. He could therefore no more remain indifferent to such an appeal than a hound could ignore the huntsman's horn. Laying down his quill pen he strove with all the eloquence and earnestness at his command to dispel Lady Skelton's doubts, begging her not to put her trust in her own repentance however lively (this would indeed be a most dangerous conceit), but to seek grace from a Higher Source. 'I would not have you abate your penitence by one thought or sigh, my lady,' he assured her, 'for this is a sweet-smelling ointment that you can offer to your Maker, but neither would I have you indulge too much in despair, for despair is of the devil.'

Lady Skelton professed herself much comforted and solaced by those godly discourses and by the prayers which Hogarth, his honest face buried in his hands, offered up on her behalf.

His zeal and fervour (on top of the household accounts), though edifying, was exhausting for them both and so Lady

Skelton, after these spiritual exercises, was accustomed to offer the good man some light refreshment which she had ready on a side table – a cup of sack or fruit syrup and a manchet of bread.[4] Hogarth partook of this standing up for, true to his word, he treated Lady Skelton, in spite of the parlous condition of her soul, with all the deference due to an honoured mistress.

It was about this time that Hogarth showed the first symptoms of his illness, being seized in the night with vomiting and cramps in the stomach. Hogarth was not a man to allow ill health to interfere with his work, and he struggled on for some time before he would admit that the bouts of sickness and pain which gripped him with increasing frequency were anything more serious than a bad attack of colic. He continued to help Lady Skelton disentangle her household accounts, to administer to her seasonable and comforting words and assist her virtuous meditations, though sometimes it was all that he could do to stand upright in her presence or to partake of the drink which she courteously offered him.

'This will not harm your stomach – poor Hogarth,' she would say, fixing her eyes on him with a look of concern. And, as he drank it down with an effort, he thought how greatly her character had altered for the better since her conversion to grace. Even before his discovery of her misdeeds he had been obliged (in spite of his natural respect for his master's wife) to regard her as a proud, light-minded and wilful lady, hardly fit, in his opinion, to be the spouse of the estimable Sir Ralph. Now there was a gentleness and meekness, as well as a pensiveness, in her demeanour that testified most pleasantly to her change of heart.

The morning came when Hogarth was no longer able to wait upon his mistress, being too much prostrated by sickness and cramps to rise from his bed. Lady Skelton shared her husband's concern over their faithful servant's illness. As lady of the manor, it was her duty to minister to the invalids in the household. As a rule she was content to leave such doctoring as was necessary to her mother-in-law, who was only too ready to try her skill on any sufferer. But now she took entire charge of the sick steward, had him moved to a bedchamber in the main part of the house where she could more conveniently attend to him, and prepared all his nourishment – the broths, paps and caudles[5] considered suitable for an invalid – with her own hands. Old Lady Skelton was disconcerted, and somewhat offended, to find herself superseded by her daughter-in-law in a sphere that she had been accustomed to consider exclusively her own. She begged Barbara not to over-tax her own frail health with this sedulous nursing and, when Barbara suavely ignored her advice, had to content herself with looking over her collection of nauseating prescriptions, and grumbling to Agatha Trimble how she would have treated Hogarth had she had the nursing of him.

Sir Ralph had nothing but approval for Barbara in her new role. Hogarth was a valued servant, a man in whom Sir Ralph had absolute confidence and trust. No effort should be spared to restore him to health. Moreover this was how he liked his wife to be – not an elusive, unaccountable creature with something disconcerting even about her beauty, but bustling, efficient, occupied in a truly womanly task.

As for Hogarth he was deeply grateful to his mistress for her care, comparing her in his mind with Dorcas,[6] and other ministering women of Scripture. For her sake, because he believed that her regenerate soul needed his continued care, he made piteous but vain efforts to get well.

Hogarth was dying. This was obvious even to Sir Ralph, who was bluffly optimistic as a rule about everyone's health except his own. Old Lady Skelton wiped away a tear as she thumbed her prescriptions. 'Take twenty-four swallows – alas, poor Hogarth!' 'I fear that neither swallows nor anything else will save the poor fellow now from great pains, a lingering death and a thousand other inconveniences,' said Agatha Trimble with lugubrious relish.

The physician summoned from Buckingham looked grave when he saw the sick man. He had seen nothing like this before – the running at the nose and eyes, the brownish colour of the skin – this was something more deadly than colic or food poisoning. He spoke learnedly and at some length about the four humours, blood, phlegm, choler and melancholy, and of how when the delicate balance between them was upset illness inevitably resulted, ordered an opiate for the patient to relieve his pain and went away shaking his head.

The weather had broken, the heavy sullen rain of late summer turned the gardens and park into a dripping greenness, darkened the old house and added to the gloom of its inmates. The household moved about with mournful steps and spoke with hushed voices. Hogarth was liked and respected. Even the younger servants, who laughed at his pious talk and ways, knew him to be a just and kindly man. He had been in charge of Sir Ralph's 'family' for so long it was hard to imagine Maryiot Cells without him.

Though everyone had given up hope of his recovery – his arms and legs were now partially paralysed and he was prostrated by vomiting and pain – young Lady Skelton never slackened in her care of him. She looked wan, there were dark shadows under her eyes as she moved about the sickroom, a gallant, gracious figure, in the opinion of the household, battling forlornly with the angel of death.

And Hogarth himself? As he lay there behind the curtains of his bed in the stuffy, darkened sickroom, submerged in awful weakness, many thoughts, some hazy, some startlingly clear, drifted through his clouded mind. He knew that he was about to die and death itself held few terrors for him. Death was a commonplace, the one great certainty in an uncertain world, and its very certainty gave it an awful dignity and reassurance. Who was he, a man of fifty, without wife or children, to shrink from death when he had seen young infants, blooming maidens, lusty young men fall like autumn leaves from life's tree? His faith, however narrow and interwoven with human complacency, was sincere and did not fail him in this dread hour. He was ready, in all humility, to submit the account of his life to his supreme Master.

But there was something that troubled him – young Lady Skelton and her reclaimed soul. Even when she was not actually bending over his bedside holding a cup to his lips, he could see her green eyes regarding him pleadingly

– with meekness – with mockery? No! God forbid – with true remorse and penitence.

He had been privileged to set her erring feet on the straight and narrow way. Would she have the spiritual strength to stay there? Soon she would have to stand alone. He would not be there to guide and encourage her, to wrestle in prayer on her behalf. He saw her eyes again staring at him – how green they were – how strangely shaped – insolent – sly – cat's eyes. No one would share her secret now. She would have to bear the burden of it alone – would have to carry it down with her to her grave. She was saying to him, 'You promise that my ugly secret will die with you?' Her voice was meek but her sleepy eyes were full of menace. And suddenly the mists of his pain and weakness cleared, and he *knew*.

Paulina, passing by the door of the sickroom, heard his feeble cry and hurried in. She parted the bed-curtains and bent over him. Sweat had broken out on his discoloured forehead, his wasted hands were clutching at the bedclothes, his eyes were full of entreaty.

'Hogarth, what is it? A drink?'

He gasped, 'No, Sir Ralph – quick. I must tell him.'

'I will fetch him at once.'

She turned and found herself face to face with Barbara.

Barbara gave her an angry look. 'What are you doing here, Paulina? Why did you not call me? I will attend to him.'

Paulina said bluntly, 'He does not need your attentions. He wants Sir Ralph.'

'Sir Ralph? Why? He is wandering in his mind. He must sleep now. Later when he is rested he shall see Sir Ralph.'

Paulina said, 'I am going now to fetch my brother.'

The two young women faced each other, tense as duellists. There was the sound of voices and footsteps in the passage. Paulina ran to the door. 'Brother, is it you? Come quickly. Hogarth wants you. There is no time for delay.'

The sickroom, dim from its shrouded curtains and the rain and falling dusk outside, seemed full of people. Old Lady Skelton, Agatha Trimble, Aunt Doll, had followed Sir Ralph. Even Cousin Jonathan, hearing the commotion, had lumbered in.

Sir Ralph, his florid face paler from emotion, had gone behind the bed-curtains. He emerged again, his prominent eyes like those of an anxious fish. 'Barbara, I cannot hear him. There is something he is trying to say, poor fellow. He is rambling about "the flinging off of all honour" – his voice is so weak, I cannot make out the rest.'

Barbara swept forward with a rustle of her silk gown. 'Let me try. I am accustomed to the faintness of his voice. I will try to catch his words. Stand back everyone! In his feeble state the sight or sound of so many people round him might be fatal.'

Her tone was commanding. Her eyes blazed with a look of power. Sir Ralph willingly stood aside. She parted the bed-curtains and drew them behind her. She was enclosed with the sick man in the muffled gloom of the bed as in a little room. She bent over Hogarth, gently drew the feather pillow from beneath his head and placed it over his face...

When she came out from behind the curtains, her face was deathly white. She answered the anxious and enquiring looks with a shake of her head.

She said dully, 'It is too late. I raised his head. I tried to hear. Too late. He has gone to his reward.'

She fell down fainting to the floor.

8

THE KNOT IS BROKEN

'False hearts and broken vows.'[1]

HOGARTH WAS BURIED, and with him Lady Skelton's secret. So she told herself, not so much in triumph or hatred (for after her first outburst of frustrated rage she had come to feel little more than a pitying contempt for the deluded steward), but with an enveloping sense of relief. The disposal of Hogarth (for so she expressed it to herself) had been an unpleasant necessity. She had hastened his departure to those heavenly regions in which he took so keen an interest, without compunction but without undue malice. Indeed, in her role of sick nurse, she had really tried to alleviate his pain and discomfort, as far as was consistent with the business in hand. It had been an irksome, exhausting and, to one of her fastidious senses, a somewhat revolting affair.

But it was over now. Sir Ralph had given him a handsome funeral, distributing gloves and scarves among the mourners as if, as Agatha Trimble had remarked acidly, he had been a member of the family. Barbara resolved to put Hogarth out of her mind, to bury him for a second time, as it were, in the dark regions below conscious thought. She felt almost deliriously safe and free. She felt, rising imperious within her, the craving to escape as soon as possible from this gloomy house, cradled in the damp, dripping greenness of its clustering trees, to the warmth of her lover's arms.

It was the saddest night of rain, the night after the funeral, that had been known that season. The rain fell steadily, stubbornly, as though the skies were dissolving into water. Not a night to venture abroad, but Barbara could not wait. When the household had retired to its rest she went up to the little hidden room, dressed herself impatiently in her man's clothes, masked herself, and stole out of the house.

Cantering along the yew hedges, she was sheltered by the thick walls of the yew hedges themselves and the interlacing branches of the trees overhead from the teeming wetness of the night. But out in the open countryside it seemed to her as if she were riding through a waterfall. The earth, squelching mud and water beneath her horse's hoofs, seemed to be trying to liquefy in sympathy with the weeping sky. The rain pelted down on to her slouched hat and ran in rivulets on to her cloak; her leather gloves were sodden as she held the reins, her hair hung wet as seaweed on her cheeks. But she did not care. She even rejoiced in the inclemency of the night, finding a savage refreshment in the raw air and the rain, after her nights of vigil in the sour-smelling sick-room, all the stuffy hypocrisy in which she had been forced to indulge. No more prayers, contrition, pious homilies for Barbara Skelton, but the highway, the pistol-shot and the embraces of her lawless lover!

She had had no time to warn Jackson of her coming, so sharp had been her impatience, but something assured her that he would be at the 'Leaping Stag' tonight. She pictured, with sensuous pleasure, his astonishment and joy as she appeared before him and threw herself into his arms.

As she drew near the inn she could see a glimmer of light through the trees. She rode up to the side door; it was unlocked and she let herself into the yard. No one was about. She went unobserved into the inn. She stood there at the foot of the staircase for a moment, the water running off her riding boots and cloak making a pool around her. A door opened and the landlady of the inn came through. She started as she saw Barbara. 'What, you!'

Excitement, feverish anticipation of delights to come, gave a sound of gaiety, almost of geniality to Barbara's voice as she replied, 'Yes, I am back. Is Captain Jackson here?' Mistress Molly looked at her sharply. Then she smiled and nodded her head. 'Oh yes, he is here. He is lying here the night. He is upstairs in the usual room. You should go up and see him. He will be mighty content to see you.'

Her smile broadened into a leer. Barbara ignored it and, throwing her cloak with an insolent gesture on to the floor, bounded up the stairs. The landlady muttered savagely as she stooped and picked it up, 'Ho, ho! my piece of imperious cruelty, I wish you joy of what you find up there.'

Barbara paused outside the door of the bedroom, savouring the passionate excitement of the moment. Then she opened the door gently and slipped into the room. It was lighted by a solitary candle. Captain Jackson was in bed and in bed with him was a tousled, fair-haired girl.

Jerry Jackson sat up with an oath, saw Barbara and stared at her with an expression of ludicrous dismay.

'Barbara! You!'

She stood quite still, regarding them, her lips smiling dangerously beneath her mask.

He blustered out excuses. 'A pox on it! I never thought you'd do the business so soon. I swear I am heartily sorry for this. This wench is nothing' (ignoring a slap and a shrill protest from his bedfellow), 'just a ramping girl I brought down from town...'

His voice failed, withered by Barbara's deadly look.

'You look very well together. Pray do not disturb yourself,' said Lady Skelton in a cool, composed voice. 'I told you that if you were unfaithful to me here our knot would be broken for ever. You may find that this strumpet, cheap though she looks, may cost you very dear. Farewell – till the next merry meeting.'

She walked quietly down the stairs, swept past the landlady who was waiting in spiteful anticipation at the bottom of the stairs, and went into the little parlour. There were writing materials here and Lady Skelton penned a brief note. She wrote hastily, for she could hear Jackson in violent altercation upstairs with his room-mate.

She passed through the hall and the landlady, cowed by something indescribably menacing in her still face and swift smooth movements, shrank back as she passed. She went out to the yard, mounted Fleury and, spurring him cruelly for the first time in her life, rode furiously out into the night.

The local constable was roused at midnight by a fierce hammering on his door. He opened the window and thrust his head out into the streaming rain.

'Who the devil is there? What d'you want?'

He could only just discern the figure of a man on horseback below the window. The rider stood up in his stirrups and, lifting his arm, thrust a piece of paper on to the window-sill.

'Stop! Hi! What is this? Who are you?'

But the unknown rider was away; the sound of his horse's hoofs came muffled through the swish of the rain, and died away.

The constable, much astonished, unfolded the piece of paper and read slowly (for he was not a notable scholar):

'Haste! haste! If you would catch the notorious highway robber Jerry Jackson, he is harboured tonight at the "Leaping Stag" inn.'

The letter had no superscription nor signature, and seemed by the handwriting to have been written in wild urgency or passion.

9

THE HEAVY HILL

'For an outlaw this is the law,
That men him take and bind,
Without pitie, hanged to be
And wave with the wind.'[1]

'LADY SKELTON, PRINTED on the River of Thames being frozen. In the 36th year of King Charles II, January 23rd.'[2]

Barbara gave a childish exclamation of pleasure as she read the little card. She slipped it into her muff and said impulsively to the young gallant by her side, 'Thank you. I will keep it always. It will be something to remind me of this prodigious sight.'

She gazed round her with eager curiosity and delight. Prodigious sight, indeed, and one that she could hardly expect to see again. It was seventy-five years since the citizens of London had been able to disport themselves in this strange way on the Thames. It might be another seventy years, perhaps a hundred, before they could do so again. A hundred years – a thousand years – it was all the same to Barbara; a shapeless, meaningless void, a nothingness, when Barbara Skelton would be no more. This present moment, this gay, exhilarating, unusual *now,* was all that mattered, and Barbara, with quickened senses and heightened spirits, was determined to extract the utmost enjoyment from each hour.

England was gripped by the greatest frost within living memory. The island lay locked in seas that were frozen for two miles from the coast. On land, town was isolated from town, village from village, snow-drifts and ice made the roads impassable. Fish, birds, beasts and even men perished in the cruel cold. Every day brought news of fresh accidents and disasters. Religious fanatics of the more extreme Protestant persuasion, rejoicing in this natural phenomenon, as they had rejoiced in the Plague and the Great Fire twenty odd years ago, cried woe upon the kingdom, upon its licentious monarch and his papist Portuguese queen and his papist French whore.[3] Enthusiastic gardeners lamented the destruction of their exotic plants. In garrets, back courts and alleys, whose foetid stenches not even the intense cold could purify, the poor suffered miserably. The streets were full of 'poor pestiferous creatures'[4] with chattering teeth and pinched blue noses, begging for alms. Lady Skelton, driving by in her coach, muffled in velvet and furs, threw a coin or two to the beggars shivering in the gutter. Their Majesties were said to be distributing relief to the needy; charity was all the vogue.

The London streets were unfamiliar, with the gables of the houses blanketed with snow, and the winter sun failing to penetrate the thick fog that muffled the city as though the intense cold of the atmosphere had become palpable. But London's great waterway, the Thames, was still more strangely transformed. Paralysed and dumb, its busy waters turned to ice, it was taking an enforced rest from its everyday occupations. The barges, wherries and skiffs lay moored by the steps, caught in the ice like flies in amber. The watermen, their tempers and language by no means improved by the frost and their pecuniary loss, had to vent their surliness on one another in riverside pot-houses. The 'shootman' at London Bridge, whose duty it was to signal the safest passage to the bridge shooters who, for a consideration, were ready to guide boats through the arches, gazed down in amazement at the frozen rapids and declared ten times an hour that he had never thought to see the like.

But if the Thames had retired temporarily from business it could still be London's playground. Londoners of all degrees and ages flocked on to its frozen surface as soon as the ice was strong enough to bear them, slipping, sliding, shouting, revelling like children in the queer sensation of being able to cross the river on foot. The frost continuing day after day, some enterprising persons set up booths, where they sold hot meats and ale. Their example was quickly followed, and soon a whole town of booths and stalls, arranged in rows like streets, sprang up on the frozen river.

There was the printing press where Lady Skelton had got her card, and which had been honoured by a visit from His Gracious Majesty; there were stalls for hot pies, roasted chestnuts and sweetmeats, miniature coffee houses where the better sort could warm themselves not only with the fashionable beverage but with 'mum',[5] and spiced and buttered ale. The tippling booths did a roaring trade among the mob, fortune-tellers, quack physicians and card-sharpers were there in force, so were the painted ladies from Drury Lane and St Giles. There were gambling booths and, in the phraseology of the respectable, 'other lewd places'. For the ladies there were vendors of ribbons, laces, combs and knick-knacks. There were puppet shows, plays, interludes, bull-baiting, cock-fighting, sledging, and even horse and coach racing, for the ice was now strong enough to bear wheeled traffic.

Torches flamed in the thick foggy air; people warmed themselves before bonfires and (as this was England) from these convivial groups came the strumming of stringed instruments, the sound of voices defying the raw atmosphere, upraised in bawdy snatches, or in the sweet plaintive lilt of a love song.

The fun continued all day, and long into the bitter night.

This was London's great Frost Fair, London's unexpected, unrehearsed Carnival, and the Londoners were enjoying it with their unsurpassable zest. Rich and poor, fashionable and obscure, no one was too grand or too humble to share in the public merriment. Ordinary life was at a standstill, the cobbled streets were infinitely more dangerous than the ice. Nature herself had granted the city a royal holiday.

Barbara, ignoring Sir Ralph's complaint that the Frost Fair was the resort of all the most 'rascally, whoring, roguing sort of people', was a constant visitor to the River. If her husband would not accompany her (and, as usual on his rare visits to London, he was occupied with all kinds of staid and tedious business and interviews with personages of state), there were plenty of lively young gallants who were eager for the privilege of acting as escort to the lovely Lady Skelton.

Barbara had been an immediate success on her appearance at Whitehall a month or so ago. Her elegance, and something unusual, even bizarre, about her beauty, caused a stir. It was asked why this vivid and alluring-looking creature had allowed herself to be buried so long in the depths of Buckinghamshire with that pompous ass of a husband. She was ogled and made love to by the men, disliked by the women, had a poem written to her nose by a Court poet, was honoured by several glances of sardonic admiration from His Majesty, and by a sweetly spiteful enquiry from the Duchess of Portsmouth as to how long she intended to stay in town. She had the exquisite satisfaction of outshining her florid Kingsclere sister-in-law at the Court revels. She was showered under with invitations to balls, supper, card and theatre parties.

As she sat side by side with some admirer in a box at the King's or Duke of York's theatre[6], waiting with shining eyes for the velvet curtains to be drawn aside, displaying the little stage with its scenery screens and tall lighted wax candles, set like an illuminated picture in the darkness, she felt, with a secret thrill, that she herself was the actress in a play of her own devising. Talented actress that she was, she played two roles with equal success – Lady Skelton, gracious lady of the manor, elegant woman of fashion; Barbara of no surname – daring highwaywoman who rode, robbed, and killed as well as any man and would endure no interference nor betrayal. No wonder that these young men, satiated with the tame beauties of the Court, hovered moth-like round the bright, dangerous flame of her personality. The pity of it was that no one but herself could appreciate her versatility. Only one man had guessed how adroit she was, and the knowledge had brought him to his grave.

This visit to London had been just what she had needed to revive and set up her spirits after that hateful night at the

‘Leaping Stag’ inn. She owed it to the deceptive fragility of her appearance, and to her indulgent, silly mother-in-law.

It had not required much ingenuity on Barbara’s part to alarm old Lady Skelton about her health. Anger, mortification, jealousy of the most primitive kind, had raged unchecked in Barbara’s bosom after her discovery of her lover’s perfidy. To these harassing emotions was added a panic fear lest by her hasty betrayal of Jackson she had also betrayed herself. If he were apprehended would he in revenge, or in hope of obtaining a pardon, lay information against her that might lead to her identity being discovered? She broke into a sweat at the thought, cursed the spasm of wild spite that had made her so unmindful of her own safety and interests.

It was the talk of the neighbourhood that a highwayman had been discovered at the ‘Leaping Stag’ inn, had escaped by jumping out of the window and had ridden away into the night. No one had heard what had become of him after that. So he had escaped after all! On the whole Barbara was relieved. She must forgo her revenge, but she believed him to be less dangerous to her at large than he would be in prison. She could not, however, be at ease till she had more sure information about his movements. He might be lurking in the neighbourhood, awaiting the opportunity to denounce her. Though she would not admit it to herself, she missed his swaggering, rollicking company. Life had become tasteless, a round of dull duties shot through with apprehension. Her nights were restless; her appetite failed. She moped in the house over her embroidery.

Old Lady Skelton warned her son that if he did not take his wife to London to consult a skilled physician he might lose her. Sir Ralph, stirred out of his usual complacency by his mother's anxiety and Barbara's pale and haggard air, agreed to spend the winter at his house in Lincoln's Inn Fields – the more readily as he had some business to attend to in the capital. It was generally acknowledged that there was nothing like a visit to London to restore the health of ailing ladies from the country. The stinks, the outbreaks of plague, the atrocious noise – the rattle of wooden wheels on cobbles, the shouts of street vendors, 'Kitchen stuff ha' you maids!' 'Buy a mousetrap – a mousetrap or a tormentor for your fleas,' milkmaids rattling their pails, apprentices shouting 'What d'ye lack?', the bawling of hackney coachmen and of footmen clearing a way for their masters and, at night, the brawling of revellers – to be sure delicate females who had wilted in the fresh air and quiet of Devonshire or Herts positively thrived on all this. Lady Skelton was no exception. The day of her arrival in London she changed into her crimson velvet and was away in a coach to choose fans at the New Exchange and, by the time that the famous physician had been summoned to attend her, had so far recovered that he declared he could see very little wrong with her.

As the weeks went by and she heard nothing of Jerry Jackson her fears died away. That episode in her life was over; the future would no doubt bring its own excitements and pleasures; meanwhile the present was very agreeable.

So she thought as her gallant, having put on his own skates, knelt down on the ice and fastened a pair on to her feet. She was a novice at this pastime, made fashionable by the exiled Cavaliers when they returned from the Low Countries, but she had taken to it with her accustomed physical verve. She was in fact already more skilled at it than she allowed to appear.

The infatuated young man by her side was prepossessing, and it was nearly as pleasant to her as it was to him to have his arm round her waist, drawing her body close to his. He bent down so low as they glided off together that the curls of his golden periwig brushed her cheek and he murmured:

'Do you know what you look like, Lady Skelton?'

His breath floated towards her in a little cloud.

She shook her head, smiling dreamily.

'Like a beautiful, pure, white swan.'

The watchman, passing outside the great house in Lincoln's Inn Fields, called out in his flat, monotonous voice, 'Past twelve of the clock and a mild, thawing morning.'

Lady Skelton, turning in her canopied and curtained bed, thought drowsily that it was a pity the Great Frost was over – it would be a long, long time before there would be anything like it again – she had enjoyed the skating, that strong young arm round her waist, the warm amorous voice murmuring compliments and endearments in her ear. But perhaps it was time for life to slip back into its accustomed grooves – one could not go skating for ever. She must visit her mantua maker, and tomorrow she had promised to wait on Lady Weston at her country house at Highgate. She sank softly again into sleep.

Twelve slow solemn chimes announced midnight from the belfry of St Sepulchre's church.[7] And as the last chime died away, there was the sound of a hand-bell tolling dolefully. The watchman paused below the walls of Newgate Prison, set his lantern down on the ground and clearing his throat, delivered the 'Admonition to the Prisoners of Newgate on the Night before Execution', as laid down and provided for, by the annual sum of 26s 8d in the will of pious Robert Dowe, citizen of London and Merchant Taylor.[8]

'You prisoners within,

Who for wickedness and sin,

After many mercies shown, are now appointed to die today, in the forenoon, give ear and understand that this morning the greatest bell of St Sepulchre shall toll for you in form and manner of a passing bell...'

The pickpocket, who was to die, looked at the Ordinary praying beside him with the blank gaze of a terrified child. He was in fact barely sixteen years of age. '...to the end that all godly people hearing that bell and knowing that it is for you going to your deaths may be stirred up heartily to pray...'

The footpad who was to die, drank off another tot of brandy and sank down again into a drunken stupor. '...there to give an account of all things done in this life and to suffer eternal torments for your sins, unless upon your hearty and unfeigned repentance you find mercy...'

The highwayman, who was to die, was giving a supper party to seven ladies of the town. He was more than a little drunk and so were they. Their painted faces and patches and curls seemed to swim before him as he raised his glass and toasted them in turn.

'Nan, Moll, Bets, Ursula, Jenny, Peggy, Fan. My pretty jades. I am heartily sorry to part with you, but no doubt I shall meet you all again in hell. Farewell then till our next merry meeting!'

Surely they had cleared the streets of slush by now? Lady Skelton lowered the window of her coach and, putting her head out, asked the footman impatiently what was causing the delay.

He said excitedly, 'A great throng of people, my lady. It seems that there is a hanging this morning at Tyburn and the prisoners are just leaving the prison. That bell that your ladyship hears is the great bell of St Sepulchre tolling for the condemned men.'

Lady Skelton said petulantly, 'Giles should have known better than to drive past Newgate. No doubt there is one of these execution processions most mornings.'

She held an orange stick with cloves up to her nose; she could smell the jostling mob from here; she did not want to catch the plague or jail fever.

The footman said with an eagerness that broke through his obsequious manner, 'Would your ladyship care to follow the procession? There must be a noted malefactor to be turned off, for the crowd is vaster than it would be for an ordinary hanging, and there are several coaches here belonging to the Quality.'

Lady Skelton laughed. 'It would be cruel, would it not, to deprive you of the pleasure of seeing a hanging? As it is, it seems that I have no alternative, and that the only way to get out of the crowd is to follow it.' Her lashes dropped, giving a partly scornful, partly good-humoured look to her face.

The footman said fervently, 'Oh, thank you, my lady,' and jumped up to his place on the box.

Barbara, in spite of her assumed air of indifference, was interested in the proceedings. She had never seen an execution. The sight might afford her some new sensation.

The crowd was growing thicker every moment as people poured out of doorways and alleys, and pushed their way through side-streets. Every window had its craning heads. There was a great deal of shouting, joking and raucous laughter. Lady Skelton's coachman, by taking advantage of a momentary gap in the crowd, and by dint of some loud whip-cracking and as much swearing as was consistent with the dignity of a coachman to a lady of rank, manoeuvred the coach into a position opposite the porch of St Sepulchre's church. Here the clergyman waited, attended by the parish clerk, with three nosegays of rosemary tied with white silken ribbons, the season being too early for the flowers which he was bound by custom to present to the doomed men.

The noisy voice of the crowd sank suddenly to a loud murmuring sound, then broke into cheering. 'The prisoners are coming, my lady,' the footman called down to his mistress. The mob, parting reluctantly, made way with ironic applause for the Sheriff's carriage and his bodyguard. This was followed by a cart in which two criminals were seated on their coffins, one a sullen ruffian of fifty, the other a sickly, scared youth. Barbara regarded them dispassionately. If this was all that was to be seen it was hardly worth the wait.

A second cart rumbled into view and the cheering swelled into a roar. Seated in the cart was the incongruous figure of a young man dressed in the height of fashion and as gaily as if for his wedding. His breeches were of black velvet, his yellow waistcoat of flowered tabby; his long-skirted green velvet coat was ornamented with big bunches of yellow ribbons, his cravat was of fine lace. A cascade of lace and ribbon fell over his wrists. His head was bare, his beautiful auburn hair hung in curls on his shoulders. He carried a black hat trimmed with feathers and yellow ribbons under one arm, in his hand a lace handkerchief which he waved in acknowledgement of the plaudits of the crowd. He held his head high, his demeanour was careless, even jaunty, his eyes defiant. Only the rope hanging round his neck showed that he was not some spark riding in a hangman's cart for a wager or a jest.

The footman appeared at the window. 'Pardon, my lady, but you might care to know that that fellow is Captain Jerry Jackson, a notorious highwayman, to be hanged this morning for robbery and murder.'

Lady Skelton said, 'Indeed! Is that his name?' Her voice came faint and breathless.

The footman, as he scrambled again on to the box, winked at the coachman and jerked his thumb over his shoulder. 'Love at first sight! They're all the same. Town wenches or ladies of quality, they all dote on a likely-looking highwayman with a hempen cravat round his neck.'

Barbara sat very still inside the coach, her fingers clenched together in her muff. 'To be hanged for highway robbery and murder.' So this was to be the end of Jerry Jackson.

Her thoughts were in confusion. An angry pity, a kind of shuddering physical horror at the thought of the violence that was to be done within the hour to her lover's body, struggled against her deep selfishness, the callousness which she had cultivated like a grace. Suddenly, crushing down every other feeling, came a terrifying apprehension for her own safety.

She leant out of the window, beckoned to a respectably dressed, elderly man standing near. 'Good sir, that highwayman Jackson – has he lain long in Newgate? Can you tell me anything of his capture?'

He doffed his hat. 'At your service, my lady. I believe that he was first apprehended in Buckinghamshire some time last summer. Isn't that so, Jake?'

He turned to his companion, who was eager to oblige this fine and lovely lady. 'Yes, that is right, my lady. What actually happened, according to the official account of his life and confession which I had a glimpse of just now – not that you can believe the half of these confessions – the criminals are always said to be "truly penitent and moved to contrition" whereas the truth is that most of them glory in dying quite unconcerned – '

Lady Skelton broke in impatiently.

'Yes, yes. But what did it say?'

The crowd was surging forward, following in the wake of the procession. Lady Skelton motioned to the man to mount on the step of her coach, and as it moved slowly forward he told her:

'Well, it seems that he was betrayed by some doxy of his – saving your ladyship's presence – when he was in bed with another woman. He escaped out of the window of the inn where he was harboured and fled northwards, but they searched the countryside and found him drinking with some companions at the "Boot" inn at Olney. They all but caught him there, but he slipped through their fingers again. He and his friends headed south after that, and were seen by some gentlemen who were out hunting near Whaddon. They rode across the fields to Winslow and gave the alarm. When Jackson and his fellow rogues came to Winslow they found the people turned out with scythes and forks to bar their way. But they dashed furiously through them, and scattering them rode to Chesham, hotly pursued by a military patrol which had been called out and a great crowd of other horsemen, and there outside the town they turned to engage their pursuers, their horses being blown. The fight lasted for half an hour – you must allow that this rogue Jackson is a man of undaunted courage – till Jackson's companions were all wounded or slain, and his horse shot under him, and then he was taken prisoner. He has languished in Newgate ever since, endeavouring to escape his just punishment, by bribery and petitions, and indeed I believe he might have escaped, for they say that his cell has been thronged with ladies of rank, but he was found guilty of murder on the highway as well as robbery, and that's a thing they daren't wink at. That is all I can tell you, my lady, but we may hear more when he makes his dying speech.'

Barbara said slowly, 'Thank you.'

'Very pleased to oblige you, I'm sure, my lady!' said the man as he jumped off the step of the coach.

Barbara leant back in her seat. Her heart was beating so violently that she felt as if she were suffocating. What she had heard justified her sharpest fears. Jackson had been captured as a direct result of her action. What more natural than that he should seek to betray her in his turn? His confession had made no mention of his mysterious female accomplice. Was he waiting to make a dramatic revelation at the foot of the gallows? Horrible though it would be she must follow him to Tyburn Tree. Only when he hung there dead, her unexposed secret dead with him, could she hope for peace of mind.

She called up to the coachman, 'Drive on and try to secure a good place.'

The order in no way surprised Giles. An interesting hanging ranked even higher than a visit to Bedlam or Bridewell among the Quality's favourite pastimes. But in spite of his anxiety to obey his mistress, on his own as well as on her account, they made slow progress. The pace of the procession was set not by the eagerness of the spectators, but by the slow rumbling of the carts which bore the chief actors in the gruesome pageant to their deaths.

Slowly the procession wended its way down Snow Hill, crawled at an even slower pace up the 'heavy hill' of

Holborn[9] and, passing St Andrews church with its tall tower, stopped at the 'Bowl' alehouse for the condemned men to have their last drink.

Her ladyship's coach was well to the fore, and she could see, over the heads of the shouting, cheering people, Jerry Jackson's tall, resplendent figure, as he stood up, a mug of ale in his hand, and toasted the mob. Some sally on his part provoked the uproarious mirth of the crowd and even louder cheers. A man standing near the coach explained to his neighbour, 'He's saying that he'll come back and pay for it later. The good plucked ones always say that. Ah, the crowd likes a rogue that dies game.'

The three doomed men had emptied their last mugs of ale. The Sheriff's carriage, the soldiers and the carts moved on. The faces of the spectators crowding the windows and balconies of the houses might have been those of an audience at a playhouse or a bull-baiting, but in the eyes of many of the women were facile tears called forth by Jackson's good looks and stylish air.

Holborn Bars, the ultimate boundary of the City, was reached. A man standing there called out, 'Friend Jackson, I wish you a good journey!' The crowd laughed at this, taking it to be a joke, but Jackson, a set smile on his lips, raised his hand in a little gesture of gratitude and farewell.

The procession bumped along the Tyburn Road. Straggling and mean houses gave way gradually to the country. And so Hyde Park, and the gallows were reached and the procession slowed down and stopped, for this was the end of the journey.

It was a mild morning. Though the ground underfoot was thick with half-melted slush there was a languor in the air that spoke of spring. In the distance a haze lay over the soft heights of Notting Hill. But here in the execution ground there was a ghastly bustle and animation. The brick wall enclosing Hyde Park was edged with spectators. More privileged onlookers filled the stands opposite. Beggars swarmed in and out of the crowd. Children cried and tumbled about; dogs barked. Orange women and sellers of ale did a brisk trade. Broadside vendors, some of them women with babies in their arms, bawled out 'Confessions of Captain Jerry Jackson,' or even 'Last Dying Speech and Confessions of the notorious highwayman, Gentleman Jackson.'

A ballad singer howled:

' "Captain Jackson's Farewell"

Farewell good friends, let not your kind hearts sorrow,
My doom has come. I shall be dead tomorrow.
Fair ladies, dry your lovely eyes
Nor pain me with your tender-hearted sighs!'

There were no tears in the lovely eyes of Barbara Skelton as she sat in her coach, her gaze fixed in fascinated horror on the three-legged gallows on which in a short time her former lover would hang. All softer emotions were extinguished by panic fear for her own safety. Repugnant though it would be to her overstrained nerves she dared not leave this grisly spot till Jackson was dead. She did not wish for his death – indeed, she assured herself, conscious of unusual and unwelcome twinges of conscience, she would gladly and generously have forgiven him his perfidy and have procured for him his release had it been possible – but, if he had to die, then the quicker and the more silently he died the better. A dreadful impatience possessed her. For his sake, as well as her own, she told herself, she wished him a speedy departure.

It seemed – and this was something to be thankful for – that Jerry Jackson was to be turned off first. The cart in which he stood was drawn up under the gallows. The Sheriff's bodyguard with some difficulty cleared a passage for the Sheriff himself. Only a little group of people – friends no doubt of the condemned highwayman – were allowed below the gallows. A woman, so disfigured with tears that it was hard to tell if she were young or middle-aged, plain or comely, seemed to be standing guard over his coffin. The hangman, who had been lounging by, smoking a pipe, pocketed his pipe and began to take an interest in the proceedings. A hush fell on the crowd as Jerry Jackson, drawing himself up, looked round on the people, preparatory to making his final confession or speech.

In spite of herself, a pang, not so much of remorse as of regret, shot through Barbara at the sight. How often he had stood before her looking just thus, waiting for her to admire some new coat or piece of finery, childish, braggart, swaggering, without force of character or unusual intellect, yet able to fire her senses and warm her heart to a semblance of love by his sheer animal magnetism. She told herself fiercely, to drive out the pity that once admitted to her heart might have brought with it compunction, even remorse, emotions that had no place in its arid soil, that his courage was mostly a pose. He would prefer to die thus, supported by the applause of the mob, the sobs of foolish women, than in the peaceful obscurity of a sick-bed. They would say of him (and he knew it) that he had died with 'undaunted courage', 'the most perfect indifference', 'very game'. Only she, Barbara Skelton, would know that he had not dared to take a man's life till she had led the way.

She saw then that he was looking straight at her and that he had recognised her. She sat perfectly still, as was her wont when danger threatened, her pale face framed in the open window of the coach. Only her eyes moved as, opening them wide, she fixed them imploringly on Jackson's face.

He smiled wryly, and bending down to the Ordinary held a whispered conversation with him. Barbara, in an agony of fear, saw the clergyman after some hesitation give Jackson writing materials. Jackson wrote for several minutes – the crowd fidgeted restlessly at the unexpected delay – and handed it to the Ordinary, who received it with several nods of the head.

Barbara could have screamed in the nervous anguish of her suspense. What unlucky impulse had urged her to follow Jackson to his death? What mighty mischief did he intend to launch against her in his last speech, or in that hurriedly scribbled confession? He was going to ruin her – the woman whom he had possessed and loved – as he stood on the very brink of eternity. Barbara was appalled by the malicious impiety of it.

But his dying speech was commendably short and to the point. 'God bless all my friends and may my enemies be hanged as I am,' were the last recorded words of Captain Jerry Jackson.

The hangman's assistant bound his arms; the hangman adjusted the noose round his neck. A sigh, a gasp of admiration and excitement ran through the crowd as, descending from the cart, Jackson with the hangman's help climbed the ladder that rested against the gallows. He was not going to wait in the usual way for the horse and cart to move away from under him, leaving him struggling in the air in the agonies of slow strangulation, dependent on the compassion of his friends to jerk his legs and end his pain. No, he was going to throw himself off the ladder and make a quick finish of it. Yes – he was a good plucked one and no mistake...

Jerry Jackson looked down at the weeping woman who stood by his coffin. Then he looked at Barbara Skelton who sat in her black and yellow coach. He jumped.

Barbara shrieked and fell back with closed eyes against the seat. A deep groan, mingled with screams and hoarse cheers, ran through the crowd. For an awful moment Barbara's unwilling body echoed the death-pangs of the man who had loved it.

She opened her eyes and saw the footman looking in at her. 'Are you all right, my lady? Ladies often come over queer at their first sight of a hanging.'

She quelled the faint insolence of his smirk with a look. He added meekly, 'Giles says, my lady, that he will have to wait till the other prisoners are turned off before he can get the coach through the mob.' She nodded and leant back again, feeling very sick and faint. Again she heard a solitary voice speaking, again the shuddering groan of the crowd – a long interval – and then again. It took longer to dispose of the other prisoners. They lacked Jackson's resolution. Barbara kept her eyes firmly shut. When at last she opened them, three bodies hung motionless from Tyburn Tree.

Shuddering, she averted her gaze, and saw the Ordinary, who had attended the condemned men, standing at the door of her coach. He said in a pompous, flustered voice, 'My lady, it was required of me by that unfortunate highwayman Jackson, shortly before his death, to give you this letter. "The lady in the black and yellow coach," he said. I trust your ladyship will forgive me if I have made some error.' His staring eyes expressed his curiosity. Curiosity too was evident in the faces of Lady Skelton's servants and of the bystanders. She unfolded the note with studied composure and read:

'Barbara! (for I have not the time at this late hour nor any longer the wish to know your other name). It makes me laugh to see the look on your face. You are afraid of me at last, aren't you, my bold little lady? It was a bad hour for me when I met you on Watling Street, but never fear! We had good sport together, and Jerry Jackson is not the man to whine now 'tis time to pay the reckoning. If it had not come through you it would have come some other way, for I was overripe for Tyburn Tree.

'But maybe you feel you owe me some kindness? If so, give a share of our earnings to the woman who is standing by my coffin. Her name is Bess Bracey – she lives at Fountain Court in the parish of St Giles. She was my doxy before ever I knew you, and she has been with me continually in my imprisonment and will see to my burial. I have bequeathed her to my best friend, but should she be left a hempen widow again I would not have her want. No woman had a greater kindness for a man than she has had for me, and she has spent all she has and sold all even to her skin for me.

'Farewell then, lovely Barbara – till our next merry meeting.'

It was signed with a flourish, 'Jerry Jackson'.

Lady Skelton said evenly, and in a clear tone that could be heard by the bystanders:

'It seems that the unfortunate man was struck by my compassionate air and, having no friends of his own, he has asked me of my Christian charity to give that poor woman yonder – some relation of his I suppose – money for his burial.' She gave a purse full of gold to her footman. 'Pray give this purse to that woman over there and tell her that I am heartily sorry for her.'

The footman pushed his way among the dispersing crowd. He was soon back, rather red in the face and the purse still in his hand.

'My lady, the woman – and a common pert jade she is too, begging your ladyship's pardon – says that she doesn't want pity or charity from you or any other woman.'

Barbara's hand trembled as she took back the purse. But she said, shrugging her shoulders, 'Poor creature. I suppose she is distracted with sorrow. Tell Giles to drive on to my lady Weston as fast as possible. We have wasted too much time already watching this tedious hanging.'

When the coach was clear of the mob and on its way to Highgate, Barbara unfolded Jerry Jackson's letter which she had held crushed in her hand, and read again with hatred, anger and a curious bewildered jealousy the words:

'No woman had a greater kindness for a man than she has had for me.'

10

SUMMER'S DATE

'And summer's date hath all too short a lease.'[1]

Summer 1684

'KING'S WEATHER' THEY called it, ignoring in their gushing loyalty all the occasions on which rain, wind and cold had marred a royal procession or party. But was it not fortunate for Sir Ralph and Lady Skelton that the neighbourhood should be basking in this spell of hot and brilliant weather just when their Majesties, accompanied by the Duchess of Portsmouth and other members of the Court, were to honour Maryiot Cells with their presence?

True, the Skeltons were not to have the privilege of having the King and Queen under their roof – that honour had been secured by even more important and influential neighbours – but His Majesty had graciously accepted an invitation to spend an afternoon at Maryiot Cells on his way from one great country house to another. The very brevity of this royal visit made it all the more important that everything should be as near perfection as possible – food, entertainment, weather.

Food was a comparatively simple if arduous matter. All the resources of Maryiot Cells were to be marshalled together – deer from the park; fish from the three fishponds, Abbot's Pool, Purgatory and Hell; peacocks, mutton, veal, calves' heads, capons, chickens and pigeons from the estate – and reinforced by such outside supplies as lobsters and crayfish brought alive in wagons from the coast. The cellars of Maryiot Cells could stand comparison with those of any of the country nobility or gentry. What Lady Skelton's cook did not know about the making of sweetmeats and comfits was hardly worth knowing. The walled gardens of Maryiot Cells produced peaches, nectarines and plums fit not only for a King and Queen but even for a royal mistress. Mrs Samson the housekeeper and Jeffreys the steward could be relied upon to see that, however frenzied the scenes in the big subterranean kitchen, all ran smoothly in Hall and drawing-room, with that seemly order and lack of commotion without which the greatest degree of magnificence would fail to be impressive.

The question of entertainment was more complicated and debatable. Would His Majesty and the Duchess of Portsmouth (her resigned, good-natured little Majesty need not be considered) look for something sophisticated, or would they be in the mood for revelry of an unpretentious and pastoral nature? Barbara and her gay young friends were in favour of private theatricals, and had gone so far as to select a play in which Barbara was to act the part of the heroine who disguised herself as a boy to escape the attentions of an elderly and dissolute admirer, with all manner of ludicrous and diverting consequences. But Sir Ralph, who could not see why a costly and heavy supper should not be enough entertainment for anyone, King or commoner, having watched a rehearsal and expressed his dislike of the idea of his wife masquerading in male attire, flatly refused to sanction the performance unless all the impertinent and immodest parts were left out. As this meant leaving out most of the play, Barbara sulkily abandoned the idea.

Old Lady Skelton suggested a masque.[2] Barbara declared that masques were old-fashioned. Nevertheless it was undeniable that Maryiot Cells would make an exquisite setting for an open-air performance of this kind, the formal gardens gaudy with flowers, the smooth grass sloping down to the glassy river, and across the water the velvet darkness of the yew glades. Perhaps after all, Barbara thought, it would be a mistake to try and imitate the sophisticated licentiousness of Whitehall; better to use the peaceful beauty of her surroundings as a background for her own unusual personality. And then it occurred to her – not a masque with its banal and tedious route of Savages, and Satyrs, Rustics, Witches and Cupids, and all the household, even Agatha Trimble and Cousin Jonathan, clamouring to dress up and take part, but a ballet danced by herself and a selected few from her younger and better-looking acquaintances, as she had heard that the nobles and ladies of King Louis' Court danced at Versailles. And so, after many arguments and discussions, the ballet was hastily evolved, the music written by a talented young man who was staying at Maryiot Cells, the dances arranged and rehearsed.

The ballet was based on the story of Diana and Actæon.[3] Barbara was to be Diana, the Queen Huntress, goddess of the Moon and of the chase. Her costume of fine white silk was to be a becoming blend of the modern and the antique. The low-cut bodice, though modish in outline, left her smooth pale shoulders as exposed as those of any classical goddess; her tight, silver-laced corsage was fashionably seventeenth century; the folds of her clinging dress, slit up the sides to imitate a hunting tunic, boldly displayed the shape, and sometimes even afforded a glimpse, of her beautiful legs. Her quiver of arrows was silver; she had silver sandals on her feet; a crescent moon of diamonds glittered in her rich bronzen hair.

A cluster of willow trees by the river bank would make an admirable grove where Diana and her nymphs could disport themselves, dancing in stately measure, till the audacious young hunter, prying upon the goddess's privacy, provoked her indignation and his doom. The nymphs would gather round young Charles Rich, while he hastily fixed on his head the antlers which were to indicate his metamorphosis into a stag. All the young sparks of the neighbourhood were eager to wear skin rugs and to be the hounds who were to fall on their master and tear him to pieces; but Lady Skelton, who had no intention of allowing the ballet to degenerate into a rough-and-tumble, insisted on their numbers being kept down to manageable proportions. The audience was to sit on the gently sloping grass facing the river, and so would have an excellent view of Diana and her nymphs as they emerged from the dark background of the yew glades and crossed the low stone-bridge.

Everything had been thought out and planned as far as time permitted; only the weather remained unaccountable. Supposing it was sullen and overcast, or worse still supposing it rained, drenching the flimsy-clad goddess and her nymphs, and the richly-clad audience? If the weather was uncertain the ballet would have to be performed in the long gallery or Great Hall, in which case it would lose much of its charm. Amid all the bustle of preparation the weather became the chief topic of conversation. On the whole there was dismay when, three days before the date of the royal visit, it became hot and cloudless. It was feared that this sudden heat could not last. 'I mistrust that bright blue sky. Depend upon it the weather will break before their Majesties arrive,' grumbled Cousin Jonathan as he puffed about the bowling-green. Still, sunny days, heavy with heat and with summer's perfumes, flamed and faded into evenings as limpid as water. The short nights were breathless, hardly much cooler than the days. But Cousin Jonathan was wrong. The dawn of the day – the King's day – was as radiant and full of promise as its predecessors. 'King's weather' everyone said, in the exuberance of their excitement and relief.

Barbara, preoccupied with preparations for the royal visit and thoughts of the success and admiration which she confidently expected to win, gave little heed to a matter which was of considerable interest to other, less self-absorbed members of the family. Paulina Skelton, who had been staying for the past six months with an aunt near Woburn, was returning to her home on the day of the royal visit, bringing with her a young man, Christopher Locksby, to whom it was understood she would shortly become engaged. Her relations were well satisfied at the prospect. The Locksbys were an old, highly esteemed and well-to-do family. The young man, who had recently returned from a prolonged tour of Europe, was reported to be all that was most amiable – good-looking, of a cheerful spirit, lively wit and agreeable manners.

Barbara, who thought Paulina dull, smiled maliciously when she heard these panegyrics. 'Our Paulina has done wisely to wait so long,' she said, making Paulina's twenty years sound like forty, 'since she has apparently secured for herself a paragon such as few of us poor women can hope to mate with.'

It was as well, she thought, that Paulina was to be married at last. She was one of those reserved, silent girls who might either remain unwed (and in Barbara's opinion there were quite enough female relations as it were at Maryiot Cells), or else suddenly elope with someone unsuitable, such as the family chaplain.

When, she wondered with a stab of jealousy and a surge of her familiar restlessness, would some new impulse set the stagnant water of her own life flowing again? Since her return from London in the spring she had gone out regularly, though less frequently than before, on the Highway. Jerry Jackson's death had been a shock to her but not a deterrent. He was, as he had written of himself, 'overripe for the gallows'. Men like Jerry Jackson, common adventurers and rogues when all was said and done, were born to die at a rope's end. Not so ladies of birth and rank like Barbara Skelton. She had no fears for her own safety. She was impressed by her own extraordinary luck. Each threat to her purpose had been swept from her path, she thought complacently.

But she had to admit to herself that she could not recapture the fevered excitement of those early days when she had first taken to the Road, nor the intoxicating delights of robbing and loving in company with 'Gentleman' Jackson. The danger remained, the momentary thrill, the secret satisfaction of her hidden life, but something was missing. What it was she did not know, for her heart, for all her crimes and passions, understood nothing, and so could not tell her that she was lonely.

People remembered afterwards how beautiful Barbara Skelton had looked. It was such a brilliant day, the epitome of summer; the air was motionless, drowsy with sunshine yet vibrant with the myriad small sounds of a summer's day. Perhaps it was the very perfection of the day that gave it an air of unreality, of expectation, as though such perfection was too great a burden to be laid on a mutable world. There was a painted look about the formal gardens, inlaid with the glowing colours of flowers, the translucent greenness of the trees and their intense lacy shadows, the lawns sloping down to the topaz river, and the rainbow-coloured silks, satins and brocades of the chattering, fashionable throng.

Then the sound of music, the lilting, plaintive voices of flutes, flageolets,[4] violins and harpsichord, pure and deliberate as drops of spring water, floated through the slumberous air and, because the day was so beautiful, it seemed to even the more critical of the audience that this was a melody more sweet than ordinary.

A hush fell on the spectators as the little group of dancers glided out from the mysterious darkness of the yew groves, a bevy of green-robed nymphs and, in their midst, the white and silver figure of the divine huntress. People had not known before how exquisitely Barbara Skelton moved, how proudly she held herself, worshipping in each fluid step and gesture her own youth and grace and loveliness. Diana-Artemis would have danced like this in the Attic sunshine, disdaining in her superb virginity any other temple than the forest solitude.

The dancers crossed the bridge, drew near the audience, sank down in attitudes of studied languor and abandon on the sward. The King leant forward and looked at Lady Skelton, his lean sallow cheek propped on his hand, a gleam of more than usual interest in his heavy-lidded eyes.

And Barbara? In this moment of triumph one man's face stood out from the crowd, caught her attention, set her heart beating wildly. It was not the King's face.

Paulina was standing near the royal party and by her side stood a young, fair-haired man. He was a good height without being very tall, well and sturdily built; his face was comely, more than strikingly handsome, but with a look of gaiety, good humour and candour in his bright blue eyes and on his wide, well shaped mouth that Barbara was sure she had never seen before on any man's face. He was looking at her in a kind of wondering and delighted admiration, and instantly, in a lightning flash, she wished to possess that amiable and candid gaiety and bask in it for the rest of her life. Paulina's hand was resting possessively on his sleeve. So this was Kit Locksby whom Paulina expected to marry. So much the worse for her.

The great day was drawing to its close. Hundreds of pounds' worth of food had been consumed in an hour or so at the sumptuous supper that had followed the ballet. The royal couple and the royal mistress had paid their gracious compliments and given their gracious thanks (His Majesty expressing a hope that he would see Lady Skelton at Court that autumn) and taken their leave. Coach after coach filled with courtiers and their hangers-on had rolled away down the beech avenue.

While the servants tried to bring order into the prevalent confusion and set the place to rights, the family, exhausted and gratified, milled to and fro aimlessly in the garden, reluctant after the excitements of the day to settle down to an ordinary evening's routine.

Young Lady Skelton stood on the lower terrace chatting in an animated manner with her mother-in-law, her brother-in-law Roger, Paulina and Kit Locksby. It was clear that she was a trifle overstrung, and who could wonder? As hostess, as principal performer in the ballet, she had carried out her exacting tasks with remarkable verve. A faint flush stained the creamy pallor of her cheeks, her green eyes glistened between the long lashes, her strange nostrils looked more than ever like wings poised for flight.

A detached onlooker, observing first her face and then Paulina's, would have been struck with the contrast between their expressions. There was a restlessness, an unstable look about Barbara's that might have repelled or fascinated according to the temperament of the beholder. Paulina's was serene, with an air of confidence that was just shy and tender enough to avoid complacency. Her looks had improved amazingly during her six months' absence. Some warm and happy emotion had thawed the reserved look which had given an unbecoming touch of austerity to her handsome young face. When she glanced at Kit Locksby it did not need much perspicacity to guess what that emotion was.

Nothing that Paulina could have done or said would have deflected Barbara now from her purpose, but if anything was needed to spur her resolution it was that tender and possessive look in Paulina's eyes. Barbara noted too with cruel satisfaction that Kit Locksby could only give Paulina a dutiful kindness in return. This was child's-play – like robbing an unarmed traveller.

She put her hand to her bosom. 'My brooch! My diamond star brooch. Great heavens! I have lost it.'

She secured everyone's solicitous attention. Paulina, her level brows drawn together said, 'But are you sure that you were wearing it, Barbara? I noticed as you were dancing that your only ornament was that crescent moon in your hair.'

'Yes, yes, I fastened it on just before I left my bedchamber. I thought it would suit well with my costume.'

They were asking her when she had last seen it? Where it might have fallen?

Barbara said, 'I had it when I was waiting in the yew glade for the music to strike up. I know that for certain, for I remember glancing down at it. It will be somewhere between the bridge and the glade. I will go and search for it, before it grows dark.'

She cast an appealing look at Kit Locksby, and he said, 'I will go with you. I am good at finding things – even my cravat ribbon in the morning!'

She had known that he would offer to help for he was that kind of young man. She said quickly in a playful tone, 'I have heard that you are a most accomplished young man, Mr Locksby. Come then, and I will see if you are as clever a finder of lost treasures as you make out.'

They walked together across the lawn and down to the river. The glowing day was dying exquisitely. The colour of the western sky was as elusive as an aquamarine; roseate and violet clouds, feather-shaped, floated in it like islands in the sea of Paradise. The colour of grass, trees, flowing water, was strangely rarefied in the sunset light, as though the earth, abashed at its grossness, was trying to imitate the ethereal beauty of the celestial world. For Barbara Skelton there was, at that moment, only one reality in earth or heaven – the presence of the young man by her side. She walked with downcast eyes, waiting in a kind of anguish of longing for him to speak.

He said, as though on a sudden impulse: 'After all, Actæon was a fortunate fellow.'

'What! to be torn in pieces by his hounds?'

'Well, everyone has to die. Few men see a goddess in *déshabille* first!'

He smiled down at her, frankly admiring her loveliness. Her heart leapt exultantly. He too then felt the physical attraction that had sprung up between them as their eyes first met. Everything about him pleased her madly – his fresh skin, his good, strong, white teeth, the generous width of his mouth, his bright blue eyes. He wore his own hair (no need to wonder how he looked in bed without a periwig) – its colour, a fine golden brown, would have graced a woman – but there was nothing foppish about his appearance. He looked clean, sweet tempered, vigorous – altogether charming. But he must feel more for her than even this compelling physical appeal. She must kindle within him her own headlong sense of their converging destinies, her yearning to be united with him body and soul for ever.

They paused in unspoken agreement on the bridge and looked down at the smoothly gliding water. He said: 'My friends laugh at me because I like fishing. They say, "Why sit for hours by a river staring at the water, when you can get all the fish you want out of your fish pond?" I like hunting and horse-racing better still perhaps, but for a summer sport I delight very much in fishing, and I believe it is the sight and sound of the running water that is the chief part of my pleasure. Do you like it too?'

She shook her head. 'I don't know. Perhaps I could learn to like it if I knew why you liked it. But it does not give me the pleasant sensation that it gives you. It seems to me when I look at this river that my life is slipping away like the water – useless – wasted.'

Her mouth trembled, her eyes filled with tears of sincere self-pity.

Kit Locksby looked down at her with startled compassion. 'Why, Lady Skelton, you must not say that. You must not give way to such a black melancholy humour. Your life wasted and useless! You who are so well-loved and beautiful. Everyone was praising your looks while you danced. You made me think of Ben Jonson's poem. You know – "Queen and huntress, chaste and fair".'[5]

She rested her fingers on his lace ruffle. 'Yes, I have had my fill of praise and compliments, but that is nothing. You can't understand. You are too young and carefree.'

He laughed. 'Young! I am not as young as all that. I am twenty-one.'

'And I am twenty-two. But grief and disappointment, such as I trust you will never know, have made me older than my years.' She sighed faintly. 'But I must strive against these melancholy humours. If I can give some pleasure to those around me I must be content.'

They walked on together, her arm resting familiarly on his sleeve. Every now and then he glanced down with tender interest at her lovely, wistful face. What were those sorrows at which she hinted? Paulina, who seemed oddly out of sympathy with her lovely sister-in-law (but he knew that the best of women were apt to be jealous of a different type from themselves) had hardly discussed her with him, beyond saying once, 'I would not buy a horse with such uneasy nostrils as my sister-in-law Barbara's.'

No doubt that self-opinionated ass Sir Ralph could not appreciate this rare and sensitive creature as she deserved to be. Could it be that he was unfaithful to her, neglectful, perhaps positively unkind? Probably he blamed her for her barrenness, made her life a misery by his reproaches. A surge of indignant pity rose within him. Almost unconsciously he pressed her arm to his side in a protective gesture which set her heart racing.

They had entered the yew glade. A deep and shadowy coolness surrounded them. It was like passing into another world, like moving about together in some dim region under the sea. They walked in a pregnant silence till they came to the open space where a carved stone urn marked the meeting-place of the yew glades.

They paused by it and he turned to her and said vehemently, 'I wish from my soul that I could dispel your sadness.' She said softly, 'You do. I felt happier as soon as I saw you. You are so kind, cheerful – and gentle. That sounds a strange thing to say about a young and robust man! I never knew before that one could love a man for that quality. But I see now that only strong people dare to be gentle. Anything would be safe in your hands – a bird, a horse's mouth – or a woman's heart.'

His face went red – partly because he was abashed at receiving this (in his opinion) undeserved and fervent praise, but also from a sudden strong emotion which he felt he ought to, but knew he neither wanted to nor could, control.

Barbara placed her hands on the stone urn, leant her head on them and wept, because for the first time since her mother's death she had found someone whom she could love as well as, perhaps better than, herself.

It was not in Kit Locksby's nature to allow a lovely woman to weep disconsolately on a stone urn. In a moment his arms were around her and her head was on his shoulder. Then as she turned her face up to him he bent over her and kissed her mouth.

When their lips parted at last he said in some confusion, 'Barbara – Lady Skelton – I don't know what came over me. You are so beautiful – the loveliest woman I have ever seen. I can't help thinking this but I suppose I have no right to say it. You are married and I am all but betrothed to Paulina.'

Barbara clung to him like a drowning woman. 'Paulina! What does she matter? She lives only for her horses and books. Oh Kit, do not be trapped as I was into a cold and loveless marriage. You cannot know the hell it is – never alone at bed nor board, yet always lonely. It is I who need you. I who love you with a pure and sincere love.' The tears were streaming down her cheeks.

He clasped her to him, submerged by his own and her desire, fondled her hair, kissed her wet lashes and her mouth again and again. 'Barbara – my moon goddess – my dear love. Never weep – your eyes are too beautiful for tears. Trust yourself to me and I will swear that I will make you as happy as you deserve.'

11

LOVERS' MEETING

'She must go fro' and she shall go fro' and she shall go whether she will or no.'[1]

'Now turn from each. So fare our sever'd hearts,
As the divorc'd soul from her body parts.'[2]

HER FACE LOOKED back at her from the mirror. She gazed at it intently, almost greedily, as though in its eyes and contours she would read the secret of her future and her fate.

She said to herself, 'This is the last time I shall ride out on the highway. I swear it. This last time and then no more.'

And so, as she sat before the mirror in the little secret room, she said, as it were, farewell to the face of that Barbara Skelton that only she and Jerry Jackson had seen. It looked out at her from between the lighted candles, like a pale mask against the shadowy background of the garret room; provocatively feminine above the mannish cravat, the bronzen curls hanging down on to the shoulders of the mannish coat; the eyes glistening, sleepy yet watchful as a cat's, between the long lashes; the nostrils eager and predatory, the lips parted – the face of a lovely and dangerous woman.

But she would never look like this again. After tonight she would strive in every wakeful moment to be the Barbara of Kit Locksby's desires and imagination – the tender, loving, long suffering woman, whom he adored and longed to cherish and protect. She would burn her man's clothes and her crepe mask, bury her pistols, give away secretly to the poor all her ill-won gains. The unknown young highwayman who had terrorised the countryside for over a year would disappear, and would never be heard of nor seen again.

Barbara had not robbed on the highway since she and Kit had become lovers soon after their first meeting. She dreaded inexpressibly that Kit might discover her secret. He was the most easy-going and tolerant of men; unassuming and modest, he was too conscious of his own failings to set himself up as a censor of morals; he would excuse much in the woman he loved. But Barbara had noticed that he had a violent, to her mind almost morbid, aversion to any form of cruelty. He had told her that when he was on his travels he had lived for a time with a Venetian courtesan, a superb red-haired creature. He admitted that he had been much under the spell of her physical attraction. Then one day he had seen her throw a newly-born kitten into a bucket of water. He had left her house at once and never seen her again. He had told the story half jokingly, as though apologising for his squeamishness, but Barbara had noticed, with a terrified contraction of her heart, that, as he told it, his eyes had gone as hard as blue stones. How would his eyes look if he knew that his sweet Barbara had not only committed robbery with violence but had also taken life on the King's Highway?

But it was not only this dread of discovery, and determination to cut loose from her sinister and dangerous secret, that had stopped her from riding abroad. She no longer felt the need for the emotional stimulation that she had derived from her nocturnal activities. Her whole soul was wrapped up in her love for Kit Locksby. If she had not found complete satisfaction and fulfilment in this love it was only, she told herself, because she could not be with him every day and every night, and take her place by his side as his acknowledged wife. She resented fiercely everything and everybody that came between them. Paulina had been a serious menace at first. Kit could not rid himself of the feeling that he had behaved very shabbily towards her, but Barbara's constant assurance that Paulina did not care for him, and had only complied with the matrimonial plans of her family, appeared to be borne out by Paulina's air of proud indifference when it became clear that Kit was, as Agatha Trimble described it, 'in a cooling condition'. She seemed so very restrained and calm beside his passionate and demanding Barbara. It was easy as well as comfortable to believe that she was secretly as relieved as he was to avoid the marriage.

He worried less about Sir Ralph. Barbara had easily convinced him of the unhappiness of her marriage. According to her he was merely taking something that Sir Ralph had not troubled to claim for a long time. All the same it was not his habit to cuckold men in their own houses. Barbara and he met secretly, sometimes by day, sometimes by night, at a small house near Whaddon which Kit had been left by an uncle, and where he went occasionally to fish, for a trout stream ran through the grounds.

Here Barbara experienced a happiness that soared beyond her most excited imaginings. She had never known before the deep delights of living for another beloved person. A new world of feeling seemed to open before her. 'No woman had a greater kindness for a man than she had for me.' Those words in Jerry Jackson's farewell letter no longer filled her with a spiteful and contemptuous bewilderment. She understood now the motive that had made the St Giles' drab strip herself of her tawdry possessions to ease a highwayman's last days. She herself – pampered woman of rank – would willingly sacrifice all her luxuries and comforts to help her dear love.

More than this, she was ready to transform her whole nature, discarding like outworn garments her craving for excitement and callous egotism. She would teach herself to be warm-hearted, clinging, sensitive, because this was how Kit Locksby imagined her to be. When she was his wife – she found it impossible to contemplate her future under any other guise – how assiduously she would devote herself to him and to the children that she would surely give him, bringing to bear all her remarkable zest for living on to the pattern of her everyday life. She had been quite sincere when she had told him in one of her letters, 'All pleasure I find is nothing without you.'

But one thing remained to be done before she could attain to this state of domestic felicity – one final risk must be taken. Sir Ralph stood in the way of her complete happiness and must be removed.

She who had so delighted in secrecy was impatient now to put an end to subterfuge where her love was concerned. For she knew that Kit would never be satisfied or at ease in the entanglements of a secret amour. Already he had suggested, with a hint of desperation in his tone, that they should abandon their families, friends and country, and flee together to the Continent. Barbara had a better plan than this, a plan, however, that she must carry out alone. Another visit to the Sign of the Golden Glove in Buckingham, a few months of patience, and she would be free to enter again into those bonds of marriage which she found so galling at present, but which, with Kit as her partner, would be the fulfilment of her heart's desire.

But all this lay in the future. At present, Barbara, all aflame with love, lived for the brief reunions with Kit Locksby. Whenever he was able to leave home – for his father was something of an invalid and upon Kit as eldest son devolved much of the management of the estate – he sent her a note arranging a meeting at the house beside the trout stream. She had been six days without seeing or hearing from him, six dragging, fretful days. Then at last he had written explaining that his father's serious illness had kept him at home, and arranging to meet her this very night. She had been keyed up to a pitch of ecstatic expectation, when a second letter had arrived with the news that his father's condition had taken a worse turn and that he could not leave after all. The disappointment had been too much for her excited nerves. She felt the imperative need to relieve her pent-up feelings in some form of violent action. Almost against her will, certainly against her better judgment, she had crept once more up the winding stairs to her garret chamber. Robbery on the highway, this was the only drug that could deaden the tumultuous longing within her.

And now, dressed in her highwayman's clothes and sitting before the mirror in a little pool of candlelight, she picked up her lover's letter, and read it again to charm and reassure herself by its loving phrases and its promises of a speedy meeting. He wrote:

'To my most passionately beloved mistress, Barbara Skelton.
'Dear heart,

I thank you for your tender letter and the lock of your delicate hair which I begged of you and which I will always carry with me. What an unhappy wretch I am to have nothing to send you in return but the news that I cannot come to you the day after tomorrow, for my father's heart is plaguing him sorely, and till I know how things go with him I dare not leave him or my mother. He is in great peril of his life I fear, and we all in sharp apprehension and distress, and so I know that I need make no further excuses to my kind sweetheart, nor tell her how much I long for her delightful company, and to kiss her sweet mouth, for if she knows anything she knows my true love and passion for her. I write in haste that this may reach you in time. Adieu my dearest dear. I shall be with you, God willing, at the earliest opportunity.

Your ladyship's passionate lover and faithful servant,

Kit Locksby.'

He had scribbled a postscript. 'I have found something to send you. This rose. It is not as sweet as you.'

Barbara laid down the letter and picked up a white rose which lay on the table beside her. Smiling gently she held it to her nose, breathed in its delicious perfume, then brushed it lightly with her lips. She began to fasten it to her coat, then, with a movement of revulsion, laid it down again. No! her lover's gift had no place in that dark, midnight life of which she was going to take final leave tonight. It must wait for her here, token of all the enchanted, candid tomorrows which she would share with him.

She opened the Dutch chest, which had once contained her wedding clothes, and put the rose in there, laying it down as softly as a mother would lay a child to sleep.

She bent towards the mirror to blow out the candles and her heart gave a jerk as she saw three candle flames reflected in its surface. What had possessed her to light three candles – dire portent – tonight of all nights?[3] A feeling of heavy foreboding weighed down on her. The sloping, shadowy walls of the attic chamber seemed to lean down menacingly towards her. The little narrow room was congested with the baleful memories of the men she had slain – Ned Cotterell, Hogarth, Jerry Jackson, and those unknown victims of the highway to whom she had never, till tonight, given a passing thought. And suddenly she was horribly afraid. Not of them but of herself. It was as though she were already dead, and watching her own lost spirit through some other person's terror-stricken eyes.

The spasm passed. She told herself, 'Love is making you a coward,' blew out the candles, and made her way furtively down the stairs and out into the moonlit night.

The superb, fantastically large moon was rising behind the trees; gradually as it soared clear of the tree-tops it would diminish in size but increase in brightness, till it sailed high, serene and brilliant in the autumn sky.

Except for a few fitful moonbeams its light had not yet penetrated to the yew glades as Barbara Skelton cantered down them. The stone urn that marked their juncture was barely visible as she passed it, a dull pallor against the darkness. It was here, as she remembered with a pang of triumphant pleasure, that she had made her bold, sudden, and successful assault on Kit Locksby's heart. In years to come other lovers might make their vows or exchange embraces by it. But it would remain sacred to her, an unknown altar to her love, because no other woman would or could love so fiercely or so wholeheartedly as she.

Out on Watling Street she roamed aimlessly to and fro, a forlorn and sinister figure. Her tingling nerves craved for action, but her mind was, as usual, occupied with thoughts of her lover. She talked in a low voice to Fleury as he paced along the roadside. 'Fleury, Fleury. This is the last time we shall ride abroad on the highway lay[4] – you and I. Never fret, we shall learn better delights when we ride beside our master. Ah, how my soul dotes on him.' She patted Fleury's arched neck, sighing to herself and longing.

The moon reigned high now in the sky, diffusing a bluish light around it. A few opalescent clouds, like the torn wings of birds, drifted idly across it.

And as Barbara Skelton sat there on horseback, her uplifted face bathed in the moonlight, she heard the urgent sounds of galloping hoofs coming along the high road.

Instantly on the alert, she took refuge behind a cluster of trees. Here was her appointed prey. Unlucky traveller, she thought with malicious amusement, to be riding along Watling Street so late, but just not late enough to be Barbara Skelton's final victim.

All unaware the solitary horseman approached her hiding place.

She took a deep breath, touched Fleury's flanks with her heels…

'Stand and deliver,' cried Barbara, flourishing her pistol. The startled horse reared. As its rider controlled it, Barbara pointed her pistol at his head. 'Down with your gold or expect no quarter.'

The man said, 'Ruffian! I have no gold, and I ask for no quarter,' whipped out his sword and lunged at her.

She sat swaying on her saddle, not from the wound but because his voice was the voice of Kit Locksby.

She turned her horse and fled.

Kit Locksby, staring after her in some surprise, thought, 'The rogue did not show much fight. Well, maybe that prick from my sword will make him shy of attacking lone travellers in future.'

He wiped his stained blade with a wry face. He thought himself a fool for it but he disliked shedding even a highwayman's blood. How his sweet Barbara would scold him for being out so late on such an ugly robbing road. But when he told her of his father's sudden, unexpected recovery, and how he had decided to travel by night so that he might spend all the next day with her, she would certainly forgive him...

Barbara rode wildly for home. That she was wounded hardly troubled her – she was only dimly aware of the pain in her chest, and the feeling that something untoward and alarming was happening to her body – only the thought, 'He must not know'. She must get home, safe, undiscovered, creep into her bed. She would find some excuse for being indisposed. Ah cruel! that she should lose, by her own folly, even a few days of his dear company. But he must never know. That was all that mattered.

She passed familiar landmarks, trees, bushes, a pond, a barn, cottages, all dream-like in the moonlight. She was riding so hard, no wonder that she was getting breathless, giddy. She heard herself give deep sighing sounds. A damp, dark trickle was creeping down her coat. He had gashed her coat, torn too the white skin that he loved – her cruel, sweet lover.

She slackened pace when she reached the yew glades, not that the urgency of her panic had abated, but because she was finding it difficult to breathe; she had grown so faint, it was an effort to sit her horse. The moon looked down indifferently. The yew glades were dappled with moonlight. She was afraid of falling off, sinking unconscious into that checkered moonshine and darkness. He might come to the house and find her lying here…

Desperately she urged Fleury forward, clinging to his neck to keep herself in the saddle. He trotted in bewildered obedience to the little back door, stood still, cropping the grass.

Barbara half slipped, half fell off his back. She must reach her room before the pain and deadly faintness engulfed her.

How dark it was in the passage, and airless as a tomb. She staggered along, leaning against the walls, appalled at the sound of her own deep, gasping sighs.

Something wet and warm trickled from her lips, her mouth was full of the acrid taste of blood. At the foot of the secret staircase she collapsed. In a last despairing effort she tried to drag herself up, clutching at the lower steps. But the blood was gushing from her mouth. She was choking, groaning. Life was ebbing from her in profound moaning sighs.

She knew that she was dying, killed by her beloved's hand. In her last conscious moments she thought in agony and also in triumph:

'He will never see me grow old.'

12

COVER HER FACE …

"Lie still, lie still but a little wee while.'[1]

THEY FOUND HER lying there, in the early morning – she who had been known as the beautiful Lady Skelton, who had been so fine, delicate and elegant – lying in the pitiful disarray of violent death, a mysterious and appalling figure in mask and man's clothes.

She was carried up to her bedchamber, divested of her masculine attire, mask, pistols, cloak hidden furtively away, her terrible green eyes closed, the blood washed from her face and tangled bronzen curls. It was given out that Lady Skelton, sleep-walking, had fallen down the disused staircase and broken her neck. No one believed it. Rumours of blood, firearms, mask, outlandish gear, a strange and sinister mystery, sped from mouth to mouth. Few, at that time or for months to come, knew the true facts, but all suspected that their mistress had died a violent and shameful death. The whisperings, the pale, scared, yet eager looks, could not be hushed nor hidden, but all the funeral pomp that rank and money could command was thrown like a pall over the hideous scandal, concealing, it was hoped, the sudden, fearful extinction of that one personality under the solemn impersonality of death.

Maryiot Cells was draped in black from ground floor to garrets. Every member of the household, from Sir Ralph to the youngest scullion or garden-boy, was clad in mourning clothes. Black coaches rumbled up to the door, disgorging relations and friends with drooping faces and lowered voices. The lower regions were filled with the smell of the funeral baked meats and biscuits. Rings, mourning scarves and hatbands were distributed to the gentry, gloves to all the retainers, money to the deserving poor.

And the principal figure in this sombre pageant – Lady Skelton herself? The law decreed that all persons, regardless of rank, should be buried in woollen. But some small but pure spring of generosity and pity welling up in Sir Ralph's heart in this hour of his profound shame and horror, reminded him how fastidious Barbara had always been in her person and attire. The rigid, strange figure lying on the sable draped bed in the sable shrouded room still seemed to him the elusive, unaccountable, but on the whole docile wife of his imagination.

The truth, so savagely incredible, had hardly penetrated yet beyond the outer surface of his shocked mind. He gave orders that Lady Skelton was to be buried in a Brussels lace 'head',[2] a holland shift, with tucker and double ruffles, and long white kid gloves. The lace and gloves were provided by Lady Skelton's favourite mercer, Mrs Munce of the Sign of the Golden Glove in the town of Buckingham.

The day of the funeral dawned crisp and bright. The haws were scarlet against the pure blue sky. A milky haze veiled the ground. Grasses and brambles were rigid and glittering as crystals in the early sunshine. The woods were copper bright, but in the distance the slopes melted to a smoky blue. High in the morning sky floated the incongruous and belated moon.

Inside Maryiot Cells all was gloom and blackness, even to the soles of the mourners' shoes, but out of doors the world sparkled with the mellow radiance of early autumn.

They buried her at night in the family vault in the churchyard of Maiden Worthy church. Twenty-two poor women in gowns and kerchiefs headed the procession, then came the household, then the family chaplain and another clergyman, a doctor of divinity, and then the coffin, the pall being borne by six young ladies, daughters of the neighbouring gentry, escorted by six young gentlemen, all with white and black cypress scarves.[3] The family followed and a great throng of relations and of other ladies and gentlemen in mourning. And last of all, a servant led Fleury, the dead lady's favourite horse. All was decent, solemn and in order.

The body of Lady Skelton was met at the lych-gate by the choristers, and borne up the same path which less than seven years ago she had trodden as a young and smiling bride.

Candles, flickering in the draught, pierced the obscurity of the church, casting a pale light on the pale and lowered faces of the mourners. The voice of the family chaplain, as he delivered the funeral sermon, seemed to flicker like the candles in the draught of a nameless spiritual malaise. He praised Barbara Lady Skelton's domestic graces and virtues, her gracious manner, her piety, her charity to the sick and needy, and his praise in its fearful insincerity was more frightening than any condemnation. He said, 'Her memory will live among us and breathe a pleasant scent,' and his voice faltered at his own words, and died away.

They shivered in the chill night air as they stood with flaring torches round the door of the vault. There was the shuffle of feet, a stifled sob, faint whisperings. They cast their boughs of rosemary on to the coffin – rosemary for the bride, rosemary for the corpse, symbol of the unity underlying all life and death. Avoiding one another's eyes they quenched their torches in the soil.

Then in darkness and in silence, bearing their smoking torches with them, they walked away believing, in their ignorance, that Barbara Skelton was at rest and would trouble her family and the neighbourhood no more.

NOTES

Introduction

1 H. Tims, *Once a Wicked Lady: A Biography of Margaret Lockwood* (London: Virgin, 1989), p. 132.

2 F.E. Smedley, 'Maud Allinghame: A Legend of Hertfordshire', in F.E. Smedley and E.H. Yates, *Mirth and Metre, by Two Merry Men* (London: Routledge, 1855), p. 1.

3 J.E. Cussans, *A History of Hertfordshire*, vol. iii (1881; East Ardsley: E.P. Publishing, 1972), p. 115.

4 Cussans, p. 115.

5 This account of Katherine Ferrers' life is largely drawn from two sources: C.W. Field, *The Wicked Lady of Markyate: Studies and Documents* (Robertsbridge, East Sussex: 1979); and J. Barber, *The Wicked Lady: The Legend and Life of Katherine Ferrers* (2014). Both are self-published works, though clearly the product of much research, and both broadly agree in their facts and their conclusions about the historical Katherine Ferrers and her connection to the legend. See also John Barber's website: http://www.johnbarber.com/wickedlady.html.

6 See Field, p. 3.

7 Ann, Lady Fanshawe, *The Memoirs of Ann, Lady Fanshawe*, ed. H.C. Fanshawe (London: John Lane, 1907), p. 95.

8 Field, p. 6.

9 C. Hole, *Haunted England: A Survey of English Ghost-Lore* (London: B.T. Batsford, 1940), p. 94.

10 I am indebted to Commander Richard Perceval Maxwell for my information regarding the life of his mother, Magdalen King-Hall, and for his hospitality when conveying it to me in person.

11 Her older brother Stephen, served in the navy before becoming an MP and a distinguished print and broadcast journalist, famous for his political newsletter which championed opposition to fascism in the 1930s. Her older sister, Louise (1897–1983), was also a writer, publishing four novels and an edited version of the diaries belonging to her naval ancestors, between 1930 and 1946.

12 D. Wallace, *The Woman's Historical Novel: British Women Writers, 1900–2000* (Basingstoke: Palgrave Macmillan, 2005), p. 79.

13 Wallace, p. 4.

14 Wallace, p. 6.

15 M. Joannou, *Women's Writing, Englishness and National and Cultural Identity: The Mobile Woman and the Migrant Voice, 1938–1962* (Basingstoke: Palgrave Macmillan, 2012), p. 68.

16 Joannou, p. 68.

17 Wallace, p. 5.

18 For Margaret Lockwood, too, the film would prove career-defining. As her biographer notes, 'the role and the title were destined to become synonymous with her', and '[f]rom that time on, for the rest of her days, she would never be allowed to forget that she was *The Wicked Lady*.' See Tims, p. 133.

19 W.B. Gerish, *The Wicked Lady Ferrers: A Legend of Markyate Cell in Flamsted* (Bishop's Stortford, 1911), p. 6.

Life and Death of the Wicked Lady Skelton

Finis?

1 The Auxiliary Territorial Service, the women's Corps of the British Army during the Second World War.

2 Air Raid Precautions, the organisation responsible for preparing for air raids during the war, and dealing with their aftermath. Their duties included maintaining the blackout at night-time.

Part I

1 A reference to 1 Corinthians 13:12: 'For now we see through a glass, darkly'.

2 From Epistle 27 of the letters of Pliny the Younger, addressed to Licinius Sura. This epigraph comes from the famous translation of Pliny's letters by John Boyle, Earl of Cork and Orrery, which was published in 1751.

Lady Skelton at Home

1 The phrase belongs to Thomas Browne (1605–82), from his *Hydriotaphia, Urne Burial, or, a Discourse of the Sepulchral Urnes lately found in Norfolk* (1658), in which he discusses the inconsistency in classical depictions of ghosts, specifically whether they can be harmed by mortal weapons.

2 A skirt with a hem so narrow that it was difficult for the wearer to walk properly, fashionable in the few years leading up to the First World War.

3 Kulanga is a small village in Northwestern Zambia, formerly within the British colonial protectorate of Northern Rhodesia. 'Ujojo' does not seem

to be the name for an actual tribe or region – it is the Zulu word for the long-tailed finch, sometimes used as a name. The inaccuracy may be part of the satire of Colonel McRoberts as a typically bigoted example of colonial attitudes, insensitive to ethnic difference.

4 A laxative made from rhubarb, ginger and magnesia, named after the British physician James Gregory (1753–1821).

The Reticence of Miss Isabella Skelton

1 From John Milton, *A Masque Presented at Ludlow Castle, 1634* (more commonly known as *Comus*), line 432.

2 A type of bobbin lace (made from braided and twisted lengths of thread, held on bobbins) which originated in Valenciennes in northern France.

3 An apple-pie bed was a type of practical joke – made with one of the sheets folded back on itself so that its occupant's legs could not stretch out.

4 A decorative certificate or scroll, probably on calf-skin vellum, to commemorate the occasion of their marriage.

5 An ulster is a thick overcoat, made of durable material such as tweed. Traditionally, in the Victorian period, it would have featured a cape around the shoulders, though in the twentieth century the cape disappeared.

6 A dolman is a wide cape or mantle worn as an outer garment by ladies, often folded over the arms in place of sleeves. It was particularly fashionable in the 1870s and 1880s, exactly when this chapter of the novel is set, so this is another instance of King-Hall's very detailed and accurate depiction of period fashions.

7 Frederic William Farrar (1831–1903) was one of the most prominent Church of England clergymen in late-Victorian England, rising to become Dean of Canterbury. He had earlier been a teacher at Harrow School and Headmaster of Marlborough College, before entering the church. His renown derived partly from his power as a preacher, and spread more widely due to his prodigious output as a writer; he was an author of fiction (particularly children's fiction) and a prominent philological scholar, as well as a theologian. Highly progressive for his time, he became a friend of Charles Darwin and argued that the church should have no theological objection to Darwin's theory of evolution, in principle, though he was not himself entirely convinced by Darwin's evidence.

Lady Sophia Met Her Match

1 Like the epigraph to the previous chapter, this is from John Milton's *Comus* (1634). In fact, it comes from line 434, a mere two lines later than the previous quotation.

2 A slightly mysterious reference, as there is no record of an actual architect by this name. The name is suggestive of Josiah Wedgwood (1730–95), the renowned eighteenth-century potter, although he was not an architect. Wedgwood's contemporary (and fellow innovator in design and marketing), the cabinet-maker Thomas Chippendale (1718–79), did take on many commissions for aristocratic patrons, helping them to redesign and furnish their grand stately homes with custom-made furnishings. 'Josias Wedgeworth' may be King-Hall's fictional merging of these two pre-eminent figures of Georgian interior design.

3 The Ionic order is one of the three orders of classical architecture, the others being Doric and Corinthian. The Ionic order originally dates back to Greece in the 6th and 5th centuries BC, the political and cultural high-point of classical Athens. It is associated with slender columns, with a distinctive scroll-like volute or capital at the top of each column, and was a popular feature of neo-classical architecture in the eighteenth century.

4 'Some foolishness'.

5 Literally, 'duck', but it can also mean a 'false rumour', as it does here.

6 'It matters little to me; I don't care'.

7 'Se'ennight' or more commonly 'sennight' is another term for a week – 'seven nights'. It has fallen out of usage, though we retain the related term 'fortnight'. In this sentence, 'Monday se'ennight' means 'a week on Monday'.

8 A 'drum' – also known as a 'kettle drum' – was a large, informal tea party, held in the afternoon, at which tea, cake and sandwiches would be served. They were popular in the late eighteenth and nineteenth centuries. Guests would dress for daytime visiting, rather than in formal evening attire. The name possibly derives from the tea party's colonial origins in parts of the British Empire such as India, when officer's wives would host such parties in military camps, and regimental kettle drums would be used as substitute tables.

9 An archaic spelling of 'sat'.

Part II

1 *The English Rogue*, by Richard Head (1637–86) is one of the earliest examples of prose fiction in English, and one of the very first English works to be widely translated on the continent. A bawdy, picaresque account of the often criminal adventures of its protagonist, Meriton Latroon, it was initially denied a publication licence in 1665 for being too indecent, but became a bestseller when Head tempered its contents a little. The popularity of the work, when it was finally published in 1667, led to the production of several sequels or further volumes of the work, some of

them authored by the bookseller Francis Kirkman. This chapter epigraph is taken from the frontispiece of the fifth volume, published in 1688, with the full title *The English Rogue, Containing a Brief Discovery of the Most Eminent Cheats, Robberies & other Extravagancies, Committed by Him*. This volume is really little more than an abridged summary of the previous four books. None of this volume was written by Head, who had died two years earlier. The presence of the epigraph suggests King-Hall's knowledge of a long tradition of English and European fiction about criminals and highwaymen, and her desire to relate her novel to this.

The Wedding

1 From William Secker, *A Wedding-Ring Fit for the Finger: Or, The Salve of Divinity on the Sore of Humanity* (London: H. Hills, 1707), p. 15. This is the text of a sermon full of earnest Christian advice for husbands and wives, as this warning about choosing a wife for her beauty suggests.

2 This is just one of many details of seventeenth-century marriage customs, food and fashions that King-Hall accurately portrays in the course of this chapter.

3 Gilded rosemary was a fashionable choice for inclusion in wedding posies in the seventeenth century, to be carried by brides and bridesmaids. Often it would have been previously dipped in scented water. Rosemary was associated with memory and remembrance, and it reappears in this symbolic capacity in the final paragraphs of the novel.

4 A coranto (also known by the French term 'courante') was a courtly dance dating from the sixteenth century, distinguished by a rapid pace ('courante' means 'running') and a pattern of short advances and retreats by the dancers.

5 Two more dances from the period. The galliard was an intricate and athletic dance involving much leaping, jumping and hopping, said to have been a favourite of Queen Elizabeth I. The pavane, by contrast, was much slower, involving a formal procession by the dancers. All of the dances mentioned here were most popular in the sixteenth century, perhaps suggesting that Barbara's wedding is rather old-fashioned, despite its extravagance.

6 The cushion dance, or kissing dance, was a popular dance from the late sixteenth century, and common at weddings and parties. A dancer would choose a partner by kissing them, and once this dance was completed, the first dancer would retire while the second dancer would kiss a new partner, and so on, until everyone in the room had been kissed and had danced.

Midday at Maryiot Cells

1 This epigraph is from the poem 'Absence', or, as it is sometimes known, 'That Time and Absence Proves Rather Helps than Hurts to Loves.' The poem has often been credited to John Donne (1572–1631), though

this attribution is uncertain. It first appeared in print in 1602, but it was not then associated with Donne, nor was it was included in any of the earliest editions of Donne's works. It was not definitely linked to Donne's name until as late as 1721, and the editors of the authoritative *Variorum Edition of the Poetry of John Donne* (1995) consider the poem to be "noncanonical".

2 Local law courts. Petty sessions were magistrates' courts, and dealt with minor crimes which did not require a jury; while quarter sessions were presided over by at least two Justices of the Peace, and were held quarterly in the county seat, at Epiphany, Easter, Midsummer, and Michaelmas. However, King-Hall is guilty of a minor anachronism here, as petty sessions were not introduced until the beginning of the eighteenth century, to alleviate the burden on the quarter sessions.

3 The Popish Plot of 1678–81 was a fictitious Catholic conspiracy to assassinate King Charles II and replace him with his brother, James. It was invented, and elaborated with ever more outrageous claims, by Titus Oates (1649–1705), and resulted in widespread anti-Catholic hysteria, the passage of numerous anti-Catholic laws by Parliament, and the imprisonment and execution of many prominent Catholics. Oates was eventually discredited and convicted of perjury, though later pardoned by King William III. The atmosphere fomented by Oates' fabricated account of the plot contributed to the passage of the Exclusion Bill by Parliament, which excluded the overtly Catholic James from succession to the throne. The bill was ultimately defeated in the House of Lords, as the anti-Catholic fever began to die down in 1681. These events would certainly have been the focus of much speculation and gossip during the period.

4 A type of clay used to bleach cloth and absorb grease or oil.

5 The New Gardens, or New Spring Gardens, at Vauxhall, were one of London's most popular sites for relaxation and entertainment, from shortly before the Restoration until the mid-nineteenth century. At this time, they would have consisted of several acres of ornamental trees and planting, with decorative fountains and numerous paths. They feature in many plays of the late seventeenth century, and the Gardens were often chosen as the site for romantic assignations. The New Exchange was a fashionable bazaar or shopping arcade, located on the south side of the Strand, which had been opened in 1608 by James I, but was extremely popular after the Restoration.

6 A King of Arms is the most senior of the officers of arms, who are appointed by the Monarch to superintend ceremonies of state, supervise matters pertaining to armorial bearings, and maintain heraldic records. The Clarenceux King of Arms specifically has jurisdiction over England and Wales to the south of the River Trent.

7 A word game based on the alphabet. The exact wording can vary, but the first participant usually starts by saying something like:

I love my love with an A because he is attractive
I hate my love with A because he is avaricious
I took my love to Andover and fed him on asparagus and anchovies
His name is Andrew and he lives in Aylesbury.

The next player does the same for the letter B, and so on.

8 A popular early-modern stringed instrument, played in a similar way to a modern guitar. It was light and portable and relatively easy to master.

9 A complex three-player card game involving the taking of tricks, an ancestor of modern-day whist. Originating in Spain, the game became highly fashionable across Europe in the late seventeenth and eighteenth centuries, and was usually played for stakes. It plays a central part in Alexander Pope's mock-epic poem *The Rape of the Lock* (1714), whose heroine Belinda is addicted to the game, much like Barbara.

10 'St Nicholas's clerks' was a term used to describe thieves, robbers, and highwaymen. Saint Nicholas is the patron saint of repentant thieves (amongst other things). According to one legend, he persuaded a group of robbers to restore their stolen goods to their rightful owners.

11 More commonly spelled 'gleek', this was a popular, thought complex, three-player card game from the sixteenth century to the early eighteenth century. It was played for stakes, and although the rules are too complicated to summarise easily, it had two main phases, the first having something in common with modern poker, and the second with modern whist. In the first phase, all cards were afforded a numerical value; players competed to gain the best 'ruff', or the highest score of cards in the same suit. Money would also change hands if players held a flush, a gleek (three of a kind), or a mourneval (four of a kind). Following a round of bidding and raising, as in poker, players then proceeded to play their cards for tricks, as in modern whist. Each phase of the game contributed points to an overall score.

Midnight on Watling Street

1 Charles G. Harper, *Half-hours with the Highwaymen: Picturesque Biographies and Traditions of the "Knights of the Road"* (London: Chapman Hall, 1908), Vol. 1, p. 134. Harper's book offers an overview of outlaws and highwaymen in England, going all the way back to the legendary Robin Hood. Drawing heavily on early eighteenth-century sources, it also contains summaries of the careers of some of England's most notorious highwaymen from the seventeenth and eighteenth centuries (though not including Katherine Ferrers, needless to say), and provides copious details of the various roads around London that were most prone to highway

robbery, of Newgate prison, and of the Tyburn gallows. Much of this material informs King-Hall's narrative.

2 A mantua was a type of robe or over-gown, designed so that some of the petticoat beneath would be visible. Sultane is a type of twilled cloth made from a combination of silk and wool.

3 Ancient road traversing England from Kent in the South East, up to London, and across in a north westerly direction through Hertfordshire, Buckinghamshire, Bedfordshire, Northamptonshire, Warwickshire, Worcestershire and Herefordshire. It was a major artery of Roman Britain and remained an important route for travellers and commerce in the seventeenth century, although, just as King-Hall depicts, its condition was extremely poor. This led to the establishment of the first turnpike trust in the early eighteenth century, to raise funds for paving the road.

4 Underworld slang term for a hangman's noose or halter. Tyburn, which features later in the novel, was the area of London where criminals were hanged (on the site of modern-day Marble Arch). A tippet was a lady's scarf.

5 Beef tongues or ox tongues. 'Neat' is an archaic English word for a domestic cow or ox.

First Kill

1 William Shakespeare, *The Rape of Lucrece*, lines 918–9. In the original poem, the line refers to Tarquin's rape of Lucrece, which robs her of her honour and leads to her death at her own hand. The reference is ironic, for Barbara has sacrificed her 'honour' voluntarily. It also hints satirically at the extent to which female virtue has been fetishized and commodified, as King-Hall transfers this description of metaphorical theft to her account of literal theft.

2 Barbara Palmer, 1st Duchess of Cleveland, Countess of Castlemaine (1640–1709), commonly known as Lady Castlemaine. She was the mistress of King Charles I, by whom she had five children.

3 A reference to the popular dice game called Hazard. One player (sometimes a banker representing the house in a gambling club), known as a 'setter', specifies the stake (in this instance £150) and also calls a 'main', which can be any number from 5 to 9. The other player, the 'caster', then rolls two dice in an effort to score the main and win the stake.

4 Hortense Mancini, Duchesse Mazarin (1646–99), was one of five aristocratic Italian sisters, famed for their beauty, whose lives became entangled in various ways with some of the most powerful and wealthy men in Europe. King Charles had actually proposed to her in 1659, shortly before he was restored to the throne, but his proposal was rejected by her

uncle and guardian, Cardinal Mazarin, who thought the exiled king had little prospect of regaining his throne. Some sixteen years later, fleeing from an unhappy marriage, she became King Charles's mistress. She was notorious both for her promiscuity and her bisexuality, engaging in many love affairs with both men and women.

5 A small prison on Poultry, a street in the City of London. One of its most famous inmates was the seventeenth-century highwayman Captain James Hind (1616–52), who was finally arrested when he unsuccessfully attempted to rob Oliver Cromwell. He was convicted of treason because of his avowedly Royalist sympathies, and was hanged, drawn and quartered in Worcester.

The Lady and the Steward

1 From William Shakespeare's *Macbeth*, Act 1, scene 7.

2 The Biblical story of Susanna and the Elders is found in chapter 13 of the Book of Daniel. It concerns a virtuous young woman who is spied on by two lecherous old men, who then try to blackmail her, saying they will falsely accuse her of meeting a lover in the garden unless she agrees to have sex with them. Daniel intercedes just as she is about to be stoned to death for promiscuity, and after cross-examination of the elders it becomes clear that they are lying, and they are executed instead of Susanna. As an icon of falsely accused, virtuous womanhood (often represented in early modern art), Susanna is clearly an ironic choice of subject for Barbara's embroidery. The story is also only considered to be canonical by the Roman Catholic church, so Barbara's association with this story places her as far away, ideologically, from the Puritan Hogarth as it is possible to be.

At the Sign of the Golden Glove

1 Proverbs 2.18.

2 A soft, delicate fabric, usually silk, used as a lining for dresses.

3 The 'Question Lay' was the very specific form of robbery described in this passage. It seems not to have been very common, and there are very few references to this term, but it can be found in the Newgate Calendar (a compendium of accounts of notorious criminals from the late seventeenth to the late eighteenth centuries, available in various editions, and enormously popular with readers of the period) describing the career of one Moll Hawkins, who was executed at Tyburn on 22 December 1703. King-Hall's description of the crime is nearly identical to that found in the Newgate Calendar, which was almost certainly her source for this detail. 'Lay' in this sense means 'line of business' or 'adventure' – see also note 4 to Part II, Chapter 1: Lovers' Meeting.

4 A type of needlepoint lace featuring elaborate designs, usually in gold or silver mixed with coloured silks. Although the name suggests it originated in Spain, it was most commonly worn at the court of King Louis XIV of France (reigned 1661–1715) and may well have been manufactured in France.

5 A pinner was a small, close fitting lace cap worn by women to accessorise their hair, popular in the seventeenth and eighteenth centuries. It had long flaps on either side which were either pinned up in the lady's hair, or worn down and pinned to the breast. A double pinner or settee was a variant on this, in which two caps were worn in combination and the pinning was more elaborate.

Dark Designments

1 William Shakespeare, *Hamlet*, Act 2, scene 2.

2 A selection of folk remedies for common ailments. Quinsy was an inflammation of the throat. 'Rew' is presumably a variant spelling of 'rue', a yellow-flowering shrub with strong-smelling feathery leaves, formerly much used for medicinal purposes. 'Madragories' is a variant of mandragora, or mandrake, a narcotic plant, the leaves and roots of which were often used to make a sedative or painkiller. 'Featherfew', more commonly known as 'feverfew', is a perennial plant with large, daisy-like flowers, traditionally used to treat all manner of ailments including headaches and fever (hence the name). 'Burnet' probably refers to the burnet-saxifrage, which was used by herbalists to make a diuretic. 'Dragons' here refers to the flowering plant often known as dragonwort or common bistort, the roots of which were used to make an astringent similar to witch-hazel.

3 'Holland' is a type of linen manufactured in the Netherlands, also called Holland-cloth. A tippet is a strip of cloth or sometimes part of a dress, usually attached to the sleeve or hood, and worn as a scarf. 'Frieze' is a coarse woollen cloth with a raised nap on one side, consisting of raised and brushed fibres of the wool. 'Pintado' was a fine cotton cloth imported from India, similar to chintz; it was painted or dyed with patterns.

4 'Sack' was a type of white wine originating in Spain or the Canary Islands. 'Manchet' was bread made from flour of the highest quality, therefore considered a luxury only available to the wealthy. 'A manchet of bread' probably describes a small, flat bread roll made from this flour.

5 'Paps and caudles' were types of thin gruel made by mixing bread with water or milk, served to invalids or to babies. Caudles were usually fortified with wine or ale, and spices.

6 In the New Testament, Dorcas (also known by her Aramaic name, Tabitha) is a Christian renowned for her kindness and charity. On her death, Peter

visits Joppa, where she lived, and raises her back to life. The story is from Acts of the Apostles, chapter 9, verses 36–43.

The Knot is Broken

1 From the poem 'Love and Life' by John Wilmot, 2nd Earl of Rochester (1647–80).

The Heavy Hill

1 From 'The Ballad of the Nut-Brown Maid', an anonymously authored traditional English folk-ballad, dating back to the 15th century. It was included by Thomas Percy in his *Reliques of Ancient English Poetry* (1765). The main theme of the poem is women's fidelity; the maid of the title is an archetype of self-sacrificial love and devotion.

2 The reign of King Charles II was calculated from the execution of his father, King Charles I, in 1649, rather than his Restoration in 1660. Hence, the thirty-sixth year of his reign was 1685.

3 King Charles II married Catherine of Braganza (1638–1705) in 1662. She was the daughter of King John IV of Portugal, and a Roman Catholic. As such, she was the object of much suspicion in England, and was accused by Titus Oates of plotting to murder the King, during the Popish plot paranoia of 1678–81. The 'papist French whore' almost certainly refers to Louise de Kérouaille, Duchess of Portsmouth (1649–1734), who became the mistress of the King in the early 1670s. She was also a Roman Catholic and was instrumental in his deathbed conversion to Catholicism. She remained an advocate of French interests throughout her time with Charles, and was greatly mistrusted and disliked by many members of the court.

4 This is a quotation from the account of the Great Plague of 1665 by the famous diarist John Evelyn (1620–1706), specifically from his entry for 11th October 1665. King-Hall here shows that she was familiar with first-hand accounts of life in London at the time, and provides a textual echo of the earlier period of the plague to reinforce her evocation of the great frost as a comparable cataclysm.

5 Sometimes known as 'Brunswick Mum'. A beer made in Brunswick, Germany, available in varying degrees of alcoholic strength. It lasted well, allowing for its wide distribution.

6 After the Restoration, King Charles II reopened London's theatres after an eighteen-year period of closure under the Puritan Commonwealth. He granted licenses to two rival theatrical companies to perform plays in the capital. The first, led by Thomas Killigrew, had Charles himself as its patron, and hence was known as the King's Company. The second, led by Sir William Davenant, had the King's brother, James, the Duke of York,

as its patron, and hence was known as the Duke's Company. They each constructed purpose built 'patent' theatres to stage their productions. The King's Playhouse was in Drury Lane, on the site of the modern Theatre Royal, Drury Lane. It opened in 1663, burned down in 1672, and was rebuilt and reopened in 1674. The Duke's Company performed in various venues in London until 1671, when it moved into the Dorset Garden Theatre, also known as the Duke of York's Theatre. This was located in Whitefriars, on the north bank of the Thames, just to the west of the modern Blackfriars Bridge. It was, at the time, the most sophisticated theatre in London, both in terms of its elegance and luxury, and in terms of the scenic technology built into its stage, allowing for elaborate and spectacular performances.

7 St Sepulchre-without-Newgate is located on Holborn Viaduct. As its name suggests, it was located just outside the walls of the City of London, by the gate known as Newgate, which had long been in use as a prison. The prison had been destroyed by the Great Fire of London in 1666, and a newly rebuilt and extended prison had opened in 1672.

8 This bequest is well summarised in an article by Francis W. Rowsell, entitled 'Charities', and published in a Victorian weekly periodical called *The Quiver: An Illustrated Magazine for Sunday and General Reading*, on November 14th 1868: "One of the most quaint in style and singular in purpose of the many gifts to charity, within the city of London, is the following, which was given to the church of St. Sepulchre by Newgate, in 1605, by Robert Dowe. Fifty pounds were left to the parish, on condition that a person should go to Newgate, in the still of the night before every execution day, and standing as near as possible to the cells of the condemned, should with a hand-bell (which was also bequeathed) give twelve solemn tolls, with double strokes; and then, after a proper pause, deliver a solemn exhortation. Robert Dowe also ordered that the great bell of the church should toll on the morning, and that as the criminals passed the wall on the way to Tyburn, the bellman or sexton should look over, and say, 'All good people pray heartily unto God for these poor sinners, who are now going to their death.'"

9 Holborn's nickname of 'the heavy hill' derived from its being on the route from Newgate and the Tower of London to the gallows at Tyburn. 'Heavy' in this context almost certainly means 'doleful' or 'grave', although it may also signify the difficulty the carts on which the condemned men were transported may have had in ascending the hill, particularly when the weather was bad and the roads muddy.

Summer's Date

1 This is a misquotation, presumably from memory, of Shakespeare's famous Sonnet 18, ('Shall I compare thee to a summer's day?'). The fourth line of the poem actually reads 'And summer's lease hath all too short a date.'

2 Masques were elaborate dramatic entertainments, often featuring music and dance, performed for (and sometimes by) members of the royal court or wealthy aristocrats. They were particularly prevalent across Europe in the sixteenth and seventeenth centuries, and many significant literary figures, including Ben Jonson and even John Milton, wrote masques. They often took a classical theme and used allegory to flatter the vanities of whichever wealthy patron they were sponsored by, though many had moral or political subtexts. Although they were often performed in private homes and gardens, it was not uncommon for masques to feature extravagant staging and costumes; Inigo Jones, for instance, one of the most important architects and set designers of the early seventeenth century, collaborated with Jonson on numerous masques.

3 In this classical myth, a young hunter named Actæon stumbles across Diana (as she was known to the Romans; Artemis to the Greeks), the goddess of the Hunt and of the Moon, as she is bathing with her nymphs. Enraged by his intrusion, Diana transforms Actaeon into a stag, and he is then chased down and killed by his own hounds. The story is included by Ovid in his *Metamorphoses*. Diana seems an ironically inappropriate character for Barbara to play, because of her association with chastity, and yet also somehow apposite, as the story demonstrates her vengefulness and power over a man.

4 A flageolet is a woodwind instrument, first invented in the late sixteenth century and widely played until the nineteenth century. It resembles the modern recorder.

5 This poem features in Jonson's satirical play *Cynthia's Revels, or The Fountain of Self-Love* (1600).

Lovers' Meeting

1 This is the refrain from the 'cushion dance'. See note 6 to Part II, Chapter 1: The Wedding.

2 The closing couplet of the poem 'The Surrender' by Henry King (1592–1669). King was a metaphysical poet, influenced in his style by his friend and contemporary, John Donne.

3 A reference to the superstitious belief that burning three candles is unlucky. This remains part of theatre lore, according to which three candles should never be lit on stage. The origins of the superstition are unclear.

4 To be 'on a lay' means to be pursuing a particular line of business or adventure. This slang phrase is most often used in exactly this construction – to be 'on (a particular) lay'. Hence, to be 'on the Highway lay' means to be out adventuring on the Highway. See note 3 to Part II, Chapter 6: At the Sign of the Golden Glove.

Cover Her Face

1 The lines are taken from an anonymously authored seventeenth-century Scottish ballad entitled 'The Wife of Usher's Well'. The poem describes how, after being lost at sea, the ghosts of three brothers return to visit their grieving mother, before having to depart when the cock crows at dawn.

2 Brussels lace was a very high quality, decorative bobbin lace made, naturally enough, in Brussels. Between 1662 and 1699, however, Parliament prohibited the importation of foreign lace into England, in order to protect the interests of English lace manufacturers. Brussels lace was therefore expensive not only because of its high quality, but also because it would have been illegally smuggled into the country.

3 'Cypress' was a light, gauzy material, similar to crape, and much used, in black, for mourning clothes. It was originally imported from Cyprus, hence its name.